3/08

D1376471

The Fiddle Game

The Fiddle Game

Richard A. Thompsom

Poisoned Pen Press

For Bud George,
who introduced me to the mystery

Acknowledgments

In real life as much as in fiction, the hero's journey is never accomplished without a host of seen and unseen helping hands. In my own journey from construction engineer to author, I have been helped enormously by the following fine people:

Ginny Hansen, who gave me the first encouragement;
Blaine Cross, who gave me the first validation;
Ellen Hart, who gave me the tool kit;
The members, past and present, of the brave little writers' group known as Murder Ink, who gave invaluable feedback and priceless ongoing fanfare—
Peter Farley, Phil Finklestein, Margaret Milne, Elizabeth Ravden, Virginia Scheff, and Ingrid Trausch;
My wonderful Canadian friends, Lyn Hamilton and Mary Jane Maffini, who first made me feel

welcome in the broader community of professional authors;
My untiring fellow traveler, Margaret Yang,
the Bard of Ann Arbor;
And finally, Roger Baldwin, wherever he may be,
who gave me a love of the lore of stringed musical
instruments that has lasted over 45 years.

Thanks doesn't begin to cover it.

Author's Note

Residents of the city of Saint Paul will be quick to point out that I have taken enormous liberties with its geography. Some of the sites and images I have used are real, or were in 1996, but are not quite in their proper location or time frame. Others, such as Lefty's Poolhall and the Happy Dragon, are purely from the back side of my mind and have never existed in the real world at all. Still others are composites of the real and the fanciful. For this, I make no apology. The story has its needs and so do I. The flavor and aura of Saint Paul, I believe, are occasionally correct, but for all other purposes, it would be best to regard the Saint Paul of this story as completely fictitious.

With the characters and events of the story, there is no such ambiguity. They are entirely the products of my imagination, and any resemblance to anyone or anything in the real world is purely coincidental.

Chapter One

Waiting for the Dough

On the day of the first killing, it rained. Not an easy rain, but the kind of endless, pounding deluge that makes people wonder if they really did throw out that old boat catalog, and if not, whether it listed any arks. Personally, I gave up looking for arks a long time ago, the wooden ones or any other kind. I like the rain. Agnes, my secretary, says that's just perversity, liking anything that puts other people in a bad mood, but she isn't always right. Not always. On that particular wet day in 1996, nobody was right.

I looked out the streaked glass of my single storefront window, past the neon sign that says "24-Hour Service" backwards, and assessed the prospects of a flash flood.

You can tell a lot about a city by what's in its old, core downtown. Across the street from me is an old time resident hotel, long ago gone to seed. There used to be a nightclub on the ground floor under it, but that's been boarded up and closed for longer than anybody remembers. Farther down is a place called Pawn USA, a hole-in-the wall deli, and a pornographic book store. They've all been around long enough to be landmarks. The pawn shop, run by a sometime friend of mine named Nickel Pete Carchetti, just expanded and got its trendy new name, which I suspect came from the title of a textbook on modern economics. Farther down the street lie a Dunn Brothers coffee shop, an upscale tattoo parlor, and a manicure emporium called Big City Nails. Kitty-corner across from me stands the newly renovated Courthouse, taking up a whole square block, and behind it, connected to it by tunnel, is the County Jail. The long fingernails, tribal markings, and chi-chi coffee are current hot-ticket items, but I don't expect them to last. The trendy shops come and go. Here in St. Paul, Minnesota, the capitol of Midwest niceness, the only really solid growth industries we have are government and crime.

Strangely enough, the cops don't have a building in downtown proper, merely one on the fringe of it, though they definitely have a street presence. Maybe that's the way it should be, since they are really just the gatekeepers to the criminal justice system. And if that's the case, then I'm the man in the tollbooth. My name is Herman Jackson, and I'm a bail bondsman.

Behind me, Agnes sat at her PC clattering keys sporadically. I could tell by the rhythm that it wasn't work-related, but since she is my chief office organizer, accountant, PR expert, and generally indispensable confidant, as well as my secretary, she's entitled to spend her time as she sees fit. The computer was making funny noises, like tinny fanfare or electronic oohs and aahs, and occasionally she would make an "ooh" of her own.

"Video games, pornography, or the stock market?" I asked, without turning around.

"Stocks. I don't do games." She said nothing about porn, I noticed. "You should look at this, Herman. Amtech-dot-com is down to sixteen and a half today. It's a fluke, has to be."

"The market is reacting to news of an outbreak of moldy sowbellies in Katmandu." Which made exactly as much sense as most of what I hear out of market analysts.

"Seriously, at that price, you could make a killing. Double your money in a couple months, tops. You could afford to take a little flier like that now and then, you know. On your latest profit-and-loss sheet, you showed…"

"I don't gamble, Aggie."

"You gamble on pool."

"That's not gambling, that's social intercourse. I never bet more than a hundred on a game, and I never try a double-back off the side rail if I've had more than two drinks." And if that isn't prudence and self-discipline, I don't know the stuff. And I do. I paid full price for it, and now it's my biggest asset.

"The market's not really gambling, either," she said. "It's more like reversible bidding at a garage sale. After all the hype blows away, there's always a real piece of merchandise of some kind there."

"Except when there isn't. How much did you lose on Enron? Isn't that why you're still driving to work in your beat-up Toyota instead of your new Lexus?"

"That's not fair, Herman. People a lot smarter than me got burned in that scam."

"And people smarter yet didn't play."

"Like you? Like that time you got arrested for somebody else's homicide and had to liquidate your business in Detroit and run off to the boonies?"

It was her ultimate weapon in any argument, and I had no defense for it. The incident she referred to was back in my high-roller days, when my ship really had come in, but I was dumb enough to torpedo it at the dock. Sometimes I let myself think those days might come back, but I don't really believe it. There aren't any big scores in the bonding business. Not usually, anyway. What you see up front is what you get, and sometimes you don't even get that. And in any case, the great god Odz doesn't forgive that kind of stupidity. St. Paul is my Elba, and if a delegation of leaderless Frenchmen came one day to rescue me from it, I would run from them in terror.

"Low blow, Aggie. I wasn't as smart then, in a lot of ways, and I admit it."

"You want a cookie for 'fessing up like a good boy?"

"You want to answer that ringing thing? It might be the phone."

She picked up the phone, and the pulse of the day's real business began.

Most of my business comes to me by phone, or at least the first contact does. I get a call from a defense lawyer or a PD, with the daily list of souls in bondage who want to buy a ticket to freedom. The logistics of paper and money flow are worked out, and the wheels begin to turn. I'm not allowed to start the process by approaching them, in the courtroom or the jail. It's sort of like ambulance chasing for a lawyer; not actually illegal, but sudden death to a professional reputation. Instead, I imitate Mohammed and wait for the accused mountains to come to me.

For most customers, it's a standard proposition: ten percent non-refundable fee and some kind of negotiable security for the rest. If you think about it, it's a crummy deal for the client. He's paying a hell of a wad of cash for a short burst of liberty that he's probably going to lose anyhow, and if he jumps bail, or even appears to, he loses the security, to boot. But of course, they're all going to be acquitted, so they don't worry about that. Meanwhile, they wait for the authorities or the gods or the odds to come around, and the prospect of a short time in jail is horrifying. The prospect of a much longer time in prison doesn't seem to bother them so much. People have no grasp of time. All they can deal with is never and forever. They don't handle cause and effect real well, either.

If the first call is from a lawyer I know, sometimes we work out some other terms. It's a quid pro quo thing. I give up a little quid, in the form of reduced or eliminated security for a trustworthy customer, and the lawyer gives me some quo in the form of telling me what his clients are really like, including which ones are going to run like rabbits the minute the cuffs are off. I could do away with this little part of the whole game, treat everybody the same, but I like the action. And that's not gambling, either.

Most of the time, I never see the actual client. But I do see a regular parade of siblings, parents, friends, lovers, business partners, and significant-whatevers, come to do the dirty job of bargaining for somebody else's freedom. They range from sensible to pathetic, and they bring me enough stories to make an endless soap opera script and put scar tissue on my soul.

While Agnes talked on the phone, doing what I always think of as making book, I watched the little wisp of a blonde cross the street in the rain and head for my door. She had a dark raincoat that hung like a crumpled trash bag, shoes that were too low for the wet streets, and one of those clear plastic rain-bonnet things on her head. She carried a violin case as if it were her first born child, pressed against her bosom, and she walked with a limp. *Nice touch*, I thought. In a business that's full of Oscar-quality performances, the limp was a perfect bit of understatement. I made a mental note not to ask her how she got it. Under the bonnet, she had high cheekbones, big doe eyes, and a prominent, sharpish nose and chin, bracketing a thin-lipped mouth. It was very dramatic and oddly attractive. Sondra Locke clutching her bundle of secret hurt and rage.

Even hunched up against the rain, she didn't have much in the way of shoulders, but she damn sure had a chip on at least one of them. I made a move to push the door open for her, but she snatched it angrily away from me, stomped in as well as one can stomp with a game leg, and shook off her bonnet at me. I was surprised. Usually, people get to know me a bit better before they're that hostile.

"Can we help you, Miss…?"

Aggie rolled her eyes. The orphan of the storm glared with hers.

"*Ms.* Amy Cox," she said, drenching the title in acid. I don't know how I could have been so politically incorrect. I must have still been thinking about *Ms.* Locke.

"What can we do for you, Ms. Cox?"

"I'm here to let you suck my blood. Probably all of it."

"I beg your pardon?"

"I think you have him confused with your lawyer, sweetheart," said Agnes. I've never figured out how she can get away with "sweetheart," when I can't even drop an occasional "Miss," but she can.

"I don't have anybody or anything confused." She tried out another glare. When nobody took the bait, she relaxed a little and did a half-hearted shrug. "But I suppose you didn't invent the system, did you? I take it nobody called? About my brother?"

I gave her my best David Carradine look. The grasshopper, waiting to be enlightened.

"I have to get a bail bond for my brother, Jimmy."

Agnes turned back to her PC and began scrolling through the list of the day's happy candidates. "Got him," she said, after a few seconds. "James W. Cox, right? Double GTA, five counts of MPD, handful of moving traffic violations. Bail is eighteen K."

GTA is grand theft auto, and MPD is malicious property damage, better known as vandalism. Two counts of GTA told me he had gotten away at least once, since it's unusual that a suspect has time to steal a second car while he's in the middle of a high speed chase with the first one. Even so, and even with the vandalism rolled in, the bail seemed high. Had he pissed off the judge? I pictured some dopey kid, hauled in for a crash-and-burn spree, maybe still lit up a bit, and stupid enough to mouth off to hizzoner. Not that I cared about any of that, except as a way of guessing how big a flight risk this guy was. So far, he sounded high-to-certain.

"Is your brother a young person?" I said. "A little on the wild side, maybe? Sometimes does a little booze, a little drugs, a joyride with some bad…"

"He's not like that."

Of course he's not. Your own brother never is. "What is he like, exactly?"

"He's a neo-Luddite."

That even stopped Agnes. I shifted to something easier.

"Is your brother underage?"

"I wish." She plopped down into my best neo-1955 motel chair, not bothering to take her coat off. "If he were still a kid, I could hope he might grow out of it. But he's pushing thirty-two now, and he's, well…"

"Crazy," said Agnes, ever eager to help out.

"Fanatical is more like it, I think. He's not really violent, at least not towards people. He thinks modern society is insane, and he imagines he's making some kind of big, heroic statement. It's his own term, neo-Luddite. The first Luddites were a bunch of people in the early eighteen hundreds who thought the Industrial Revolution was ruining the world, so they went around smashing power looms, burning mills, that sort of thing. Jimmy goes out and steals fifty-thousand-dollar SUVs and crashes them through the windows of Starbucks."

I looked out the window to see if perhaps little Jimmy had been to visit my neighborhood while my attention was turned elsewhere. Nope. The brown and green storefront seemed to have all its glass intact.

"What he imagines he's accomplishing is beyond me. Other than bankrupting the entire family. Mom and Dad disowned him years ago. I'm all he's got now. And the judge wasn't just being mean with the bond amount, Mr. Jackson."

Wow, a "Mister." Did that mean I was no longer the vile bloodsucker or the chauvinist pig? Was I about to get the inside dope? "I take it he's done this before?"

"Five times, in three other states."

Bingo.

"What you will need, Ms. Cox, is…"

"I know what I need. I can give you a check for the eighteen hundred. It wipes out the last of my savings, but if my stupid little brother doesn't care, why should you? Our lawyer explained that in a flight-risk case, I'll have to post something for security for the full eighteen thousand, as well."

If she was hoping I would disagree with her, she was about to be disappointed.

"All I have is my violin," she said.

I wanted to say, "Must be one hell of a fiddle," but it didn't seem to fit. My expression must have said it for me.

"It's an Amati," she said. "It's over four hundred years old."

Silly me, I thought the Amati was a car that Studebaker quit making in 1965. I didn't want one of them, and I didn't want a fancy antique fiddle, either.

"It's probably priceless," she said, "but it's been appraised at sixty thousand dollars. And that was almost twenty years ago."

On the other hand, old violins spill very little oil on the floor and never, ever rust out. Maybe I'd been a bit hasty.

She produced a much-folded paper from her purse and handed it to me. It appeared to be a professional appraisal, and as I scanned it, I began to assess the situation. And all the possible combinations and permutations. There was still the question of possession. "Is there a title document of some kind?"

"None. Never was. My grandfather brought it home after the Second World War. We never knew how he got it, and probably wouldn't want to. When I took up playing the violin seriously in high school, he put me in his will to receive it. After he died, it was something of a family joke at first, then the source of a lot of bad feelings. It turned out the whole rest of his estate wasn't worth that much. But I kept it. It was the first really fine instrument I ever got to play, and I swore I'd never give it up."

"Until now," I said.

"For your stupid little brother," said Agnes.

"Yes." It was a word, but it sounded more like a sob. She stood up, put the case on my desk, and opened it for my inspection.

I leaned over and took a look, not touching the instrument, in case it was ready to crumble into dust. It looked a lot like a violin. Not very shiny, I thought, but after four hundred years, what is? I tried to remember something about a secret varnish formula. Maybe that was Stradivarius.

"You understand that for something like this, with no title, I can't just attach a lien against it? I'll have to actually take possession, or have some mutually accept-able third person do it."

She nodded. "The problem is, I have to have something to play. It's what I do. I play for the Opera, and sometimes for the Chamber Orchestra, and I teach a little. I have to have an instrument."

I glanced over at Agnes, and she shot me a look that said "Don't you dare even think about it." But I was thinking about a different angle than waiving possession.

"What's a run-of-the-mill, professional-quality instrument cost?"

"Two, maybe three thousand. I already told you, the eighteen hundred is all…"

I held up my hand. "I'll have to get somebody else to take a look at the Amati anyway, to tell me if your certificate is really talking about this exact instrument. That's as good a place as any to do it." I gestured at the window and the street beyond, towards Nickel Pete's. "Maybe we can work out something with a loaner, while we're there."

She looked, and her face fell. "A pawn shop? My God, have I come to this?"

Trust me, sweetie, there's lots worse places to come to. I put on my trenchcoat, grabbed an umbrella, and we headed out into the rain.

The streets were empty except for a dark Ford LTD parked at the curb a half block down, so we crossed against the light and hurried down to the emporium of discarded dreams. Pete's shop was a mixture of traditional and new, with a modern, open sales floor up front, to display all the bulky stuff like exercise machines and huge TVs, and the old-style teller's cage in the back, guarding the cases of the smaller and more precious goods, as well as the firearms. Pete greeted us the way he greets everybody, sitting owl-faced at his cage with both hands under the counter. I knew that he had one hand poised to push an alarm button, while the other gripped a sawed-off shotgun. When he saw it was me, he folded his hands on top of the counter.

"Herman, old friend." His ancient troll's face morphed into what passed for a smile. "How's business? Mine's great. You ever get ready to expand, take on a new partner, I got the capital and the disposition for it. All's I need is the referrals."

"You've got the disposition of an undertaker."

"Then we'll get along fine, won't we?" He laughed, went into a coughing spasm, and finally treated himself to a pink antacid tablet from a bottle that he kept next to the cash register. It was a regular ritual of his. The ball was back in my court.

"This lady," I said, "needs a professional violin. You got anything of any quality?"

"One or two, I think. The good ones are in the back."

"Let's see them. And while she's checking them out, I want you to take a look at the one she's carrying, give me your opinion."

"Is this a professional consultation? Do I get a fee?"

"Yes, it is, and no, you don't."

"You always were a cheap sonofabitch, Herman." It wasn't true, but I let him get away with it, and he went into the back room and emerged with one violin whose case said it was a Yamaha and another, older-looking one that had no label. He passed them over to Amy Cox, and then proceeded to have a look at the maybe-Amati and the appraisal document. Then he took out his jeweler's loupe and had a real look, and an attitude of reverence spread across his face.

"I don't usually deal in goods of this quality, you know. I have no market, no contacts. The best I could do on it..."

"I'm not asking you to do anything on it, Pete. Just tell me if it's the Amati the paper talks about."

"Oh, it's the violin in the appraisal, all right. As to whether it's a real Amati, that's not such a simple question."

"Is it worth twenty-one grand?"

"The paper says sixty, plus inflation."

"It doesn't have to be worth sixty. The bond she needs is for eighteen, plus she needs enough to get one of those fiddles you just showed her. Is it worth that much or not?"

"Absolutely. You want I should advance it?"

"No. We'll do it a little different."

Amy Cox picked out the Yamaha. Pete said it was worth twenty-seven hundred, Amy said twelve, tops, and we all knew we were eventually going to settle on eighteen, if only for the beautiful irony of the number.

Pete put the Amati away somewhere in the back and wrote a pawn ticket for eighteen hundred, made out to me. The deal was that I would issue the bail bond for the wayward, neo-Luddite Jimmy. If he showed up at his trial like a good little boy, and the bond got released, then his sister could come and get the ticket from me and redeem her own violin by bringing back the Yamaha and paying the interest. If little Jimmy reverted to type and took a hike, then I was out eighteen grand to the Sheriff's office, but the Amati was mine for the eighteen hundred, plus interest. In that case, Amy could keep her substitute, so she wouldn't have to go to her job at the Chamber Orchestra with a kazoo, but she lost first rights to her heirloom. It was the deal of the century. For somebody, anyway. She took it. We went back to my office to have Agnes draw up the formal papers.

The length of time it takes to mortgage all your past dreams to pay for tomorrow's reduced hopes is heartbreakingly short. Before Amy Cox had time to feel the cold lump in the pit of her stomach spread to the rest of her soul, or to look at her new violin and cry a bit, she was signed, notarized, wished the best of luck, and sent back out into the rain. I stood in the same spot where I had been when I first saw her, looking through the neon letters, watching her go. Once again, she had her shoulders hunched against the rain, but now she held her violin case under one arm, at her side.

"Cute, wasn't she? In a prickly sort of way."

I turned around to see Agnes looking disgustingly smug. "Was she?" I said.

"Oh, listen to him. The ice man. This is me you're talking to, okay? If she'd put her hooks into you any deeper, you'd need sutures."

Had she? "You are obviously mistaking my professional manner of…"

I was interrupted by the sound of a loud thump, out in the street, and I looked back that way in time to see Amy Cox flying through the air like a rag doll. She hit the wet pavement with a sickening second thud and lay motionless. Behind her, the dark LTD I had noticed earlier was braking to a stop.

"Call 9-1-1!" I screamed over my shoulder. I ran out the door and into the street, where the rain hit me in the face like a slap with a wet towel. The LTD was at the scene ahead of me, and the driver's door opened to disgorge a large man in a dark overcoat. He bent over the victim briefly, then ran back to the car and got in. He immediately floored it, spinning the tires on the wet pavement, running over the crumpled body, and fleeing into the mist. I couldn't believe I had seen him do that. I think I screamed again, something obscene, but I'm not sure.

I tried my damnedest, but with the rain spitting in my eyes, I couldn't read the departing license plate. I kept running until I got to where Amy Cox lay like a pile of broken sticks, one leg bent the wrong way, an arm thrown over her head, blood trailing from her mouth and ears, wide eyes staring at nothing. I bent down and felt for a pulse in her throat, but I was already pretty sure I wasn't going to find one. She looked as dead as anybody I've ever seen. I hunkered down beside her, not sure what to do.

Down the street, Sheriff's deputies and cops were running out of the courthouse, and I could already hear an ambulance siren. I was surprised to also hear myself moaning. I rocked back on my heels and let somebody pull me up and guide me off to one side. I looked around, dazed. Twenty yards down the road were the shoes that were too low for the wet streets. The speeding car had knocked her right out of them. Closer to me was her small purse, from which she had produced the certificate of appraisal. Here and there were a few scattered papers and what may have been some gouts of blood. I looked all around, scanning the area in progressively widening sweeps, zoning it off, making sure I missed nothing. That seemed important, for some reason.

There was nothing, anywhere, remotely resembling a violin case.

Chapter Two

Picking Up Sticks

Someplace far away, a boom box was playing an odd, slow version of white rap. Or maybe it was a call-in radio show.

"Anybody see the accident?"

"That guy might have. He was the first one on the scene, far as I could tell."

"The dopey-looking one, standing around with no raincoat? What's his name?"

"We didn't talk to him. He was bent over the body when we got there. Groaning, sort of."

"Is he okay?"

"I don't think he got hit or anything. He's just shook up. But if anybody saw the vehicle, it'd be him."

"Excuse me? Sir?"

There was a hand on my upper arm, I realized, not pressing hard, but insistent. I guessed the dopey-looking guy they were talking about must have gone someplace else.

"Sir?" Blue and brass, the square bulk of an armored vest showing, even through the uniform jacket. Lots of black leather pouches and snaps, like a bunch of fanny packs from the Harley store. A cop, not a Sheriff's deputy. Right. That was the way it should be. We weren't in front of his courthouse, but it was still his street, his case. Only, if it turned into a real case, they would take it away from him and give it to a couple of plainclothes detectives. That made me sad, for some reason. Maybe I just wanted to be sad.

"Are you all right, sir?"

The paramedics had zipped Amy Cox up in a body bag and were taking their time loading her into the meat wagon. I don't know how long I had been standing there or what I thought I was doing.

"Hey, fella, I asked if you're all right?"

"I'm not injured, officer."

"Did you see the accident?"

Was it an accident? What little I saw looked awfully damned cold-blooded and deliberate to me. "I didn't see the actual impact," I said. "I saw her flying through the air, and I saw her hit the pavement. Then I saw the bastards run over her a second time. They stole her violin."

"They?"

I thought for a minute and blinked. "I only saw one, come to think about it. But it was a big car, with blackout glass all around. There could have been a small mob in there."

A notebook came out of his upper pocket, and he hunched over, trying to keep the rain off it. When he tipped his head down to write, a stream came off the brim of his hat, onto the pages.

"They make waterproof notebooks, you know, officer. Nickel Pete, down the street there, showed me one once. They make them for surveyors. He gets all kinds of strange merchandise, but never the same kind twice. It was his violin, too, come to think of it. He traded it for…"

"I'll need your name, sir."

It was as polite a way as anybody had ever told me that I was babbling, and I shifted down a gear or two, and told him my name and what little I knew. I could see his disappointment grow at every key point, like no description of the driver, no license number, and inexact year on the car.

"Did you know the victim, Mr. Jackson?"

"Just met her. She was a customer, came to me to get a bond for her brother." I told him the gist of the situation, including the name of the yuppie-hating brother. The pencil scribbled on the wet pages, and the cop made a face when it didn't work right.

"Maybe you should try circling the drops first, so you don't run into them and get the lead wet," I said. He didn't.

"You say she had a violin?"

I nodded. "Carrying it under her right arm. The guy who got out of the car must have taken it." I noticed that the pencil had stopped moving altogether. Fair enough. Why struggle with wet paper, trying to write a statement that didn't make any sense? And it didn't. If somebody's going to mug you for a lousy violin, they don't hit you with two tons of metal first. Even if they don't give a damn about you, they could smash the instrument that way. And if the accident really is just an accident, then they don't get out and steal the violin, just to have a nice souvenir of the event. And finally, if it was purely a case of opportunistic theft, why hadn't they also taken her purse, which was right out there in front of God and everybody? I wouldn't write it down, either.

"Why would this guy stop to steal her violin?" said the cop.

My intellectual peer, obviously. Went right to the key question without even being led. A perceptive fellow, this beat-pounder.

"Because he thought it was valuable. Very valuable. It wasn't, really, because it wasn't the right one, but somebody thought it was supposed to be." Somebody who wasn't paying attention when Amy Cox and I went in and out of Nickel Pete's, or who couldn't see well enough in the rain, or was confused because there were two of us, or was busy taking a leak in a plastic bottle or using his fantastic cell phone technology to argue with his mother or his girlfriend. But by the time Ms. Cox left my office the second time, that somebody was back on the job, with a vengeance. But what was the job, exactly? Killing her?

"That still doesn't make any sense," said the cop.

I hate it when people steal my own arguments. But he was right, it didn't, and I had pushed my thinking as far as I could. I suddenly became aware of being very wet. There was a hissing sound in the back of my head that I gradually realized was a passing car, tires spraying road water. In the front of my head, my mouth was sticky-dry.

"Maybe you should get out of the rain, Mr. Jackson, sit down and collect your thoughts a bit."

Too damn right I should. But not with him. If I needed a ventriloquist's dummy, I'd go see what Pete had on hand. I pulled a soggy card from my pocket and gave it to the cop. "You can get me there most of the time if you have any more questions," I said. I pointed at my office. He looked at the card and nodded, and that was the end of the interview.

I have a room in the back of the office with a cot and a kitchenette and a closet with some spare clothes, for times when I'm sweating a round-the-clock skip-recovery case. I went straight there, without talking to Agnes on my way through the front.

I took off my tie and looked at it briefly, holding it out at arm's length. It used to be maroon, I think. I thanked it for long, if undistinguished, service, and threw it in the trash. I hung my suit coat on a hanger to dry, dumped my wet shirt on the floor, and toweled off my hair. Buttoning up a fresh shirt, I went back out into the reception room and poured myself the last of the toxic waste from the Mr. Coffee in the corner. I think it was a blend called Refried Dreams. After steeping half the day, it tasted the way corroded batteries look, but I barely noticed.

"Is the bond ready yet for Jimmy Cox?"

"All set," said Agnes. "You want me to take it over? You look like you could use a little down time."

I shook my head. "I'd rather be moving around a bit, while I'm trying to sort things out. Besides, delivering the bond is the closest thing to a dying request that I've ever had laid on me. Seems like I ought to do it myself."

"I saw the body bag. Did she suffer much?"

That was a very nice way of asking me if I had

botched up giving first aid. Suddenly everybody was being nice to me. Did they think that blunt trauma was contagious and I might have caught some? I shook my head again. "Bastards smashed her all to hell, squashed her like a nasty bug. Even a doctor couldn't have done anything for her."

"I wasn't accusing you of anything."

"You didn't have to. I'll probably do enough accusing for both of us. Just give me the bond."

I put the document in a zippered vinyl pouch with several others, put on my trenchcoat, grabbed the umbrella, and headed for the door.

"Maybe you ought to comb your hair."

"What for? The cops think I'm dopey-looking, anyway, and Amy Cox and her brother damn sure won't care."

Most arrests in the metro area are made by city cops, but the City, as such, has no courts. So the cases are charged and tried in the Ramsey County court system, and bail bonds are delivered to the County Sheriff's office. It's in one corner of the County Jail, which is a multi-story affair hung on the face of the stone river bluff. You can enter via a little pill box at street level or through a tunnel from the basement of the courthouse. I usually do pill box. I'm a regular customer there, and a tall, cute brunette deputy named Janice Whitney smiled at me when I came in. She used to be even cuter, before body armor became part of the regular uniform. Now she has no waist, and not much in the way of a bosom, either. Hazards of war, I guess. She logs in the bonds the same, either way, but it's not as much fun as it used to be. Nothing ever is.

"Hey, it's the ticket master," she said. "Neither rain nor sleet, and all that other bullshit."

"Hey, yourself, Jan. How's business?"

"Business is good. Maybe we should quit advertising."

"Maybe you should. Take that budget and use it for an office golf outing or something."

If I'd suggested a prayer meeting, I'd have gotten the same look. "I've been known to do a little swinging with my fellow workers," she said, "but not with any stupid golf club. What have you got for me?"

I opened the vinyl case, pulled out the stack of bonds, and dropped them on the counter. She took each one in turn, shoved it in a machine that stamped the date and time, then manually logged it into a green, hardcover day book. The Cox bond was the last one in the stack.

"You might be sticking your neck out a bit on this one," she said. "He only got arraigned this morning, and already I've heard about him. If he was any nuttier, they'd chop him up and make Snickers bars."

"Just a high-spirited kid, Jan. Misunderstood. Doesn't like Luds. Or maybe he does like them, I forget which way it works."

"Like Timothy McVeigh didn't like concrete?"

"McVeigh was a flat-earther, as I recall. Didn't like anything vertical. But he did like really big bangs. The two guys are nothing alike."

"You're right about that. McVeigh knew enough to keep his mouth shut in court. Not Cox."

"Well, it doesn't matter now, anyway. The bond is paid for, and I can't refund it, so you might as well go ahead and log it in."

"Your funeral. I'm just saying, watch this one. You want me to have him mustered out through here, so you can meet him, maybe give him a little pep talk?"

Her eyes flashed wickedly. What she really meant was that she would give me a chance to slip a tracer bug into the guy's pocket. It was something she never officially knew about and I never officially did. After-wards, I sometimes took her out to a fancy candlelight dinner, just to keep her feeling unofficially rewarded. It pays to have friends in the working end of the power structure. Better than in high places, any day.

"Thanks anyway, Jan, but they've probably already pulled him out of the lockup. His sister just got run over by a Ford tank, and they'll be looking for some-body to ID the body."

"Are you serious?"

"Happened right out there, less than an hour ago."
I pointed at the now-deserted street.

"Oh, wow, that one? I was outside having a
smoke, and I saw the paramedics come. That was the
Monkey-boy's sister, huh? What a funny world. Makes
you think, doesn't it?"

"It made Amy Cox stop thinking."

It didn't have that effect on me. The Sheriff's office
was not the place for heavy meditation, though, and
neither was my own place. I mumbled some kind of
farewell to Deputy Janice and wandered back out into
the rain. Five blocks and three corners later, I found
myself at the entrance to Lefty's Billiard Parlor.

Lefty's is a real, old-fashioned pool hall, where
you buy time on the tables from a teller, rather than
constantly stuffing coins in a slot. That means you can
still play straight pool, and you can abide by the clas-
sical rules for scratch shots, whatever game you play.
The place is also one long flight of rickety, dark stairs
up from street level, a tradition in pool halls that I've
never understood. A regulation table weighs over a
ton, so why put it on the second story, where you have
to reinforce the floor and hoist the table in through
a skylight, with a crane? Maybe it makes it harder to
break the lease, is all I can think. And it damn sure

discourages anybody from stealing a table.

Anyhow, Lefty's is a walkup joint, in strict violation of the federal handicap access laws, and it's as good a place as I know to go practice on a quiet corner table and let the click of the balls knit your unraveled thoughts back together. Unlike Ames' in *The Hustler*, it also has a bar and a decent grill, though Lefty will watch you like a hawk and charge you if you spill grease or ketchup on his precious green felt. Beer he doesn't seem to mind. There's also a sign by the upper entry that says, "This is a Smoke-Free Establishment. Any Smoke You Find Here is Absolutely Free." Lefty isn't real big on regulations, other than his own.

It was late afternoon by the time I walked in, and some guy I didn't know was tending bar and keeping time on the tables, all by himself. I ordered a shot of vodka and a Guinness. I downed the shot and took just a sip of the stout, to give it a bit of after-flavor. Dark brews, I have always thought, are for sipping and contemplation. If your pint doesn't get up to room temperature before you finish it, you're drinking it too fast. White liquor, by contrast, is for impact, to start the negotiating process with the back of your mind. It has no other qualities, and there's no point in savoring it.

I got a rack of balls for an empty table by the windows and another shot to take with me. I told the bartender to take his time getting me a California burger with extra onions and some lattice fries. Then I laid out the balls on the table, planted my drinks on the window sill, and picked out a house cue from a rack on the wall. It was a bit heavier than I usually like, but it was only warped in one direction and looked like somebody had actually chalked the tip now and then.

Two tables over, Wide Track Wilkie was shooting a game of nine ball with some Asian kid, while the kid's girlfriend watched. He looked like he was doing some serious hustling and didn't need any interference, which was fine with me. Wilkie is a three-hundred-plus pound movable barrier of African and Puerto Rican descent, with more in the mix. I was just as glad he was in St. Paul, because I occasionally like to hire him as a bounty hunter. Besides that and hustling pool, I have no idea what he does for a living.

In another part of the room, some teenagers were doing a bad imitation of playing snooker, and clowning around about their own ineptitude. Otherwise, the place was empty. There was no jukebox or piped-in Muzak, just the click of the balls and the whir of overhead fans and whatever the players had to say. In that respect, Lefty's is just like Ames'. You want to be surrounded by sound, go to a rave.

I put the belly of the warped cue stick downward and stroked a nice, clean break. Not a money break. I almost never sink anything on the break, and I've given up trying. That's why I like the longer games—rotation or straight pool—where there's time for a few wild cards to emerge and enough pauses to work the opposition's head a little. I studied the spread after the break for a while and decided I was shooting eight ball. Ten shots later, my burger came, in a cute little basket that looked like it was made for holding a fancy wine bottle. The no-name bartender put it down on the window sill, next to my drinks, along with another basket that had napkins, salt and pepper in heavy glass shakers, and ketchup in a wide-mouthed jar instead of one of those plastic squeeze bottles. Lefty's is a classy place.

I ate about half of the burger, punctuating the last chew of each mouthful with a little bit of alcohol and foam. It was good stuff, and my body was grateful for it, but my eyes kept wandering back to the table. I didn't consciously decide to put the food down, but pretty soon I was back to staring down the cue stick, sizing up a long, single-cushion shot on the ten ball. Going into my spatial meditation mode.

Shots with a lot of open green are a kind of Zen thing for me. At first, I can't see the angle and can't compute my way to it, either. Might as well shoot with my eyes closed. But if I wait, take my time, and sort of *identify* with the space of the setup, suddenly the line will reveal itself to me and I absolutely can't miss. When I drop the ball, it will look like a lucky fluke, but luck has nothing to do with it. I did a few practice strokes and waited for the line to appear. Did luck have anything to do with Amy Cox? A lot of long green on that table. Much less on Jimmy Cox's bond. Eighteen K is little people's dreams, not the stuff of conspiracy or murder. Sixty gets a bit more interesting, but whoever killed Amy wouldn't actually get their hands on even the eighteen, much less the big money. *Did I use enough chalk? You have to put it on before you go out in the rain. Otherwise it won't stick, and you'll wind up like…*Jesus, where did that come from? And why couldn't I see the line yet?

The felt turned a slightly darker shade of green, and I looked up to see two guys blocking the light from the window. Closest to me, looking as if he expected something, was a big, shapeless, forty-something guy with an oversized head and puffy, babylike features. The kind of guy that will still look like Baby Huey when he's eighty. Scowl marks by the mouth and eyes told me that he worked a bit too hard at overcoming that image. The other guy was smaller in every dimension, with dark, stringy hair and a gaunt face that looked like a poster for European famine relief. As if he had read my mind, he made a show of eating the rest of my burger.

Both guys had brimmed hats pulled low and semi-respectable topcoats that were bulky enough to hide all kinds of hardware. And they were both working very hard at looking mean and serious. Was I about to be leaned on? What the hell for? I looked over to where Wide Track was still shooting with the Asian kids. If he had picked up on the situation, he made no sign, but then, he wouldn't. Hollow Cheeks spoke first, while Babyface continued to stare me down.

"Good burger. Get me another one, will you?"

"You think so?" I said. "I put it down after I thought I saw something moving in the onions, but maybe that was just my imagination."

"Bullshit." Obviously, not the captain of his high school debating team. I continued to bend over and sight down the pool cue, only now I was visually measuring its length against the distance between me and the big guy.

"You Herman Jackson?" Babyface, this time.

"Who's asking, exactly?" Too far. I needed to get about two feet closer, for a really effective swing.

"Detective Evans, Homicide. My partner over there, with the tape worm, is Stroud. We gotta show you our badges?"

"If we're talking business here, that would be the professional way to proceed, wouldn't it?" I stood partway up, but I didn't let go of the cue stick.

Evans made a show of looking put out, but he pulled a gold badge out of an inner pocket and gave me all of a three-second look at it. His partner gave me an even shorter look at his. I tried to think of a recent homicide case that I had carried a bond on, but I was coming up empty. "Did one of my customers show up missing?"

"Not as far as I know. We're here about the woman who got killed in front of your office today."

I finally let go of the cue and stood up. "Amy Cox," I said. "You've decided to call it a murder?"

"Yeah, we call it murder. But we don't call her Amy Cox. And we're very interested to know why you do."

"How about because that's who she is? Get a clue here, detectives. Haven't you talked to her brother yet?"

"We talked to a James Cox, recently released on a bond provided by you."

"And?"

"He says he doesn't have a sister."

"What?" Now it was my turn to say "bullshit," but I didn't want to sound just as lame as Detective Stroud. "Did you make him go look at the body anyway?"

"You're not too bright, are you, Jackson?" Stroud was shifting away from the window, towards me. I think he was trying to be menacing, but he didn't have the stature or the presence for it. "If he doesn't have a sister, he can't exactly tell us if that's her, can he?"

"We made him look," said Evans, ignoring his partner.

"And?"

"Says he never saw her before."

"Then why would she hock her heirloom violin to bail him out?"

"Well, we don't really know that she did, do we?"

"No," said Stroud, now moving around so he and his partner flanked me at the table. "Alls we know is what Jackson here told the officer at the scene."

"Officer Krupke?" I said. That wasn't the officer's name, of course, but it seemed like a clever thing to say.

"Yeah, Krupke," said Stroud. "Good cop, but he don't always know to ask the right questions."

Oops. If that didn't clinch it for me, it should have.

"So we're thinking," said Evans, "that you maybe ought to just show us the contract you had the woman sign."

"And maybe the violin you say she gave you for security, too," said Stroud.

"And maybe you'd like to show me a warrant," I said.

"Maybe we could get one."

"Maybe you couldn't, too. What do you think you have probable cause to suspect, anyway, issuing a bond to the wrong client?" I bent back down and took the shot on the ten ball, missing it badly. *Wait for the Zen moment, Jackson?* But the new lie of the balls gave me an excuse to move out from between my new friends and take a stance by the opposite rail. As I moved around the table, I looked over at the ongoing nine ball game. Wide Track Wilkie was nowhere to be seen. I began to get a very bad feeling in my gut that had nothing to do with Lefty's onions.

"Murder," said Evans.

"We agree about that," I said, bending down to sight the new shot, again measuring the geometry of space and bodies. "So why aren't you guys out checking body shops and outstanding traffic warrants?"

"Because the car didn't kill her," said Stroud.

"Excuse me all to hell," I said, mentally adding *you dumb shits*. "I was there, remember? I saw them put her in a body bag."

"Oh, she was dead, all right. Wasn't she, Detective Stroud?"

"Dead, Detective Evans. Broken neck. But it wasn't broken by any car. According to the M.E., somebody did it to her with his hands, real up-close and personal, like."

"We think maybe it was you," said Evans. "So, like we were saying, we think maybe you better show us that contract."

"And that violin," said Stroud.

The room was starting to feel very small. "I think

you're both so full of shit your eyeballs are brown," I said. "I don't believe the M.E. has even looked at her yet. I want to see the medical report."

"Oh, we'll do better than that," said Evans. "We'll take you down to the Morgue, and you can see for yourself. We'll go there on our way to the precinct, to talk it all out."

"After he gives…" began Stroud.

"Shows," corrected Evans.

"…yeah, shows us the violin."

They were single-minded goons, I had to give them that. "Am I under arrest?" I said.

"You want to be?"

I thought about it for a minute. Forcing them into one more formality might slow them down a bit, but I didn't need the extra handicap of wearing cuffs. And I now had no doubt that I was going to have to go with them, whether I insisted on formalities or not. "No," I said, "but I want to call my lawyer."

"Be our guest."

They would say that, wouldn't they? Especially since we all knew we weren't going anywhere near any cop station. I went over to the bar and asked non-Lefty for a phone. He produced one from somewhere in or near the sink and plonked it down on the polished top with his dishwater-wrinkled hand, saying, "No long-distance."

"The least of my needs," I said.

I figured they'd notice and cut me off if I dialed 9-1-1, so I called my own office instead, and mentally cursed when I got my voice mail. After the piercing little beep, I said, "Listen, Agnes, get ahold of the cops as fast as you can. I'm about to be abducted from Lefty's Poolhall by a couple of thugs posing as police detectives." I gave her a quick description of my companions, including the names they were using. "After the cops, call Nickel Pete and tell him not to give the Amati to anybody, including me, unless I'm alone. Then call every damn bounty hunter we ever use and tell them…"

"Done yet?" Evans loomed over me like a glacier about to calve.

"Not quite."

"I think you are." He pushed the button on the receiver cradle, and the phone went dead. I hung up and shrugged into my trenchcoat, which he had thoughtfully brought from the back of the hall, and we proceeded to the door. There wasn't a lot else I could do. I began to wonder if I had any of my electronic tracer gizmos in my pocket. They wouldn't help my present situation much, but I thought it might be nice if somebody found my corpse.

Chapter Three

The Zen Moment

The stairway to Lefty's is too narrow for three people to go abreast, so the skinny guy went ahead of us while Babyface Evans stayed tight to me, on my left and slightly behind. He didn't poke a gun in my ribs, but I figured he had one handy, if not already out. Stroud didn't use the handrail, and I thought about how easy it would be to reach my foot out, tap the back of one of his knees, and send him crashing down the rest of the flight. Then I would only have the big guy to take out.

Tempting. A lot of people assume that since bonding is a nonviolent, even sedentary profession, all of us are flabby little wimps who haven't been in a fight since the age of seven and would faint dead away at the sight of a gun. In a lot of cases, it's true. "Nothing but Milquetoast, on the gravy train," is the saying.

I grew up in a neighborhood where people thought *The Godfather* was a sitcom. Becoming a bondsman was a way of graduating, not running away, from my own violent past. If these two thugs didn't know that, it could give me a significant edge. But only once. Not yet, I decided, since I couldn't see what Evans was doing until I was already committed to a move. But soon. It had to be soon, or it wouldn't work at all.

We clumped down the sloped shaft and out onto the street, where both the daylight and the rain were running out of juice. Somewhere in the distance, some noisy pigeons were announcing the end of the deluge. I don't know if any of them had an olive branch in his beak. Parked at the curb was a massive Chevy of the kind the cops use a lot, a Caprice or some such model, but without the extra bells and whistles. What it did have was a right rear tire that was flatter than my Aunt Hannah's bra. When Evans and I came out the door, Stroud was already looking at it, fists on his hips, as if he had never seen such a calamity before. Evans acted more like he had seen a lot of them and took them all as personal insults.

"Look at that, man. Is that all we need, or what? I mean, my God."

"I see it, Stroud. I'm sharp on that kind of shit, you know? Picked right up on it."

"So, what do we do?"

"We? What I do, is I babysit our friend here. What you do is, you change the tire. That's what *we* do."

"Why's it always me that's got to do the hard stuff?"

"Yeah, why does he?" I asked. Not that I gave a damn who changed the stupid tire. I just liked the way the partnership was coming unglued, and I thought I'd help it along a bit.

Evans ignored me and glared at Stroud. "Why?" he said. "Because you're a sneaky, lazy, stupid Rom who isn't worth the powder to blow you to hell or the match to touch it off with, that's why. Because you've screwed up this operation from day one, and you probably drove over something to blow that tire, too. And because if you don't, I'm going to kick your skinny little ass around the block a few times, just to keep my foot from going to sleep. Is that enough 'whys' for you?"

I wondered what a Rom was, but I figured it wasn't a good time to ask.

"Your time's gonna come," said Stroud. But his voice had no conviction, and he was already putting the key in the trunk lock.

"And when it gets here, I'll kick your ass, then, too," said Evans.

He had taken a step away from me, to intimidate his partner better, and I was considering what to do about that when Stroud popped open the trunk on the Chevy and got instantly sucked into it like a dust bunny into a vacuum cleaner pipe.

"What in hell…" said Evans.

I didn't care what in hell. I clipped him in the back of the knee, the way I had wanted to do to Stroud on the stairs, and as he was dropping to the pavement, I pretended his head was a soccer ball and the car was a goal net. I didn't know how hard I kicked him, and I didn't care. Three seconds later, I was around the corner and running like a scared rabbit.

I turned into an alley a couple of blocks away and chanced a look back. Nobody was following me. I slowed down to a trot and then a walk, looking for a place to hide among the trash bins, piles of junk, and service doors. I liked what I saw. Lots of back doors in that alley, and lots of fire escape ladders. Too many places for a pair of pursuers to check by themselves, unless they already had a glimpse of their quarry.

The smell of fresh rain mixed with that of old garbage, plus something else that took me a minute to identify, something sweet and vaguely oily. Glycol, I decided. Antifreeze.

Parked tight to a brick wall a half block away was an ancient ton-and-a-half truck with the back of the cab cut off and a square, homemade, windowless van body crudely grafted to the frame. The sides were badly warped plywood, covered with faded-out slogans and biblical quotations, done in an amateur sign-painting hand. Or maybe they weren't exactly biblical. One said,

"He that bloweth not his own horn, Neither shall it be Blown." Another was something, mostly unreadable, about strumpets sounding at "the crank of dawn" and the "Horn of Babylon" having something to do with the "Car Lot of Jerusalem." Across the back was one that had been renewed several times, in several colors. It simply said, "Yah! Is My God!" The plywood looked grateful for any paint it could get. Near the front of the vehicle, green fluid trickled down onto the pavement and formed a small stream that meandered towards the center of the alley, producing the smell I had noticed. If the truck wasn't already a goner, it was definitely bleeding to death. Yah, with or without exclamation mark, was clearly not the god of radiators. I decided the truck looked like a good blind, and I followed the slimy green path.

Sitting on what was left of the rear bumper was a black man who could have been any age except young, reading a battered paperback that had no cover, and absent-mindedly stirring a pot of something on a Coleman camp stove. He looked up at my approach, huge, fierce eyes peering through a tangle of dark locks.

"Praise Yah!" he said, putting plenty of breath into it.

"Yeah?"

"You pronounce it wrong, pilgrim." His voice had a rich, melodic quality. It wasn't strident enough for a preacher, but it definitely got your attention.

"There's a lot of that going around."

"You making fun of me, asshole?"

"No."

"Lucky for you." He grinned, the whitest teeth I've ever seen accenting his dense beard. Then he chuckled. "But you're right, too. There is a lot of that going around. A lot of damn heathens in this valley of sorrows." He took the pot off the fire and stood up, offering his hand. "I'm the Prophet," he said. "No doubt, you've read my work."

"No doubt." His hand was frail, almost bird-like, but his grip was firm. "Listen," I said, "I need…"

"I knew you were coming here."

"Of course you did." I turned to watch the alley behind me. I was still clear, but I absolutely did not have time for this kind of crap.

"Yah! told me."

"Well he would, wouldn't he? Listen…"

"A man in a shitload of trouble, said Yah! A man in need of sanctuary. A man with a riddle."

"Right. I don't suppose Yah told you what to do about him?" I didn't bother to ask if Yah had told him all that before or after he saw me out of breath and looking over my shoulder.

"Yah! does not meddle in the affairs of Caesar."

"What the hell does that mean?"

"Twenty bucks to hide in the truck for an hour."

"Seems like sanctuary is a pretty good business."

"It has a trap door in the floor and spy holes in all four sides."

"Deal."

While he unhooked the padlock on the flimsy door, I reached in my wallet and pulled out two twenties. "If trouble is still following me," I said, "it's going to be here a lot sooner than an hour. When that happens, I could use a bit of diverting bullshit, okay?"

"I am a prophet and a holy man, brother." He straightened up and solemnly laid a palm against his breast. "Bullshit, I got." He took the twenties and ushered me inside.

I stepped into a cluttered space lit by a tiny plastic skylight that doubled as a vent. When the Prophet closed the door again, I could see that each wall had not one, but two spy holes, one with a wide-angle lens, like a hotel or apartment door, and one that was just a plain hole. There was a four-legged stool on the floor, and I put it by the back door, planted myself on it, and looked out. The Prophet went back to reading his book and cooking his potion. When I didn't see any other action for ten minutes or so, I looked around the interior a bit. The trap door was easy enough to spot, if you were looking for it. It was off to one side, presumably to miss the drive shaft. That's if the truck still had a drive shaft. It looked like it hadn't moved for several decades and if it did, about half a ton of junk would immediately wind up on the floor, along with the flimsy roof. It smelled like dust and brake fluid and old, damp paper. Somehow, that seemed right for an ersatz holy man's cave.

I looked again at the spy holes. The plain ones were about an inch in diameter and just down and to the right of those with the fish-eye lenses. Just the right size and location for a gun muzzle, I thought. Did my man the Prophet go in for holy wars? I was about to turn away from the hole and have a closer look at the cabinets on the walls, when I saw something move outside.

The big Chevy nosed into the alley, bouncing heavily on its springs, stalking, sniffing. It straightened out and cruised straight at us, taking its time.

"Tally ho," I said through the hole.

"Trust in Yah!" said the Prophet. "And keep your ass down."

When the car got within twenty feet of my hidey hole, it stopped. The driver's door opened and a shape emerged. And emerged some more. A bigger shape than the phony cop, by at least a hundred pounds. Apparently, Wide Track Wilkie hadn't abandoned me, after all.

"Praise Yah!" said the prophet.

"What's he done for me lately?" Wilkie wasn't big on chit chat, as a rule.

"He has led you to me."

"Yeah? Well, you better hope he doesn't tell me to stay. I'm looking for a guy might have run by here fifteen minutes ago."

"Might have. You can build a universe on 'might have,' pilgrim. Perhaps you've read my theological work on islands of alternate consciousness in the bicameral…"

"Look into my eyes, asshole." He came close enough for the man to do exactly that. "Do I look like a philosopher, to you? Do I look patient?"

"Up," said the Prophet, backing against the truck.

"Up what?"

"A hunted man always goes up. It's a primal instinct." He stretched out a bony arm to point at the fire escapes on the other side of the alley, and Wilkie backed off a half a step.

"Which one?" said Wilkie.

"On the back of the locksmith shop."

"That's more like it." He turned on his heel and strode away, his tent-like coat billowing out behind him like the wake of a garbage scow.

I decided the show was over, so I opened the door and stepped out. "Nice to see you, Wide," I said.

"Hey, Herman." He spun around and smiled. "I thought you looked like you didn't like your blind date much, up there in Lefty's, so I stowed away in the limo. Was that okay?"

"Much more than okay."

"Glad you think so, because that was a really horseshit little space. I don't know why they can't make a vehicle with a bigger trunk."

"Like a Euclid truck?"

"Just like that." He came back over to the truck and gave me a bear hug that fractured a rib or two. "You all right, man?"

"I was, until you did that. Where's my two new friends?"

"The big guy is having a little nap in the trunk. I took his gun and the other stuff out of his pockets, just so he wouldn't be too uncomfortable."

"Very considerate. What about his partner?"

"He took off, after I made him change the tire. Never saw a man so scared of a little bit of work."

"You think that was smart?"

"Making him change the tire?"

"Letting him go."

"Well, I thought if I bopped him one, he might just get chickenshit later on, and finger me for assault. He looked like that kind of wuss. And he isn't going anywhere very far, right away. Seems to have lost all his clothes, poor bastard. Also his money and ID."

"Shoes, too?"

"Hey, am I a thorough professional, or what?"

I laughed out loud at the image of Stroud padding

down the sidewalk in his bare feet and skivvies.

The Prophet seemed to like it, too, and he added, "The wolves shall devour each other, and the loin shall lie down with the limb."

"I got my twenty bucks' worth of bullshit already," I said.

"Me, too," said Wilkie. "Go preach to a stone, or something." Turning to me, he said, "So, what's the story, Herman? I could see you needed some cavalry back there, but that wasn't your usual kind of action, to say the least."

"Tell me about it," I said. I filled him in on the high points of the day's events. The Prophet also leaned into the conversation, as if he were an old conspirator. Wilkie gave him a dirty look now and then, but otherwise left him alone. I decided it couldn't hurt to have a possibly crazy person listening in on a definitely crazy story, and I left him alone, too.

"What the hell is going on?" said Wilkie, when I had finished.

"Well put," I said. "I haven't a clue."

"What's in the trunk?" said the Proph.

"An unhappy camper," said Wilkie. "The other stuff, I put in the back seat."

"And it is…?" I said.

"Interesting," said Wilkie. He led us over to the car and opened the back door.

"The little guy…"

"You mean Stroud," I said.

"Stroud, my ass. The guy had a briefcase full of phony ID, some of it pretty good, and his own little printing press and art supplies for making some more." He pointed to a pile of papers and cards in an open case. "He's got more damn names than a downtown law firm. Look at this: James Stroud, Strom Jameson, Tom Wade, Wade Thomas—you see a bit of a pattern here?—James Cox…"

"James Cox? Are you sure?"

"Sure, I'm sure. That's one of his better sets, even has a real-looking driver's license. Is that important?"

"Son of a bitch," I said.

"Which one?" said the Proph.

"That's the name of the guy I wrote the bond for."

"I take it, you don't believe in coincidence," said Wilkie.

"Do you?"

"Never," said Wilkie.

"Always," said the Proph.

"There's more," said Wilkie. "The little guy was carrying, a great big nine-millie Browning High Power, looks like it weighs more than he does. Only it's a phony."

"It's not a real Browning?"

"Hell, it's not even a real gun. All plastic, shoots gumball pellets or some damn thing. His badge is also phony, but it's an awfully good one. A casting, probably. An exact replica of the one the big guy had."

"I don't think I like where this is going," I said.

"You're right. You don't like it at all. As far as I can tell, your other guy, Evans, is a real cop. Real badge, real gun, and probably real mad when he wakes up."

"Oh, shit."

"That's about it, all right."

"How's your workload these days, Wide?"

"You owe me two hundred."

"How's that, exactly?"

"That's what I figure the Korean kid was good for, if I hadn't had to leave the nine ball game early."

Wilkie was a lot better pool player when he was figuring than when he was shooting, but I let it pass. Two hundred for an impromptu deliverance was a good deal, any day. We were sitting in the Chevy, me and Wilkie in the back seat and the Proph behind the wheel, pretending he was Yah's road warrior, making motor noises in his throat. Nobody seemed to know what to do next. Is it the Navy, where they teach people, "Do something, even if it's wrong?" One of those fanatical outfits, anyway. I was starting to feel that way. Somebody had sucked me into a game without telling me the rules, and it was pissing me off. I wanted to be the shooter, for a change, even if I couldn't see the Zen line.

"I'll tell Agnes to cut you a check," I said.

"I like the other stuff better, if it's all the same to you. The green stuff that the government doesn't know about."

"No problem," I said. "You need it right away? If so, I've got to go run an errand."

"Tomorrow's good enough. Leave it with Agnes, if you're not around."

"Fair enough. Besides that, do you need a job?"

"Like checking up on a real cop who travels with a phony one?"

"Maybe."

"I can't do that."

"You've worked for me plenty of times before."

"Yeah, but only bounty hunting. Any fool can do that. But to do investigating, you need a PI license. A carry permit is nice to have, too. You get caught with an unregistered gun when you're chasing a bail-jumping scumbag, they might not even take it away from you. But you get caught carrying heat while you're investigating somebody, you're in deep shit, dig?"

"For somebody who just stuffed a cop in a trunk, you're awfully scrupulous, all of a sudden."

"Hey, you're the one who kicked him. Anyway,

I've been officially warned, okay?"

"Ah. But only warned about doing PI work?"

"That's it."

"I'm hip."

"Vroooom," said the Proph.

"Shut up," said Wilkie.

"So, how's your workload?" I said.

"I could use some."

"I've got some for you. You don't know anything about the fiddle or the phony-cop-real-cop affair, okay?"

"What affair is that?"

"Exactly. This is a bounty hunting job."

"That's what I do, all right. Who am I hunting?"

"Amy Cox."

"Not her brother?"

"We seem to be able to find him, easily enough. Whether we want to or not."

"Her, too. Isn't she in the morgue?"

"You don't know that, and you're going to forget to look there. Assume that's somebody else. I want the real Amy Cox. Find her and bring her in, and I'll give you five thousand."

"And if she can't be found?"

"Then give me some progress reports, and I'll give you a partial payment."

"What kind of progress reports?"

"Detailed ones. What you found out along the way."

"Written?"

"Absolutely not."

"Herman, my man, you are definitely on."

"Are you going to be wanting this car anymore?" said the Proph.

We thought about it for a minute.

"I got my own wheels," said Wilkie. "Three blocks back. What about you, Herm?"

"I never did like Chevrolets." I looked at the gleeful figure behind the wheel. "What are you going to do with it?" I asked him.

"There are some truths that even a pilgrim should not seek. Vroom!"

"I don't think he trusts us," said Wilkie.

"Look, Mr. Prophet…"

"The Prophet is only the Prophet," said the prophet.

"Fine," I said. "Listen, Prophet, I couldn't care less what happens to the car, but I'm not going to be party to a murder here, of a cop or anybody else."

"Trust in Yah!"

"I'd prefer a statement of intent."

"The karma of the man in the trunk is mystically linked with the sidewalk in front of the emergency entrance at United Hospital."

"Will his karma get him there?"

"If not, his car will. But it will not wait around to rejoice in his enlightenment."

"That, I can accept."

"He will learn much from it." He quit making motor noises and nodded solemnly.

"What do you want to do with all this other junk?" said Wilkie.

The proph looked at me hopefully.

"Leave Evans his badge and gun," I said.

"That works," said Wilkie. "Cops get vicious as hell, you take that stuff away. Better leave him his wallet, too."

"I am not leaving him any bullets," said the proph.

I was impressed. Pearls of wisdom come out of the oddest shells, sometimes.

"Throw the rest of the stuff back in the briefcase," I said. "I'll hang onto it for now. Maybe there's a clue in there somewhere."

"So that's it?" said Wilkie. "Are we done for now?" He hoisted his bulk up from the back seat and started making departure motions.

"One other thing," I said. "Ever hear of a Rom?"

"You mean, like a computer thing?"

"I don't think so. I think it's some kind of a person."

"Never heard of the bum. I'm out of here, okay?"

"Later," I said. I watched him walk down the alley, then looked back over at my new Chevrolet owner, who seemed to be pondering some deep truth.

"It's not a person," he said, "it's a scourge."

"You mean Wilkie? He's okay, when you get to know him."

"Not him. The Rom. If they are here, then truly, the barbarians have breached the gate."

"Would you care to elaborate on that?"

"I'm in the elaboration business, Pilgrim."

"Call me Herman."

"Then, let me tell you how the world will end, Herman."

"Is this going to take long?"

"Absolutely."

"How about a short version?"

"Okay. If you meet a Rom on the road, kill him."

Chapter Four

High Road to Chinatown

I wanted to hear what the Proph had to say about the Rom, but I really didn't have the time. I suddenly remembered the phone message I had left with Agnes, and I could think of a hundred good reasons why I wanted to stop her before she acted on it.

"Listen," I said to the Proph, who was still behind the wheel, "I need a quick lift back to my office. You think you can come down from the mountain long enough to handle that?"

"Chauffeuring is not a path to spiritual enlightenment. It'll cost you."

"In a Buddha's eye, it will. I already gave you forty bucks and a car. You can afford to spot me a freebie."

"Your karma must be high. You are profound."

"I'm also right."

"That, too. Pull in your feet, shut the door, and navigate."

He was off before I had time to do any of those things. He drove like a kid playing a video game of the kind where you get three free crashes before you're really dead. But I noticed that he also checked his mirrors a lot and kept his hands on the two-and ten-o'clock positions on the wheel. In some ways, at least, he was not the lunatic he seemed. I gave him directions and advice which he mostly ignored, and three minutes later, we were in front of my office. I was ready to leap out, commando-style, in case he forgot to stop, but he came to a normal halt and even waited around for a minute and talked to me through the window.

"Do you really want to know about the Rom?" he asked.

"You tell me. Do I?"

"A good answer. The true pilgrim does not know the name of his own quest. Yes, you do want to know. But you don't want to mess with them, no, no, no."

"Exactly how would I go about learning without messing?"

"You would need a guide,"

"And I'll just bet I know where I'm going to get one, too, don't I?"

"It's possible I know somebody. Only possible. Give me a day to see if I can set up a meeting."

"All right. Do I check back with you in the alley, or what?"

"I will find you."

I thought about the undead body in the trunk and what it might do when it became reanimated. "In a day, I may have to be making myself hard to find."

"Yah! will tell me where you are."

"Silly me. How could I have forgotten?"

"Keep the faith, Herman." And he was gone in a cloud of very nonspiritual exhaust. I think he was aiming for a lightpost in the middle of the next block. I wondered what faith it was he wanted me to keep.

I turned back to the office and saw Agnes standing in the doorway, her face the image of sisterly concern and possible disapproval. It's not always her most attractive expression, but this time, it looked terrific. Or maybe I was just glad to be alive to see it.

"Is everything all right, Herman? There were two detectives here looking for you earlier. Pushy, nasty types. I told them I thought you were gone for the day."

"I thought I was gone for good, for a while there. I take it you haven't listened to your voice mail?"

"Not lately. Should I? I always check the email first. It's so much easier to sort."

"I left you a message, telling you I was in a lot of trouble."

"You should have left me an email. You can highlight the urgent messages with a little picture of a red envelope, you know."

"I'll remember that next time I'm stranded in the jungle. Erase the voice mail, okay?"

"Should I listen to it first?"

"Probably not. It would just upset you."

"Then I'll erase it tomorrow, if it's all the same to you. I was just going to lock up for the day. I'm late as it is."

I gave her a raised eyebrow that said, "You have a date?" and she gave me one raised even higher that said, "None of your damn business." Did I mention that I don't cope all that well with the fairer sex?

"You go on, Aggie. I'll close up shop. Wide Track Wilkie will be in sometime tomorrow, by the way, and…"

"You mean Wendell?"

"He's a Wendell? Wow. All these years, I never suspected him of anything of the sort."

"I really am late, Herman."

"So you said. Okay, Wendell, if you insist, will be by tomorrow. If I'm not around, give him two hundred dollars, cash, and copies of all the stuff we got from Amy Cox."

"Including the ID?"

"Especially the ID."

"What's going on, Herman?"

"That's what he's going to try to find out. Go keep your appointment, why don't you? We'll talk tomorrow."

We said good night and she headed down the street towards the Garrick Ramp, where her Toyota waited to thank her properly for keeping it out of the rain. I went inside the office, locking the door behind me and throwing Stroud's briefcase on the desk. Suddenly, it was feeling like an awfully long day, and I killed the main lights, closed the safe, and headed for the cot in the back room. I think I got my whole body on it before I fell asleep. If not, it was close enough.

It was more like falling into a bottomless hole than sleep. When I woke up, it was full-blown night, and the room was lit only by a bit of spilled light from the neon sign in the front office. It took me a while to remember where I was, even longer to remember why. As the pieces of the day came back, first grudgingly and then with greater ease, I went to the sink and washed my face, then changed out of my rumpled clothes and thought about what to do next. Going home seemed like more trouble than it was worth, and there wasn't anybody waiting for me there, in any case. I went into the front office to see if Agnes had shut down her computer for the night. Stroud's briefcase was where I had left it, and I flipped it open and rifled idly through the contents, looking for some inspiration. Not finding any, I put the phony badge in my pocket, to look it over later, and went over to the computer.

The screen on the monitor was dark, but when I fooled with a few keys, it came to life, showing the in-box on the email. It reminded me of what Agnes had said, and I wondered if we might be on the brink of an age when an arrested criminal will demand a laptop, rather than a phone. Brave new squirrels.

There were several unopened new messages. As far as I was concerned, they could stay that way until morning. Except for one, that caught my eye because it had the little red envelope-picture that Agnes had told me about. It also had a return address that included COX in the middle of a lot of other jumbled letters. I sat down in front of the monitor, grabbed the mouse, and did a double click on that line. I don't know how to do much on Agnes' machine, but what I do know, I know all to hell. The incoming message, what little there was of it, filled a new window.

> *mr. jackson,*
>
> *i believe you are in possession of a certain valuable musical instrument that is the rightful property of my family.*
>
> *i understand that you acquired it in good faith, and i am prepared to reward you handsomely for its return.*
>
> *can we talk?*

That was it. No name, no phone number, no particulars at all. It didn't even come right out and say the word "Amati." From whom were we keeping secrets, I wondered? I stared at the message for a while, not sure how to react. My first instinct was that it had "Phony" stamped all over it. But my instincts have been wrong before, so I decided not to erase it just yet. I might decide later that I wanted to reply to it, after all, so I left it where it was and shut down the machine. I forget why. Agnes must have told me once that it was a good thing to do.

By now, my stomach was waking up also, reminding me that I hadn't had anything to eat since the half hamburger at Lefty's, about two years ago. It was pushing eleven-thirty. Joe Bock's hot dog cart, which he fondly referred to as "Bock's Car," would have been rolled away for the night a long time ago, and Lew's Half-Deli and C-store down the street and The Downtowner Café would likewise be closed. There were a few bars downtown, besides Lefty's, where you could get a sandwich or a microwave pizza, but I didn't feel like bar food. And I definitely didn't feel like Lefty's. I decided to take a walk. This isn't a big enough city to have a Chinatown, but we do have an area of mixed Asian, Italian, Irish, and Unaligned Redneck, where some of the joints are open late, and I thought a stroll in the night air might clear my head. I put on a light windbreaker and left, locking the door behind me.

I headed west, past the Courthouse and the County Jail, past high-rise offices with selective blocks of floors lit up for the night cleaning crews, past the Central Library that looks like the Bank of England and the Catholic soup kitchen that looks like nothing at all, towards the oldest part of the city. The semaphores got farther apart after a while, the street lights were replaced by antique replicas that worked just as badly as the originals, and the canopy of dark sky got closer to street level, trying to take over completely. Past Seven Corners, it had almost succeeded. But then an island of light appeared in the distance, a jumble of color and glitter, like a beacon across a dark sea. West Seventh, calling to all the wandering barks of the night, all the lost vessels laden with the pilgrims of the square world. Jesus, I was starting to sound like the Proph. So much for the night air clearing my head.

The jumble of lights resolved itself into a strip of shops and restaurants, and my stomach urged me to up my pace a bit. I didn't have a favorite place here, but I wasn't feeling all that fussy. One that was open for business and served food would be good. If the food was good, that would be even better. The nearest one had a red-painted storefront with curtained windows and a neon sign that proclaimed it to be Shanghai. And it had seemed like such a short walk. Across the street was a place with only incandescent lights and a no-color front. It was called the Happy Dragon, and it had several hand-lettered signs in the windows:

Cantonese, Viet Namese, and American
Breakfast All times, bacons and eggs
No Sushi, Thank You Please

No wonder the dragon was happy. I was about to follow the wonderful smells of hot oil, soy, and ginger across the street, when two cars, one a regular police prowl car and the other an unmarked sedan, came tooling up from behind me and did an assault-landing at the very curb I was headed for. Doors flew open and bodies piled out, some with and some without uniforms, all very full of their own importance. They left the car doors hanging open and pushed each other into the restaurant, like a bunch of frat boys who heard a rumor of free beer. One of the without-uniforms was a big figure in a baggy topcoat and a wide-brimmed hat. I couldn't tell for sure if it was Evans, but it definitely could have been.

Since I didn't see any jackets with INS written on them, the most likely explanation was a raid on an illegal gambling operation in some bean-curd cellar. Our current mayor was very big on cracking down on crimes that the people who elected him never indulged in, like cheating at mah-jong. But I didn't feel like finding out. Even if the Proph was right about my karma being high, the stuff could have worn itself out by now. I did a one-eighty without breaking my stride. At the first cross street, I headed away from West Seventh, as fast as I could walk without looking like a fugitive.

Two blocks later, I started changing direction at every corner. Half an hour after that, I decided I was alone, and I slowed to a more casual pace and tried to figure out where I was. Somewhere in an area of mixed blue-collar housing and assorted old industrial buildings. The neighborhood hadn't been "discovered" and gentrified yet, so it didn't have a name, but I vaguely recognized it. There were streetlights only at the intersections, and the dark sidewalks and streets in between were deserted, except for me. This was good.

With my adrenalin back to maintenance levels, I could again afford to think about my stomach, which was becoming vocal in its complaints. Somewhere nearby, a commercial bakery was saturating the night air with the smell of fresh bread, making me giddy with longing. Maybe they had an outlet shop. If not, I might have to catch an alley cat and roast it over my cigarette lighter soon.

The street dead-ended into a five or six-story brick building that could have been built as a factory or an office. Now it was occupied by a lot of small businesses, each with its own logo or lighted sign. A lot of them had their lights on, and a tattoo parlor on the second floor had a neon sign that actually said, "OPEN." If it was, the building had to be, too. I decided to go in and look for the Keebler elves or the Tastee bakers, whichever came first. Before I got to the front door, though, something caught my eye down at one end of the building.

Under a harsh, sodium floodlight, a truck was backed up to a loading dock, and some guy with a gray uniform was wheeling pallets of flat, openwork, plastic crates into it. Crates of fresh bread that smelled like heaven. As I got closer, I could read "Cottage Bakers," on the side of the truck. The guy with the pallet jack stopped and gave me a pained look.

"We don't sell out of the truck," he said.

"That's too bad." I reached for the phony badge in my inside pocket. I was debating whether to impersonate a health inspector or a cop when the doughboy made up my mind for me.

"Oh, a cop, huh?"

"Well, see…"

"Yeah, I see. Undercover. You should've said something."

"We don't like to draw attention to ourselves."

"Got you." He gave me an exaggerated conspiratorial wink that made me want to smack him one, just for being so insufferably cute. But I managed to keep my mouth shut and my hands to myself, and he pointed to a stack of blue crates in the corner of the truck box.

"Frosted cinnamon rolls and filled Danish," he said. "Help yourself."

"Right." I stopped myself short of saying, "thanks." If I had, I figured he'd know for sure I wasn't a real cop. I was finding this impersonating business a lot easier than I had ever imagined. I took a plastic-wrapped package of something warm out of one crate. Then at the urging gestures of Mr. Wink, I took two more out of another crate. Maybe the Proph had been right about my karma, after all. I headed into the building to look for a coffee machine.

Over my shoulder I heard, "You part of the stakeout, then?"

"I guess you figured us out, all right." *What stakeout?*

"Share some with the guys in blue, hey?"

"You got it." I hoped the man was hallucinating.

The main lobby was half a flight above the loading dock, and almost a full flight above street level. It had no reception desk, just a tenant directory, a pair of elevators, and signs directing people to the restrooms and phones. I decided the vending machines, if any, would be near an easy source of water piping, and I followed the signs. A wide corridor had storefront windows looking into some of the tenant spaces, and as I passed one of them, I did a double-take, backed up a half step, and stopped altogether.

The sign said "G. B. Feinstein, Luthier: Fine Musical Instruments." Did I know that name from somewhere? Inside, a man was carving a large piece of wood that was attached somehow to a pedestal. He was peeling off long, curly shavings as if he had a plane, but he used only a large chisel or gouge, pushed with one hand and guided artfully with the other. Must have been one hell of a sharp chisel, I thought. The piece he was working on was the face or back of a bass fiddle, and he bent over it with total intensity and focus, a dead cigarette hanging from his mouth and drops of sweat clinging to his forehead and eyebrows. He would be tall if he stood up, I thought. He had bony elbows and shoulder blades poking out in every direction, a nose that may have extended further than his cigarette, and wire spectacles perched on top of it. Ichabod Crane with a leather apron. And quite possibly, just the man I wanted to talk to.

I knocked on the door, but he didn't look up from his work. A louder knock worked no better. I tried the knob, found it unlocked, and let myself in. I walked past formal glass display cases and walls lined with dark, gleaming violins. Toward the back, the space got more shop-like, with heavy wood benches cluttered with tools and strange-looking parts. I went up to the chisel-master, who still had not acknowledged my presence.

As I got closer, he spoke without looking up.

"I don't sell out of the shop," he said. He must have belonged to the same union as the bakery-truck driver.

"You'll have to go to a dealer, one of the better ones." When that didn't get rid of me, he added, "I do some commissions, but right now, I'm booked three years in advance."

"I'm not looking for an instrument," I said.

Finally, he put down the chisel and looked up. "Then why are you here? Feinstein is the master. Everybody who comes here is looking for an instrument." He spoke with a slight accent that might have been German. It made him sound dignified and maybe important.

I held out a package of warm cinnamon rolls in their steamed-up plastic wrap.

"Got any coffee?" I said.

"I can make some *macht schnell*." German, it was. "You are proposing an exchange?"

"More like share and share alike."

"Sharing is good." If his eyes had been heat lamps, the plastic wrap would have melted. "What is, as they say, the catcher?"

"I'm also looking for some information."

"I got out of the spy business years ago. What kind of information?"

"Information about old violins," I said.

"Ah, yes. Well. Now, that would be quite another matter. What I do know about old violins could fill books. How much time do you have?"

I thought about the alleged police stakeout, and the fact that wherever it was, it did not appear to be in this workshop.

"For once in my life," I said, "time is not a problem."

Chapter Five

Cinnamon Rolls and
Other Weighty Topics

I followed Feinstein to the back of the shop, where he cleared glue pots and strange-looking tools off a counter and fired up an industrial gas ring burner. He brewed his coffee in a way I had heard of but never seen before, boiling the grounds, all unfiltered, in an enameled metal pot and then throwing in a raw egg to collect the grits. He measured the grounds with his hand, and the water not at all. Four fistfuls to a splash or two. I didn't want to know what he did with the egg afterwards.

"For the instruments, I have precision, instinct, and soul," he said. "But first and always, precision. For coffee, however, one needs only instinct."

"Was I complaining?"

"You looked skeptical."

"Sorry. Sometimes, that's the only look I've got. Probably comes from the Scottish side of my family."

"Poor fellow. I'll ignore it, then. Now, let us see if those rolls are still hot enough to melt butter."

He opened a drawer in a wooden parts cabinet and took out a dish with a slab of pale yellow stuff and a small spatula. My heart threatened to rat me out to my doctor later, and I told it to shut up and enjoy itself. I can always give up doctors, but real butter, on hot rolls, is a biological imperative. The rich smell of the boiling coffee began to overcome the atmosphere of hide glue, varnish, and musty-sweet wood dust, as we ripped open a package of rolls and performed the definitive melt-test. The butter didn't go all the way to drizzly-flowy, but it slumped down agreeably, mixing with the white frosting, and we pronounced it a success. I inhaled the first roll, I think. Never even put a tooth mark in it. Then I slowed down and savored the next one a bit. The instrument man looked me over between bites and talked around a mouthful of dough and topping.

"You will forgive the possible presumption, *mein Herr*, but I don't see you as quite seedy enough to be a musician or wealthy enough to be a serious collector. What is your interest in old violins, exactly?"

"No apology needed. I should have introduced myself before." I wiped off my hand on my pocket lining, gave him a business card, and told him my name. "I'm a bail bondsman, and I seem to have acquired an old violin as a security forfeit. I don't know what it's worth on the open market, but one person may have literally died for it, and at least two others are willing to break the law to get their hands on it. I'd like to figure out why."

"A good story."

"You don't believe it?"

"Oh, I didn't mean it was a lie. Fine violins often have an air of intrigue about them. The great ones, tragedy and perhaps even death. So a good, preferably dark, story is appropriate. It's no guarantee of quality, mind you, but it's a start."

He took a rag from the bench top and used it to protect his hand while he poured boiling coffee into two battered mugs. I was surprised at how gritty it did not look, though it was certainly dark. He left about an inch of space at the top of each mug, and I was about to tell him that I didn't take cream, when he produced a bottle of cognac from another cabinet and held it out inquiringly. I gave him my best "why not?" expression, and he topped off both mugs, adding a spoonful of sugar from a bag in another cubbyhole. Now we had all the major food groups: alcohol, sugar, caffeine, and fat. I blew on the hot liquid, took a sip, and remembered what it used to be like to believe in heaven. He bit into another roll and went on.

"You say this violin is very old?"

"All I said was 'old,' but it's supposed to be four hundred years and counting."

"Supposed to be."

"It has an appraisal document"

"Does it also have a label?"

I shook my head. "I'm told it's an Amati. I don't know where to look for a label."

"Ah," he said. He wiped his hands on a wet rag and passed it to me to do the same. "Come over here. I show you some things."

He selected a smallish, light-colored violin from his wall display and took it over to a bench, where he turned on an intense fluorescent drafting lamp.

"This is a Roger Baldwin," he said. "Not a great instrument, but certainly a very good one."

"So you're a collector, as well as a maker?"

"All makers are also collectors and repairers. That's how one learns the possibilities of the art. That's also why one locates in a city like this, with a famous chamber orchestra and a symphony nearby. It means there are lots of available examples. Now look at this one."

"Is this the same Baldwin as the pianos?"

"It is not. This violin is from a one-man shop of some obscurity. It's about a hundred and fifty years old."

"It's sort of small." That was as close as I could come to perceptive observation.

"Very good. It is what was once called a knapsack fiddle. For wandering musicians, you see. Quite possibly, it was carried by some soldier in your Civil War. This one is better than most of the type, though. Look here." He pointed out the little stripe around the edge of the top, which he called the "purfling," and told me what kind of wood it ought to be made of, which it was. Then he talked about the arch of the top and back. "It's like the curve of a beautiful woman's buttock," he said. "Every one is slightly different, a subtle variation on a timeless theme. But even so, there is good and there is not so good. A true connoisseur learns to feel the quality of the line, even though he cannot define it. This one has a fine, if somewhat flamboyant character. Now take a look inside." He handed me a tiny flashlight and a little mirror on a stick, like dentists use.

"What am I looking for?"

"Just tell me what you see."

I slipped the mirror down through one of the f-shaped holes and panned it around. I really needed another set of tools and at least one more hand. If I used the mirror to direct the light, then I couldn't get my eye anyplace where I could see what it was reflecting. I decided I was not on the threshold of a new vocation here.

"What do you see?"

"I see the dark, dusty inside of a very complicated-looking box."

"That's a start. What else?"

"Some kind of stick going between the top and the bottom."

"That's the sound post, to keep the tension on the strings from collapsing the top. Ignore that. It's most unlikely to be the original."

"They wear out and have to be replaced?"

"The sound box changes shape slightly, with seasoning, and it needs a different size post."

"Good thing, since I can't get a good look at it, anyway."

"Tell me what you *can* get a look at."

"There's a piece of paper that could be a label, but I can't make out any of the printing on it. It isn't under the hole."

"It shouldn't be, it should be in the center. Symmetry is important in a thing that is made to resonate. It would have been put on before the box was assembled. But it could be a fake, anyway, or a later addition. The real maker's mark would be a brand, literally, scorched into the wood, under the label. Paper eventually crumbles, and nothing is easier than to add a new piece. Sometimes there are several layers, just accumulated. You wouldn't believe the inscriptions I find on some of them."

"Like, 'If you can read this, you're very, very small'?"

"More often a blessing, or a curse to scare off

thieves. Sometimes something about the owner. This particular one identifies the maker as one R. Baldwin, and it's actually written backwards, meant to be read with a mirror."

I moved my eye to the hole that didn't have the mirror in it, shined the light in the other one, and made out the faint capitals R and B in the reflection.

"I'll be damned."

"It dates it, you see, but only forward. It means that we're well into the industrial age, when specialized mirrors would have been widely available. What else do you see?"

I felt like quitting while I was ahead, but he seemed most insistent.

"There's a lot of little ridges and grooves in the back," I said. I wondered if the rolls were getting cold yet.

"Tool marks, from gouges and scrapers. You see? You are more observant than you think. The marks also date it, this time the right way. It means that the production predates the invention of sandpaper. You can tell that from the outside of the instrument, too, but it takes a more practiced eye. You have to learn to look for something called 'truing lines.'"

"And those are good?"

"Not necessarily, but like your story, they are a start."

This whole conversation was starting to drive me

crazy, and I turned away to have some more laced coffee and break open another package of rolls. The last one seemed to have evaporated. Feinstein topped off our cups and started another pot brewing. For a while, we ate and drank in silence. I looked at the walls covered with violins and decided I was no closer than I had been to knowing why one was worth three grand and another one twenty times that, much less why one would be worth killing over. Feinstein might have read my mind, or at least my face.

"It's a funny market, the market in old instruments," he said. "It's like the art market, only it isn't."

I must have been feeling the alcohol, because that made perfect sense to me. "Of course," I said.

"A certain Van Gogh, say, or a Michelangelo is worth such and such many million because there is only one of it and there are never going to be any more and the world has been taking care of it for a very long time now."

"And because somebody is willing to pay that much for it."

"Just so. It has nothing whatever to do with anybody getting a million dollars' worth of uplifting inspiration from looking at it."

"I personally think the same argument can be applied to a Mercedes Benz."

"That's not as stupid as it sounds."

That sounded stupid? How strong was that cognac, anyway?

"They are both a matter of assigned value." he said. "But with a violin, there is such a thing as intrinsic value, as well. It is, after all, made to play music. Sadly, the people best able to judge the real quality are those least likely to be able to afford it."

"Musicians."

He nodded and took more coffee. "Scum of the earth. Steal from their own mothers to buy a set of strings. Cash in advance for them, always."

It was hard for me to see Amy Cox in that light, but I nodded anyway, to encourage him. Or maybe the evening had just started to turn mellow.

"So musicians get hired to evaluate instruments they can't afford to buy?"

"Mostly, they do not. Nobody wants to take the chance that the Stradivarius they just paid half a million dollars for sounds like a cigar-box fiddle. And it can happen. So the serious buyer settles for pedigrees and proofs of age. Nobody argues with age."

"They just don't make them like they used to," I said.

"Utter rubbish," he said, spilling coffee with a dismissive gesture. "We make them as well or better than they ever did. And there's no secret varnish, either. No secrets of any kind, just the finest workmanship you can get out." He calmed down, refilled his mug from the new pot, and took another sip. "But a new instrument is a new instrument, and there's no arguing with that. It won't find its true voice for at least twenty years, sometimes twice that long. And its soul? Well, if it's going to have one at all, it won't acquire that for at least a hundred."

"Or four?"

"Four hundred years is better, sometimes."

"Why only sometimes?"

"Sometimes it destroys itself before then. You know anything about engines, Mr. Jackson?"

"Engines? You mean like in cars?"

"Exactly like that."

"I turn the key, and mine goes. If it doesn't go, I call a garage."

"How nice for you. When I was a young man in the Army, before I had a vocation, I worked on engines. I learned that diesel engines, specifically, have a peculiar trait. They are the easiest to start, smoothest, and most powerful when they are at the end of their natural life span, ready for a complete overhaul or a trip to the junkyard. The same thing is true of violins.

"It is said that the sweetest sound ever heard from a set of strings was once when Jascha Heifetz played the Tchaikovsky concerto—there is only one, you know—on his Stradivarius, at Carnegie Hall. People who don't even like Tchaikovsky wept and cheered and gave him a fifteen-minute standing ovation." He took a bite of Danish and a gulp of coffee and got a far-away look in his eyes, picturing the scene. "After the concert, he put the instrument in its case, the same as always, and it immediately fractured into a thousand splinters, impossible to repair. The timing of its life, you see, was exquisite."

"This is true?"

"True? Probably not. I have heard the story many times. Sometimes it is Heifetz and the Tchaikovsky and sometimes it is Isaac Stern playing a Bach partita or Itzhak Perlman and a Paganini caprice. It is most likely a professional myth. But the heart of it is true enough. The instrument, any stringed instrument, is at its sweetest just before it dies."

"And they all die?"

"Just like you and me, my friend." He leaned over to clink his mug against mine in a toast to the essential sadness of the universe. It seemed like the right thing to do.

"But not just yet," I said.

He nodded solemnly, then smiled. "But not just yet."

"Of course," he added, "some come to an earlier end than others. Getting put in a museum or a private collector's case is a kind of early death, rather like being embalmed while you're still walking around. Then there are accidents and weather and just general lack of care. And of course, there are always the Gypsies."

"Gypsies kill violins?" I tried to picture some swarthy, mustachioed type, like Omar Sharif, with a bandana on his head and a billowing peasant shirt, plunging his dagger into the f-hole of an old fiddle, but it just didn't work.

"They don't kill them, exactly. Not right away, at least. A Gypsy could take that Baldwin, scrape down the inside to sweeten the tap tone, loosen the purfling, and make it sound like an Amati, for a while. But it wouldn't last long after that."

"A mere hundred years or so?"

"If it did, then it would be truly a fine violin, a real collector's item, but that is most unlikely. Who knows? I, myself, do not know the exact life of the violins I build. But I know that a Gypsy would take one, make it sound like an instant masterpiece, and shorten its life dramatically. You never heard of a Gypsy violin?"

"I thought that was just an expression, like Dutch courage or a Chinese fire drill. I didn't know Gypsies actually made violins."

"Make? No. They do not make, they fake. The point of all effort with them is fraud. And they are very good at it. Throughout history, they have complicated the lives of both serious luthiers and their customers. And they have destroyed many fine instruments and many lives. The Nazis should have left the Jews alone and concentrated on the damned Rom, and the world would have thanked them for it."

I almost choked on my coffee. "What did you call them?" I asked.

"Is something wrong, *Herr* Jackson?"

"Just tell me what you called them."

"Damned Rom? What of it?"

"What does that mean?"

"It means I don't think much of them."

"Not the 'damned,' the other."

"Oh, you mean Rom? It's what they call themselves. Also their language. Rom, Gypsy, all the same thing. Horrible people. Worse than musicians, which many of them are, as well. If you meet one, grab your wallet and run for your life."

"Or kill him?"

"That would be better, yes."

"*Déja vu.*"

"I don't understand."

"I don't either, but I'm starting to."

I took my mug and strolled over to the outside window, deep in thought. A wind had come up while we were talking, and the thrashing branches of an elm tree made monochrome kaleidoscope patterns with the corner street light. Now and then, they illuminated a squat, dark shape in the middle of the block.

"Is this a tough neighborhood, Mr. Feinstein?"

"We are old drinking friends now. Call me G.B. And no, I don't think this is an especially bad area."

"Is there always a squad car parked across the street, G.B.?"

"No. It has been there since late this afternoon."

"Do you know why?"

"I think they are waiting for you, *Herr* Herman."

So much for karma.

Chapter Six

Flight to Avoid

I suppose most people would have made a mad dash for the rear exit then and there, but I had used up my panic reflex for the day. I moved away from the window, had another sip of coffee, and looked at the man who had been my host for the past couple of hours.

"Why do you say they're looking for me, G.B.?" But even as I said it, I suddenly knew the answer. *The name on the shop door, that I hadn't quite recognized, was also on the certificate of authenticity for the Amati.* It was an automatic connection, and I had walked right into it.

"I'm not positive, mind you. They didn't tell me a name, only that I should be watching for a man who was looking for a very old violin."

"Looking for one? Are you sure they didn't say he would be bringing one for you to look at?"

He shook his head. "They said what I just told you. But then, they didn't strike me as the sharpest tools on the bench, either. They could have got it wrong. They fooled around with my instruments, like a bunch of obnoxious little children, and then they tried to act serious and important. I didn't like them very much."

"Are they still here, in the building?"

"Only the uniformed officer out in the car, I think. Maybe another one out in front. I haven't looked there for a while."

"So what do you intend to do?"

"Do? Why would I do anything? I already told you, I didn't like them."

"And that's it?" I said. "That's all you need to be willing to harbor a possible fugitive?"

"I have lived in places where the police know how to intimidate people, Herr Herman. Intimidate and hurt. I assure you, these fellows are amateurs, and not very talented ones at that. I don't like them, and I do rather like you. Yes, that is all I need. What do you need?"

I thought about it for a while and then told him.

When I went over to the squad car at the curb, the officer inside was busy tapping something into the keyboard of his big onboard computer, which left him looking away from me and the building I had just come from. That explained a lot. He seemed to have a computer instead of a partner, and I had to wonder how much comfort that was when the shooting started. It was the coming trend, though. Robo Friday, virtual partner.

"Are things as dull out here as they are inside?" I said.

He whirled around to face me and began to reach for his pistol. Then his eyes registered the phony badge that I had carefully placed just peeking out from behind the lapel of Feinstein's raincoat, and he relaxed and gave me a more leisurely look.

"I didn't know we had a man inside," he said.

"It figures, doesn't it? It wasn't enough of a bullshit operation to start with, so they threw some more manpower at it."

"You got the 'bullshit' part right, anyway."

"Yeah, well, it all pays the same, they say." I stuffed my hands deep in my pockets, the way I hoped a bored detective would.

"That's what they say, all right," said the cop. "And it all counts for thirty." What a stimulating conversation. It even made me feel like a cop. So far, so good, but sooner or later, he would…

"I don't think I know you, detective."

That, right there, is what he would do. And with his hand alarmingly close to his weapon again, too. Well, there was nothing for it now but to pick a name and try it out.

"Hanes," I said, offering my hand. "I work with Evans." *And in my off-duty time, I manufacture underwear.*

"Bunco, huh? I don't get over there much. Been on the strawberry wagon a lot lately. Lots of action, but no weight, if you know what I mean. I'm Benson." He took my hand and, to my astonishment and joy, shook it, rather than cuffing the wrist it was attached to.

"Yeah," I said, "I know exactly what you mean. Pleased to meet you." I had no clue what he meant. But the information about Evans being on the Bunco Squad was certainly interesting. Not Homicide at all, but the division that dealt with con games and grifts. My, my, my. I would also have liked to find out what case Evans was officially working at that exact moment, but I figured I had pushed my luck far enough. Time to wrap up this little bit of street theater, before the set fell apart on me.

"How long you been out here?" I said.

"Three and a half hours, but who's counting?"

"Nobody relieved you?"

"Do I look relieved?"

"That really sucks, man."

"Tell me about it."

"Tell you what, Benson," I said. "I'm on my way out, but if you want, I'll stay with the unit for fifteen, while you take a code seven." I may not know what a "strawberry wagon" is, but I do know that a car is a "unit," and a "code seven" is a rest break. In this case, it was also the magic phrase.

"You sure about that?"

"Absolutely." If he only knew how sure.

"You're on." He hoisted himself out of the car, dropped his flashlight in its holster, and motioned to me to take his place.

"Use the computer, if you want," he said. "But don't forget, CIS can tell every site you went to, even if you erase it, okay?"

Still more unsolicited information. I was starting to like this guy a lot. Maybe I wouldn't steal his squad car, after all. I nodded and climbed in the driver's seat, and he went off toward the building, walking like a man who has just remembered he has a bladder he's been neglecting. I figured he wouldn't be gone long, though. After all, I never did find a coffee machine in the building, and Feinstein damn sure wasn't going to give him anything.

I decided to leave the car, and the sooner the better, but first I wanted a look at that computer. I'm not even slightly proficient with these things, but it was an opportunity I couldn't resist. The screen was full of dialogue between Benson's unit and at least two others, mostly in some language known only to cops. Not what I wanted, even if I could decipher it. I looked around for a mouse and found none, but I did find a cute little black pad that made the cursor move when I fingered it, and I figured the bar at the bottom of the pad was the equivalent of the mouse-clicker. Or whatever the hell it's called. I sent the chit-chat display off into some electronic Never Never Land and looked at a screen full of icons. I didn't see any that might be a gateway to homicide or bunco files. I tried opening something that called itself Day Book, but found that I needed a password. Seeing none written on the windshield or dashboard in magic marker, I gave up on that. I looked instead at the little bars at the bottom of the screen that showed what files were already open. One of them was labeled APBs, and I clicked it into a new window.

There were about twenty listings of outstanding warrants, a couple of which had added notes about recent apprehensions. When I scrolled down, I could see the lists from previous days, too. A lot of familiar names there. Some good, long-time customers and some I wished I had never heard of. Hector Ruiz, a regular of mine, was wanted for smacking his grandmother around again, and Henderson the Pain King was wanted for smacking anybody he could find. Willie Martin, better known as Whisper, was wanted for murder one. That would make the fourth time, if memory served. No bond there, and that didn't break my heart in the slightest. That guy gave me the creeps.

I went on down the list of candidates for County housing, smiling at the predictable repeaters. Actual and potential scenes of confrontation or flight, fight, arrest, and even death, were all laid out in a crisp shorthand that was positively chilling. One officer had been shot that day, though not fatally, and one drug dealer named Slick Cicero had gone down, rather than go in. My man Benson hadn't made a high-profile arrest in days, poor soul. But then, as we had both just said, it all pays the same.

My own name was about halfway down the list. *Shit.*

I was only "wanted for questioning in connection with…," which wasn't too bad, except that I was listed as "armed and extremely dangerous." Get *real* here, folks. Maybe Evans just didn't want to admit he'd been taken out of the play by an unarmed amateur, but the other cops reading the list wouldn't know that. Or maybe he just wanted me to get shot. Too many maybes to contemplate, and I had already tarried too long behind enemy lines. The simple fact was that I was wanted. It was a different game now.

I closed the APB window, left the real window on the real cop car open, and got my wanted body out of there. A glance back at the building told me that Officer Benson was still making the most of his break, while at one of the windows, G. B. Feinstein was giving me a thumbs up. I gave him a quick wave back and melted into the shadows between the nearest two apartment buildings. I trotted for a while, putting several blocks and a freeway ramp between me and the abandoned "unit." Then I slowed to a more leisurely pace, switching to alleys and backyards. The Stealth Bondsman vanishes again. What a guy. I could hardly wait to see what he would do next.

A man on the run needs three things: money, transportation, and a destination, which is not the same as merely a place to lay low. All three of those needs are possible traps.

A lot of wanted felons don't make it past need number one. They get picked up waiting around for their bank to open, or going into a traceable cache, or just talking to somebody who owes them money or might conceivably loan it to them. Or if they're really dumb, which most criminals definitely are, they get nailed adding an armed robbery or two to the list of performances they're already wanted for.

Those who manage to get some operating cash without blowing the whistle on themselves may still get caught by driving their own car too long or traveling on plastic. And of the ones who avoid all those pitfalls, a large percentage are picked up at their homes, their girlfriends' pads, their favorite bars, or Mom's place. Especially that last one. It is a wonderful bit of trade irony that the more dangerous and desperate a fugitive is, the more likely he is to go to Mom. I've never even tried to figure that one out, but I've seen it enough to believe it absolutely. Jackson's Theorem Number Six:

If a man goes to hide with his mother, apprehend him with extreme prejudice and a lot of firepower.

I have also observed that if a man commits none of the above acts of criminal stupidity, travels without using plastic, and goes to a place he has never been and has no reason to ever go, he is virtually impossible to catch. Until he comes back, and there's the rub. That's why a place to lay low is not the same as a destination. If your ultimate plan involves getting your old life back, then any hiding place that doesn't let you work on that problem is just a dead end. Most fugitives do come back, and so would I, but not until I had arranged a better script for my reception party. Meanwhile, it was definitely time to go to ground.

The stakeout with Patrolman Benson was most likely an informal operation, set up on Evans' personal authority. If he was only Bunco, he wouldn't have enough clout to set it up for multiple sites. So I could probably risk one trip back there, if I didn't linger. Also on the plus side, the computer listing for me had not included any mention of my car, so it should be safe for me to drive it around for a few hours at least. After that, I had better be financed and gone.

I headed back towards downtown, keeping to alleys and poorly-lit streets. Walking past the back of a block of tenements, I was surprised at how many lights were still on in the shabby apartments, despite the late hour. Jumbled black and gray background, with dim little windows of yellow light, floating in space, showing film clips of other people's lives.

My instinct was to stare, and I felt a bit dirty about it, like an intruder, even though there was nothing very interesting to see. In one dingy kitchen, some men sat around a table, playing cards and drinking beer. In another, a frail white-haired woman was feeding a scrawny cat on top of a similar table. Several windows were filled with the flickering blue light of TV sets. The TVs were animated, but the black silhouettes in front of them were not. In yet another kitchen, a man and a woman were standing in the middle of the room, holding each other. Not hugging and kissing and fondling, just holding. Each one claiming the other as a sole ally against the night. The reason could be deliverance or tragedy, joy or unbearable sorrow: the phone call from the hospital, the telegram from the Army, the layoff slip or the bonus in the pay packet, the good or bad numbers in the lottery, the check that was or wasn't in the mail. All with the same result. That's what couples do, I thought, if they're real. They hold.

Watching them, I suddenly knew. I didn't have a mom to get me trapped, or a woman to hold, or any other family that anybody knew about, but I knew where I needed to go.

I got back to my office, cased it front and back from a block away first, and then went in, leaving the lights off. The floor safe under Agnes' desk had a little less than a thousand dollars in it. I left the two hundred I had promised to Wilkie, plus another two for operating capital for Aggie, and took the rest. I threw it and some clothes into the briefcase I had gotten with Stroud's stuff, locked up again, and left without a backwards glance. No phone calls, no notes, no computer nonsense, just in and out in less than five minutes. The streets were still empty, the night quiet, and I held back premature thoughts about being home free. Two blocks away, I cased the parking ramp as carefully as I had my office. The place was deserted, and I quickly found my old BMW on the third level and took it out, driving neither fast nor slow.

I drove straight to the Amtrak depot on Cleveland Avenue, where I parked in the long-term part of the lot and locked the car up. Inside, I bought a ticket on the morning train to Chicago, with a connection to Seattle on the Empire Builder, complete with observation car and diner. But I didn't get a sleeping compartment. People with sleepers get catered to and remembered. Coach-class passengers might as well be cattle, for all the notice that's taken of them. I paid for the ticket with a credit card. The train didn't board for another three hours, and I made a point of asking the ticket agent if there was a good coffee shop nearby. I have no idea what he told me, but we had a nice chat about it. This was good. I also went to the lobby ATM and drew another $500 out of two separate accounts.

Outside, I found a vacant cab to take me to the Hertz agency at the main Twin Cities airport, where I rented a Pontiac sedan. I used the Cox credit card and driver's license from the briefcase, the ones Wilkie had said were really good fakes. They had better be.

"You don't look much like your photo, Mr. Stroud," said the agent at the counter.

"It's old," I told her. "I've put on a lot of weight since then. The disease, I'm afraid. Probably terminal."

"Oh, my God, I'm so sorry." She began doing busy, important things with papers. Nice kid, but a bit on the ditzy side.

"My problem. Don't trouble yourself about it."

"Geez, that's so brave." Then she paused and got a thoughtful look, which may have been a bit of a strain for her. "I thought most diseases made you thin, not fat."

"You think I'm fat?"

"No, I didn't mean that, at all. I think you're actually, kind of, um. Well, I just meant…"

"When I get depressed, I eat a lot."

"Oh, yeah. Sure. I can see doing that. Me, too." She did some more important things with papers, working even harder at being helpful now. "Great, then. Just sign here, and initial here, here, and here. I don't suppose you want the supplemental insurance? I mean, I'm sorry, but I have to ask, you know?"

"How much is it?"

She told me, and I said, "Sure."

"Really?"

"You can't have too much insurance."

"I guess. But I mean, well…wow."

Two minutes later, I was headed out of the lot, having kicked the tires, inspected all the existing scratches in the paint, and assured the agent that she really didn't have to worry about me. It almost seemed a pity to go. I think she wanted to take me home with her. Probably not the holding type, but she did a good "wow."

The Pontiac had kind of a rubbery ride, I thought, and it smelled of air freshener, but it had pretty good sight lines and plenty of power, and it looked like a million other cars on the road. It would do. The clock on the dash read 3:22, which was just fine. It was about six hours, plus rest stops, to where I was going, and there was no point in getting there before mid-morning. Upstate, they call it, and every state has one. Way upstate. So far, in fact, that it was in a different state altogether. There, the only real family I ever had, my Uncle Fred, was doing his third stretch in a prison called the Bomb Factory.

Chapter Seven

Upstate

It wasn't called the Bomb Factory because it was full of anarchists, but because that's what it had originally been. It was built in World War II to make bombs and artillery shells. Maybe napalm, too, though only the people who worked there knew for sure. They were very big on secrecy back then. A slip of the lip could sink a ship, even a thousand miles from any ocean. They were also very paranoid about saboteurs. The high concrete walls that ringed the complex were built to keep people out, not in. The machine gun towers at the corners were also original, and a mile of open marshland in every direction gave them a free field of fire. Against whom, your guess is as good as mine. Neo-Luddites, maybe.

Its first name was the Redrock Munitions Facility. Now it's called the Redrock State Penitentiary, and it's a medium-security prison for nonviolent repeat offenders, like my Uncle Fred. The old smokestacks are still there, and the open lowland, the cost of wrecking and reclaiming being astronomical. The stacks lean a bit now, and the walls that surround them are cracked and crooked in places. Someday, the whole complex may simply sink into the surrounding marsh, which would leave nobody either surprised or sad. Meanwhile, it's actually not the worst place in the world to do time, I'm told. In any case, nobody has ever escaped from it. Maybe nobody has ever tried. Least of all, Uncle Fred.

I think Redrock is where he always wanted to be, though I can't tell him that to his face. If it isn't, I'll never figure out how somebody so street-smart couldn't manage to stay on the outside. "Some things just aren't worth worrying about, Hermie, my boy," he used to say. Like keeping two sets of books for his front business and washable numbers sheets for his real operation. Uncle Fred was a bookie, a numbers man, and a loan shark, and he was very successful, except for when he got caught. I always thought he just couldn't take the rarefied air of freedom for too long. But with respect to other people and the pitfalls and traps of the cruel old world, he is absolutely the wisest man I have ever known. He could figure out everybody and everything except himself. And if you think about it, that's really not such bad odds to be playing with. He's also the closest thing I ever had to a real father.

I grew up in a Rust Belt slum of blue-collar Detroit. If I knew my father, I don't remember him anymore. Uncle Fred would, of course, being his brother and all, but he never spoke of him. My mother, I would just as soon forget, though I can't always manage that. I don't know what it was she wanted out of life, but a son definitely wasn't it. I spent my childhood running away from foster homes and orphanages, and working small street scams, always trying to build up enough of a stash so I could run so far I would never have to come back. Uncle Fred took me under his wing and made it more or less moot. He didn't actually let me live with him, but he gave me a job and made me sort of an unofficial apprentice. Everything I know about money, numbers, and odds, plus a lot of what I know about human frailty, I learned from him. He gave me an identity. I became a numbers man. In any way that really counts, I still am.

And he was proud of his student. He wasn't big on the whole idea of family, but I often felt that he saw me as the son he never had. When he went away to prison the first time, he let me run the business for him in his absence. I rewarded this amazing display of trust by liquidating the whole operation and using the capital to start my first bonding agency. He didn't like the idea much at first, his favorite nephew going legit, but as the money started to flow in, with no penal risk attached, he grudgingly approved and eventually even admired. Before he got out from his first stretch, I had salted away enough cash to repay him, and I was off and running on my own. Playing with the house money, they call it.

The business worked, but my life didn't. I got involved in the wrong way with one of my own clients and wound up having to flee Detroit permanently, walking away from a lot of money and a nominal wife who in any case was not the holding type. Also from my Uncle Fred. That's the short version. I'm not especially fond of telling the longer one, though I have no bitterness about it. If there's anything I learned from my apprenticeship, it's that you play the hand you're dealt and don't whine about it, even to yourself.

I'm 43 going on ancient now, reestablished and in some ways reborn. New business, new part of the country, new life. I might as well be in the Witness Relocation Program, except that I was never a witness to anything that I admitted. I seldom risk contacting Uncle Fred, though I think of him often. I've never been to Redrock to visit him before. It just wasn't worth the worry. My friend Nickel Pete sometimes takes vacations in exotic places like Mexico, Hawaii, and Italy, and while he's there, he mails cards and letters to Redrock for me. I like to imagine that my uncle knows perfectly well what kind of fraud is going on and laughs his ass off about it. It's as much as I can do for him. And without any help from me, he himself had also managed to build up a new business and lose it again by going back to the slammer, not once but twice. So how much help could he stand? Maybe I'll ask him someday.

I stopped twice for gas and coffee on the road, and once for ham and eggs with some of those terrific fried potatoes that only small town diners know how to make. I also bought half a dozen candy bars and a carton of cigarettes at a truck stop, a standard visitor's gift. I was feeling tired but eager as the blacktop road broke out of the autumn landscape of scrubby farms and small groves and into the last mile of low, blighted land that still surrounds Redrock. It loomed black and ugly on the horizon, and its leaning chimneys made it look like a set from a bad horror movie. The big archway through the outer wall had a rolling steel gate that was open, and the courtyard inside had a visitor parking lot where a big sign told me to lock my car, take my keys, and leave no valuables in plain sight. I guess they don't get a very classy clientele there. Mostly lawyers, probably.

Another sign told me that all visitors had to register at the front office, but it didn't say I had to have a photo ID. I rummaged through the phony credentials in the briefcase and decided I would be Samuel Hill,

Attorney at Law. A lame joke, maybe, but who was going to complain? I locked the Pontiac, leaving no valuables in plain sight, and went in. Five minutes later, a uniformed guard had searched me for lethal substances or devices and was escorting me into the compound. When I heard the massive steel gates clang shut behind me, even though I was just a visitor, I knew what doom sounded like. I decided to avoid it a while longer.

The visitor area was just a big gym-sized room with a lot of tables and chairs. The tables were bolted to the floor in neat rows, and guards strolled the aisles between them. The fluorescent lighting was just a little brighter than the sun, and the place smelled of Lysol and cigarette smoke. It also had several video cameras, up high in the corners, but none of the glass separators with phones that you see in the high-security joints. Visitors and cons could actually touch here, as long as they didn't get carried away about it.

It took them about half an hour to find my Uncle Fred and get him there. I suppose he didn't believe them at first, telling him he had a lawyer for a visitor. When they led him in, he looked confused and crabby, but when he saw me, he smiled slyly and gave me a wink, and the years since we had last seen each other dropped away. That was my uncle, all right. We shook hands just like a real lawyer and client would, then sat down to talk.

"So, what's up, Mr. Shyster?"

"Hey, Mr. Con. Good to see you, too. Yes, I've been well thank you. How about yourself? Bernice and the kids send their love. We're all praying for your appeal."

We sat down and leaned together, and he lowered his voice a notch.

"Who the hell is Bernice?"

"I just made her up."

He chuckled. "Cute. You just playing to the cameras, or are you trying to make me think you care about me?"

"You trying to pretend that I don't?"

"You don't visit me here, ever."

"If I did, I could wind up joining you."

"A smart guy like you? Never happen."

"Yeah, well, some days I'm smarter than others."

"Ain't we all, though?" He laughed, then, and visibly relaxed. "God*damn*, it's good to see you, Hermie."

"You, too, Unc. You look pretty good, for a geezer and a lifer." Actually, I thought he looked like nine miles of bad road. His salt and pepper hair had gone to full white, his moustache had no shape to it anymore, and he seemed about two inches shorter than I remembered him. If he still had a jaw, it was lost now in the folds of his shapeless neck. The glint was still in the eyes, though, the hard intelligence and spirit of a game player who would die playing.

"I'm only a borderline geezer," he said, "and I get one more shot before I'm a lifer."

"Really? I thought three times down and you were out."

"Nah, that's all political bullshit. Us nonviolent types get a little more slack. It's not like they got a big shortage of inmates, you know? I'm figuring on parole in a couple years. Meanwhile, I keep my manly physique ready for all those eager women out there, by eating only organic foods and pumping iron every day, which I'm sure you can tell. What do you do?"

"I pump wood at a place called Lefty's Pool Hall."

"That's better. We had a pool table here, I'd be a rich man by now. You bring any smokes?"

I pulled the paper bag from under my chair and plopped it on the table. He opened the top and peered in. "What the hell are these?" he demanded.

"They're called cigarettes. Old Golds, your usual brand. Remember?"

"Yeah, but they're regulars. I can't take that kind no more. I got to have the sissy ultra lights, or I go all asthmatic, have to give up my daily marathon training and everything."

"I'm sorry."

"You wouldn't know, I guess. Well, they're good for capital, anyway. Thanks, kid."

"Do I need to ask what you need capital for?"

"If you do, I didn't teach you much. Book is a good business here. Cons will bet on any damn thing, and they got no clue what the odds ought to be. You gotta stay away from craps, though. Guys get crazy over craps, make me forsake all the nonviolent training I got from Hot Mama Gandhi. What about you? You still writing GET OUT OF JAIL FREE cards for exorbitant fees?"

"That and pool are the only games I know anymore."

"And I'm up for sainthood next year. So what's the problem?"

"Did I say there was a problem?"

"Don't try to con an old con, Hermie. You didn't come here just to listen to me lie about my health."

"Well, since you mentioned it…"

"I mentioned, already. Give."

So I gave. I told Uncle Fred everything that had happened, from the time Amy Cox had first walked into my office until I had walked into the visitor lobby at Redrock. Shortly after I got started, he lit a cigarette from the carton he had said was the wrong kind, then offered me one. I figured he was letting me know that the video cameras were high-resolution. I took the offered smoke, and whenever I came to the parts about running afoul of the law, I made sure I had the cigarette and my hand in front of my mouth, to stymie any lip-readers. He sat back in his chair, crossed his legs, and listened. Once in a while, he would make a note on a little lined pad he had in his shirt pocket. He looked comfortable, and so was I. Focused. Talking business was more natural to either of us than talking sentiment.

After I finished, he looked at his notes for a while, scowled a few times, and massaged his chin with his scrawny hand.

"It's a con," he said.

"Hey, no kidding? What gave you the first clue?" Sometimes Uncle Fred talks to me as if I were still a little kid, and since real fathers everywhere do that, too, I don't even try to break him of it. Sooner or later, he would get to the paydirt.

"But it's not so simple," he said.

"Oh, I see. Did it look simple at some point? Somehow, I missed that part."

"You ever hear of the 'old fiddle game?'"

"Sure," I said. "Of course. Everybody has, but it doesn't apply here."

He was referring to a classic, two-man short con, the kind that doesn't give the victim enough time to think things over before it's already sprung.

It works this way: Grifter Number One eats a meal in a fancy restaurant, then tells the manager he can't pay because he just realized he left his wallet in his hotel room. But if the manager will wait for him to go get it, he will leave his violin for security. He opens an old-looking violin case, flashes the violin around a bit, and leaves, acting hurried and embarrassed. After he goes, another customer, Grifter Number Two, comes up to pay his own bill and asks to have a closer look at the instrument. He's a collector, he says, and would like to buy it. He offers a huge chunk of money, at least ten times what the restaurant is likely to have for cash on-hand. The manager, of course, says it's not his to sell, but if Number Two will wait a bit, the owner will be back shortly. Number Two says sorry, but he has to catch a hot flight to Timbuktu, and he splits. But he leaves the manager his business card and asks him to have the owner of the fiddle call.

When Number One comes back, the manager, if he's as greedy as the grifters hope and trust, negotiates a quick purchase of the violin. Grifter Number One doesn't want to sell, he says, but he finally agrees to do so for all the money in the place, cash only. Then he, also, suddenly remembers a hot date somewhere very far away, and he takes the money and runs. The "collector's" business card, of course, is as phony as the two grifters, and the violin turns out to be worth maybe fifty bucks, tops. But by the time the manager knows he's been had, both players are long gone. There are lots of variations, but that's the purest version.

"I thought of it right away," I said, "but the only thing I can see that it has in common with my situation is an old violin and a security arrangement. What are you seeing that I'm not?"

"I'm seeing two completely different operations, Hermie."

"You want to lay that out for me?"

"Look, when you wipe away all the byplay, like the limp that the cute broad had, and…"

"Did I say she was cute?"

"You didn't have to. You wipe away that, and the business with the kneeled tights…"

"Neo-Luddites, Uncle Fred."

"Will you cut that shit out and listen for a minute?"

"Yes."

He glared at me for a bit, daring me to interrupt him again. When I didn't, he lit another cigarette and continued. "You sift through all the byplay, I'm saying, and if the scam still looks too complicated, then there's something else going on."

I waited. He made a gesture with his hand that said, *Your turn.*

"Like murder?" I said.

"Just like that. The killing wasn't part of the grift. Con men aren't hit men. If they were, they'd give up conning and go to armed robbery or extortion or murder for hire. Something with a lot more loot and a faster payoff."

"Excuse me for being a little slow," I said, "but I don't see where there's any payoff in this scheme, fast or slow. If I have to give eighteen grand to the court, that doesn't help anybody else."

"You won't have to. You got a bent cop in on the scam..."

"Evans."

"Yeah, Evans. You watch. When the time comes for the Cox kid's trial, something will show up in the police records, makes the whole thing go away, null and void. The arrest was just to get your attention, get you to look at the violin."

"Why me?"

"Because bondsmen have more money than restaurant managers."

"Fair enough. But I still don't see where the payoff comes in."

"That's because we haven't seen the hook yet, only the bait."

"But I don't have to buy the violin from any phony musician. I already have it."

"Do you?"

"Well, Pete does."

"Does he?"

"Sure, he does."

"If you say so."

"What are you saying, Unc? That Pete's in on the con?"

"He wouldn't have to be. You trust him, that's good enough for me. I'm just saying I'd look, that's all. Maybe there's a little pigeon drop going on here, too."

The "pigeon drop" is another classic short con, in which the victim literally winds up holding the bag. The bag is supposed to be full of money, but it turns out to be stuffed with worthless paper. I sighed.

"Couldn't just one thing be what it looks like?" I said.

"In this sorry old world, probably not much."

"What about the killing? You figure Evans for it?"

"Could be, but I don't think so. If he did it, it was a mistake, and he's trying to pin it on you. But if he's clean, then he might really think you did it. Either way, you've got some running time."

"How's that?"

"I figure Evans is in on the con, no matter what. He'll let you be a wanted man for a while, just to keep you off balance, but he isn't going to let you go down until the game plays itself out and some money changes hands. If Plan A didn't work, he'll go to Plan B or Z, but he won't give up on it. There's too much invested at this point, and the gang has its little hearts set on the payoff."

"Which I'm not going to give them."

"Are you sure? People who do this for a living are awfully good at it, you know. You might not see the hook until it's too late. At this point, you probably haven't even seen all the players."

"So what do you suggest?"

"Well, you can't turn State's evidence, because you don't have any evidence."

"This is true."

"So the only thing to do is see another card. Then turn the hook back on the grifters, if you can. If you can't, at least you might find out who killed the girl, get clear of it yourself."

"Play the hand I'm dealt? Where have I heard that before?"

"Play the hand out, damn straight. But keep a gun under the table, you hear? This thing is going to get ugly before it's done."

"You think so?"

"I know so. Murder by automobile is not the professional's method of choice. It's a caper with a lot more rage than thought. Believe me, there's still plenty of it left floating around for you."

"Okay, so I need a gun."

"An untraceable gun."

"Absolutely. Who do I shoot with it?"

"Well, that's the art of it, you know? If it's not

clear by the time the last card's turned, you could be in deep shit."

"You're just full of good advice today, aren't you?"

"You remember the story I used to tell about the horse trader in Constantinople?"

A guard was going around the tables, telling people their time was up.

"You mean the one with the little kid who saw…" I began. Uncle Fred motioned to me to cut it off.

"Yeah, that one," he said. "You keep that one in mind, and you'll be fine."

"I don't see how it applies here."

"Then you'll just have to find a way to make it apply, won't you?"

The guard was about to come up and poke one or both of us, so we preempted him by standing up and shaking hands again.

"Twenty miles south of here," said Uncle Fred, "there's a little dump of a town, has a diner on Main Street. The house specialty is pecan pie. You ought to stop and try it."

I didn't for a minute take that to be a casual suggestion.

"Pecan, you say?"

"That's the stuff. You got to ask about it. Rosie, the waitress will know." He gave me another wink and a final squeeze of my hand.

"You take care of yourself." I stopped myself short of calling him "Unc" in front of the guard.

"Count on it." He thought for a moment. "Count on it, Mister Sam Hill. And you watch your back."

Chapter Eight

Pecan Pie at the Last Chance Café

The rush of being on the run and the pleasure of seeing my uncle were long gone by the time I headed the Pontiac back through the blighted lowland, and the road back seemed longer than it was on the way out. But I was in no hurry. I needed a solid block of sleep and then a solid plan before I went anywhere. First, though, I needed to check out the locally famous pecan pie.

The town didn't look much different from the one where I had stopped for breakfast: tiny, tired, and nearly deserted. Norman Rockwell might have painted it once, but even he wouldn't look at it now. Thomas Hart Benton, never. The sign at the city limits said NEW SALEM, pop. 312, and I suspected the number included cats and dogs. Even counting pets, it was probably an exaggeration. But there was, as promised, a diner on Main Street, between a grain elevator and a boarded-up creamery. The sign over the door simply said CAFE. I guessed they didn't have to worry about being confused with the competition.

Down by the grain elevator stood a couple of dirty pickups and one ton-and-a-half stakebed parked nose-in to the curb. By the café, there was only a rusted and battered old Trans Am that looked as if it had been painted with a brush, bright blue with crooked white racing stripes. The rear lid was popped up, and a hay bale took up all of the trunk space, and then some. I thought it looked hilarious. The rest of the street was deserted. I parked ten yards away from the Trans Am and went into the café.

The door's old-fashioned jingle-bell ringer woke up the two or three resident flies and sent them spiraling up to do battle with a lazy ceiling fan. There were high-backed booths along one wall and tables in the rest of the place, with a counter up at the end. In one of the booths, a couple of well-fed rural types in Big Smith overalls and DeKalb baseball caps were hunched over heavy china plates, mopping up gravy with small loaves of bread. When I walked in, they gave me a look that openly asked if I came from another planet. I gave them one back that said I certainly hoped so. They didn't look away and I didn't waste my time trying to stare them down.

The rest of the place was empty, so I went to the back and sat on a stool, hoping a Munchkin named

Rosie might be lurking behind the counter. She wasn't, so I grabbed a menu from behind a paper napkin holder. The regular house special was something called the Whole Cow Steakburger, while the special of the day was a hot turkey sandwich with mashed potatoes and sage dressing and savory cranberry sauce. Both of them came with gravy. Apple, cherry, and blueberry pie were also listed, but no pecan. If I were really feeling daring, I could try something called Aunt Mary's Chocolate Bombe. A misspelling, no doubt.

After I had read both sides of the plastic-coated menu and put it back down, a double-action door with a porthole in it swung toward me. A coffee pot emerged from the secret room behind, followed by a shapely arm and a thirty-something blonde. She was maybe five foot six, not really heavy, but with a solid look, like a somewhat softer version of one of those Amazons from the cover of a body building magazine. She had watery blue eyes, flat cheek planes and the strong jaw and mobile mouth of a Norwegian or Finn.

Fifteen years earlier or so, she must have driven the local 4-H boys wild. Now she still bulged and receded in all the right places, but she was on the threshold of losing it. In another ten years, she could go to either purely voluptuous or just plain fat, depending. Her expression told me she didn't really care. But like my uncle Fred, she had a glint in her eyes that implied too much energy for a place like this.

"Coffee?" she said, flipping a mug from under the counter.

"Sure."

"Hey, Laurie," came a noise from the booth, "you got other people want coffee, too, you know. Real customers, not some half-assed tourists." The voice was gravelly and lazy, like that of a long-term drunk, and there was no humor in it.

"Any that ever tip?" she said, without looking over.

"We decide to tip you, babe, you'll walk funny for a week." The other hayseed had a younger voice, but no friendlier. He guffawed at his own crude joke. The waitress ignored them and calmly filled my cup.

"If you want to hit one of them upside the head with the coffee pot," I said, "I'll swear it was self-defense."

She gave me a funny, crooked smile. "You won't have to swear to anything. The law around here is like everything else: mostly homemade. But if I need any help burying the bodies, I'll let you know."

"My doctor says I should avoid heavy lifting."

"Yeah, I bet." Her look said she knew all about me, them, and just about everybody else, and had had just about enough of all of us. I've seen that look in some of my clients. It's not exactly the thousand-yard stare, but it's at least five hundred of it. It's not a good sign. "Be right back," she said.

She took her time strolling over to the booth, where she plopped down two green paper checks and splashed coffee into two mugs. The younger cornball got a sly grin on his face and started to reach around to grab her ass, but she moved quickly out of range, put a hand on one hip, and gave him a look that would kill jimson weed to the root. That's a weed they have in the crops around there. I learned about it from a radio commercial, on the way out. A lifelong student, that's me. The guy dropped the grin and stared into his coffee, muttering, and the waitress came back over to me.

"What takes your fancy?" she said, pulling a pencil from behind one ear.

"You want to be careful who you give that line to."

"I am. You want anything on the menu, or not?"

"I was hoping to talk to Rosie."

"I'm not rosy enough for you?" She gave me about a half-second flash of a phony stage smile, all teeth and dimples, and instantly reverted to her expression of studied indifference. I laughed in spite of myself.

"You're probably enough of anything for any man, but I was told Rosie could get me some pecan pie."

"Who told you that?"

"A guy named Numbers Jackson."

She raised both eyebrows. "He's in Redrock."

"That's him."

"Yeah, huh?" She tapped her pencil rhythmically on the order pad and looked at me as if for the first time, sizing me up, deciding something. She suddenly looked tougher than before, and it looked good on her, like a piece of animation that had been missing. "What's your name?" she said.

"Herman." I can't imagine why I didn't tell her "Sam Hill," but I didn't.

"You're kidding, right?"

"Afraid not." More afraid than she could imagine.

"We all have our problems, I guess." She shook her head. "I'm Laura. Rosie left years ago."

"Maybe she got tired of riveter jokes."

"That and a lot of other things. Wait until the others leave, okay? We'll talk. Meanwhile, pick something off the menu, look like you belong here."

"That could be tough."

It was her turn to laugh. "Picking something, or looking like you belong?"

"Either one."

She gave me the crooked smile again, this time with bit of warmth in it. It looked better than the stare. "I know that tune better than you do," she said.

"It shows."

"It ought to. Tell you what: have a fried egg sandwich. It's the cheapest thing on the menu, and even the dumb kid we've got out in the kitchen can't mess it up."

"I had eggs this morning. How about a plain burger?"

"Your funeral. Onions?"

"Absolutely."

"A man after my own heart." Why did I know she would say that? "That comes with French fries or hash browns."

"How about a salad?"

"How about sprouts and hollandaise sauce? Where do you think you are, civilization? The fries aren't too bad."

"Okay, fries, then. If they're no good, you can eat them."

Again the smile. "I can be had, Herman, but I'm not that cheap." I never thought for a minute that she was.

She went up to the pass window, impaled an order slip on a spike, and slapped a little bell. Then she went back through the kitchen door. While she was gone, Homer and Jethro came up to the counter to pay their bill. They glared at the dark porthole for a while, then at me. They were good at glaring. Finally, they left some money on the counter and turned to go. I concentrated on slurping some coffee, which wasn't as good as G. B. Feinstein's, but wasn't bad, either. The older one, with the cheap-booze voice and beer belly, looked like he wanted to start something but couldn't remember how. The younger one did it for him.

"We don't get a whole lot of strangers around here."

"Sounds right to me," I said, without looking up.

"Sounds right to us, too. Better, we don't get any."

"Somehow, I don't think you have to worry about that."

"I gotta spell it out for you? You ain't wanted here. I'm telling you to get out whilst you can still do it under your own power."

"I see." And I looked and did see, all the while thinking, *I absolutely do not need this shit.* The guy fronting me had a lot of muscle under the fat, but he didn't look either quick or smart. His buddy looked as if his chief contribution to any fight would be sitting on people, plus nasty little chores like gouging eyes and spitting on them. Neither one of them was worth messing up my plans over.

"Well, since you're so nice about it," I said, "I'll tell you something, too. You have no idea what you're fucking with here." Of course, neither did I, but this was not the time for that kind of timid thoughts. I slipped half off the stool, planted my feet in an easy intro to a half-stride fighter's stance, and pushed my right hand deep into my pocket. "I'm going to have a hamburger and then I'm going to go. If you want to make that a problem, that's up to you. But I'm never coming back here, and that means I don't care what kind of mess I leave behind for the cops or the ambulance. Think about it for a minute." And I gave them what I hoped was a cold smile.

I closed the hand inside my pocket, as if I had grasped something, and slowly began to bring it back out. Hayseed Junior stuck his finger at me as if he were going to poke it in my chest, but the older guy pulled his arm away. Too bad, in a way. That finger was practically begging to be broken.

"Leave it alone, Ditto," he said. "Come away."

"Aah…"

"It ain't the time. And I ain't backin' you up against some big city street fighter."

"We don't know that he is."

"And we don't know he ain't, neither. Come on, now."

"Oh, fuck it all, anahow." The belligerent one snatched his arm indignantly away and let himself be herded to the door, making a show of refusing to be hurried.

At the door, he turned and said, "She ain't going with you, no ways. She ain't never going with nobody but me."

So that's what it was all about. "That's right," I said. "She isn't." I began to think about how many hours of roaring tractors, bellowing cows, fertilizer commercials, and whining, hard-lard music it took to induce permanent brain damage. However many it was, he'd had a lot more than that.

He glowered at me for a while longer, then got bored with it and stomped out with his pal. I took my hand back out of my pocket, glad that I hadn't been forced to show that it had nothing in it but a pack of smokes, a Zippo lighter, and a lot of lint.

The waitress came back in a few minutes with my food and some utensils. "I made a call," she said.

"I'm happy for you."

"You carry a lot of weight with this Numbers guy."

"We go back a long ways." I salted the burger, put some anemic-looking pickle slices on it, and closed the bun. *How did they manage to make the bun greasy?*

"You must. The word is, don't charge you."

"For the burger?"

"For the pie."

"Oh, that." How could I have forgotten?

"Yeah, that. You like it heavy or light?"

I began to seriously wonder what we were talking about here. "What have you got?" I said.

"I've got a .380 semi-auto, a .357 revolver, and a couple flavors of nine millimeter. Anything else, we have to go someplace to get. It's a ways from here."

Oh, that, indeed. "Give me the three-eighty," I said. "Something that's easy to conceal. If I'm far enough away to need the heavy artillery, I'll run instead of shoot, every time."

"I like that in a man."

"Cowardice?"

"Sense. There's not much of that around these days."

"Seems to me Plato noticed that, too."

"You read a lot of Plato, do you?"

"No, but I thought it sounded more impressive than saying I picked it up from Rocky and Bullwinkle."

"Uh, huh." She did not sound impressed, and when I thought about it, that was just fine with me.

"You want a holster?" she said.

"With a belt clip, if you've got one."

"I've got." She went in the back again and returned with something that really did look like a pie box, heavy white cardboard with tricky fastener tabs.

"You've got a box of shells in there, too," she said, "but only one extra magazine. Also a velcro strap, in case you want to carry it on your ankle. Have fun."

I spared her my standard lecture on guns and fun. She pushed the box across the counter to me, then scribbled on one of her green slips and put that on top. She had charged me $12.85 for pie. With the burger and coffee and taxes, the whole tab came to $20.32. And people think it's cheap to live in small towns. I put a twenty and a five on the counter. She rang it all up on a genuine non-electronic cash register, along with the slips from the two hayseeds. She started to hand me change, but I waved it away, so she shrugged and dropped it into the pocket on her faded pink uniform. Then she poured herself a cup of coffee, came around the counter, and sat down next to me. She helped herself to one of my fries. I concentrated on chewing my burger.

"Take me with you."

I'd been half expecting that, but not this soon and definitely not this straightforward. It served me right, for flirting with her. "No," I said.

"Just like that? Just 'no'?"

"Just like that."

"I'll make it worth your while."

Was she really talking about what it sounded like? If she was from my uncle's world, it was a distinct possibility. His people made and dissolved relationships on just that whimsical a moment, and some of them turned out to be tight and durable. Uncle Fred himself lived for over twenty years with a woman he claimed to have won in a card game. She had never seemed cheap to me, but she never disputed the assertion, either. Whether or not they held each other against the night,

I'll never know. In any case, I could hardly judge them. I personally went the route of conventional marriage, and that turned out to be the biggest catastrophe of my then-young life.

I thought about how long it had been since I had touched a woman. Agnes is really like a sister to me, or maybe a buddy, and Deputy Janice is business. And business is business, another irrefutable little lesson from my long apprenticeship. Having a real woman again could be a fine thing. But it was a luxury I couldn't afford right then. It was already too much that she knew my real first name and that I had been to Redrock to see Uncle Fred. If she also saw where I lived, it would be a disaster.

"You're a big girl," I said. "You can leave any time you want, find a man any place you go. What do you need me for?"

"That's easy for you to say. It's not so easy for a woman, you know?"

"No, I don't."

"There are places you can't go unless you at least look like you're with a man. Being alone is like having a sign on your forehead that says 'Victim.'"

"And what makes you think I'm going any of those places?"

"Hey, I give up. Where are you going, anyway?"

"If I'm honest about it, I don't know."

"That's a good place. I can help you find it."

"No." I tried to make it sound more final this time, but it didn't come out that way, so I tried something else.

"You don't know anything about me," I said.

"I know enough."

"Oh, really? For all you know, I have a body in the trunk of my car."

"Better than a bale of hay." She had a point.

"I could be a psycho-sadist, with half the cops in the country looking for me, and a compulsive gambler and woman-hater and a closet vegetarian, to boot."

"You could be, but you're not. You're on the run from something, but you're not an asshole or a loser."

"Is that what you found out from your phone call?"

"No, I figured it out, all by my lonesome. I'm not stupid, Herman."

"I didn't think you were. So what are you doing in a dump like this? You from here, originally?"

"For a while. I ran away when I was sixteen, to the big city. You know, to get the things you can only get in a real city?"

"Including an abortion?"

"You're not stupid, either, are you, Herman? See? I was right about you, from the get-go. Anyway, I kept moving for fifteen years. Good times or bad, I never even thought about coming back here. My asshole of a father died, and I sent a THANK YOU card to the funeral parlor. Then my mom died, too. I came home to bury her, and I got suckered in by the prospect of inheriting this joint, free and clear. It seemed safe, you know? Easy, for a change. Like safe and easy is something you should give a rat's ass about. Now I can't even spit in the owner's eye and walk out. I'm losing my edge, big time. If I don't get out soon, I never will."

"I can see that," I said. "But it's not my problem, and I can't let it be."

"Sure you can. It's simple: when you get your own little problem solved, you're going back to where you come from. You can leave me wherever we happen to be when that happens, no complaints. Meanwhile, we help each other down the road."

"Really? And how are you going to help me, exactly?"

"Can you travel on plastic?"

"Don't have any."

"Bullshit. You have it, but you don't dare use it. That's why Numbers said not to charge you for the heat."

Well, I did say she wasn't stupid, didn't I?

"We can travel on mine," she said. "I've got a lot of it, and the bills all come here, where I'm never coming back, where I want a reason why I can't come back. It'll work, Herman. I don't exactly have a Sunday-school past, but I'm not wanted anywhere."

"Except by the doofus with the bad haircut and the Trans Am."

"Put your finger right on it, didn't you? That should be his problem, entirely. But he's trying hard to make it mine, and sooner or later, he'll do it. When that happens, I'm going to have to kill him, no choice." She turned and studied my face. "You believe that?' she said.

I looked in her eyes and saw about eight hundred yards of stare now, the threshold of the place where consequences don't matter any more. "Yes," I said.

"Much better all around if I'm just not here, wouldn't you say? Come on, Herman, what have you got to lose? Don't you ever need somebody to hold, just to keep away the night?"

I had to admit, she knew which buttons to push. But that didn't make the whole proposition any more sensible. "It's not a good time," I said.

"It's never a good time, unless you make it one."

"I'm sorry. I really am."

"You'll be sorrier when you're a hundred miles down the road, in a world of trouble, and all by yourself."

"Could be, but that's the hand I was dealt."

"You trying to break my heart?"

"See you, Laura."

"You could, but you won't. And that is definitely your loss."

"I'm prepared to believe that."

"And?"

"Goodbye."

"I was wrong; you are a loser." She flung the plate of fries away with an angry flick of dark-enameled nails. They crashed against the kitchen door just before she went back through it for the last time.

I didn't call after her.

Chapter Nine

Travels With Rosie

I chewed on the gristly burger for a while and argued with myself. I had definitely done the right thing, but why did I feel so shitty about it? *Herman, my man, what you feel and what you've got to do are two completely unrelated topics. You learned that a long time ago, remember?* I remembered. *So, why are you still here? Do you really like that burger?* No, I didn't, much. *Then get your sentimental ass out of here.* I picked up my pie box and got.

I hadn't noticed that the café was especially dark, but when I stepped outside, the sunlight hit me like an industrial strength flashbulb. I stopped on the sidewalk and fished in my jacket pocket for my shades. Over by my rented car, I heard the unmistakable noise of the gravel-voiced hick, telling me I wasn't going to get away completely clean, after all.

"There he is, Pud."

"I see him, Ditto."

Well. Not Homer and Jethro, after all, but Pud and Ditto. Very original, these rustic folk.

"Hey, Slick," the fat one again this time, "You're pretty good at sniffing around old Laurie in there. You any good at anything out here?"

I swear, the little one, Ditto, said, "Hee, hee, hee." Gomer Pyle, psychopath. Just what I needed.

"I'm good at leaving," I said. "And that's what I'm going to do, okay?"

"Not with her, you ain't."

With the shades on, I could see that they both had knives, ugly, curved things, too big to have been in their pockets. I wondered if they were called "corn knives." It would be a shame if they weren't. They had gone out to the car to arm themselves, apparently. And along the way, they had run into the waitress. The young goon had her pushed up against my car now, a meaty hand folded around her throat and an ugly knife held against one cheek. The knife didn't worry me so much, but a cop once told me that going for the throat was a very bad sign. On the ground nearby was a small suitcase that I assumed was hers. Not such an easy woman to brush off, after all. Her eyes were wide, but she looked more outraged than afraid. Outraged and determined.

And that, I have to admit, made all the difference.

I composed myself and gave them the same smile I had used in the café. Then I turned and walked away from them.

"Hey, where the fuck you think you're going?"

I reached in my pocket again and grabbed my lighter.

"We're talking to you, asshole."

I didn't turn around or pause, refusing to let them show me what they wanted to do to the woman. Instead, I went straight over to the blue Trans Am.

"What in hell does he think he's playing at?"

"Oh, dear, sweet Jesus, no. Not my car!"

There were some grunts and squeals then, and some scuffling noises, but I still didn't turn around. The hay bale was nicely dried out, and it lit like fine kindling. I had been going to start on one end and work my way across, but one spot turned out to be enough. The whole thing went from wisps of white-blue smoke to a full inferno faster than you could say, "Gaw-lee gee, Pud."

When I turned back, the fat man was running towards the Trans Am, eyes bulging and belly bouncing, gravelly voice shouting something incoherent. The younger guy was still back by my car, only now he was lying on the ground in a fetal position. He had blood on his face, which matched a blotch on the waitress' elbow. She stood over and behind him now, fire in her eye, methodically kicking his kidneys and spine. Enough of anything for any man, yes, indeed. Quick and possibly lethal, too. And God help me, I was about to go down the road with her.

I unlocked the rental car and got in. "You coming?" I said. "Or have you got better things to do now?"

"Just one little spot I missed," she said. No need to ask where that might be. I heard a meaty "thunk" and a prolonged, "Aaagh," and then she and her bag were in the car with me and we were gone.

Three minutes later, I slowed at a blacktop crossroads and asked her which way the nearest big town was.

"South," she said, "the way we're going, but I don't want…"

I hooked a hard left and put the pedal down.

"This is east," she said.

I nodded. "If the gas tank on that wreck was going to blow, it would have done it by now, and we would have heard it. If it didn't, your two fine friends might come after us for a bit of instant replay. We'll go a direction they won't expect you to pick."

"Nice," she said. "Always a pleasure, dealing with a professional."

"I'm a bondsman."

"Are you, really?"

"For years."

"What a trip. We've only just met, and already you never cease to amaze me."

"There's a lot of that going around."

We drove in silence for a while, and finally I said, "Your name isn't really Laura, is it?"

"That's what they know me as, back there. Your friends at Redrock know me as Rosie. I've had a lot of names over the years. Changing them seems to come naturally to me. Maybe I'm part Gypsy."

"Good Lord, not you, too."

"Not me too, what?"

"Everybody I meet lately seems to have something to do with Gypsies. All my problems keep pointing me back to them, and until a couple days ago, I didn't even know there were any left in the modern world." Or was it a couple of years?

"You want to learn all about them?"

"No, but I'd damn well better."

"Well, then, there's only one place to go: Skokie."

"Is that a place or an adjective?"

"Three fourths of the Gypsies in the country live within ten miles of Skokie, Illinois."

My turn to be amazed. "Why on earth?" I said.

"Beats me, but they do. I learned that from a bartender at a strip jo…um, a place in Chicago where I worked for a while. He wasn't exactly my type"—she made an exaggerated limp-wrist gesture—"but we were friends, and he knew a lot of things, and nobody else ever talked to him. He was sort of a disinherited Gypsy. Or excommunicated, or something like that."

I couldn't think of a thing to say to any of that.

"Didn't I tell you I'd help you find your way?"

"Oh you told me, all right. You have any idea where this Skokie place is?"

"More or less. North of Chicago."

"Then you can more or less drive."

I pulled over onto the gravel shoulder and changed places with her. She adjusted the driver's seat, fastened her harness, and checked the mirrors. Then she peeled off like a stock car driver. All around, a formidable woman, this former prairie flower, gun moll, stripper, café owner, martial arts expert, and God knew what else. "So, what do I call you?" I said.

"Call me Rosie. That's the one I always liked the best."

"Good night, Rosie." I tilted the seat back as far as it would go, pulled my jacket up over my chest and chin, and closed my eyes. Except for the nap in my office after the Proph brought me back, I hadn't had any sleep in the last thirty hours or more, and it was starting to weigh on me. "If you decide to drive into Lake Michigan, wake me up first, will you?"

"Herman?"

I opened my left eye and looked over at her. She had the crooked smile again, this time with wrinkles in the corners of her eyes to match. She was having a good time. *A lunatic fleeing the asylum. Wonderful.*

"I'm unconscious," I said.

"I did good back there, didn't I?" The way she said it, it was a gleeful boast, not a question. I didn't know if she was talking about kicking the hick in the nuts or about getting me to take her along, and I decided not to ask.

"You did good, Rosie." *Do better: let me sleep.*

"You're going to be glad you took me along. I know it."

That made one of us.

"Where do you want to stop for the night?"

"Someplace near an outside phone booth and a terminal where I can get on the Internet," I said. "Other than that, I couldn't care less."

"Sounds like you have a plan."

"It does sound like that, doesn't it?" Sometimes these things just sneak up on you.

The subdued hum of the machine, the road noise, and the gentle breeze from Rosie driving with her window down were better than a hot toddy and a massage. Magic. I felt my consciousness drop like a submarine on a crash dive, and I made no attempt to slow its descent.

Somewhere on the way to the bottom, it passed some whales that looked a lot like violins with flippers and tails, and a mermaid that looked a lot like Rosie, but we plunged on past, to the depths that even the light can't penetrate. Somewhere down there, answers were waiting for me. Answers and a real plan. And oblivion. And even if I was wrong about the rest, the oblivion was enough for now.

We stopped at least once for gas and whatever, I think, but it didn't seem worth waking up for. Later I cracked an eye open briefly to see the light dying on a landscape of featureless prairie that probably looked better in the dark anyway. *Land that only a farmer could love*, I thought. *A place where he's got lots of room to park his two-acre, all-in-one rolling factory that Cyrus McCormick would never recognize.* It made me miss the city more than a little kid at summer camp. I had never been to summer camp myself, but I figured I knew the feeling. St. Paul wasn't exactly Detroit or Chicago, but at least it wasn't open flatlands. I drifted back off. After a second stop, I woke slowly to the smell of coffee and garlic, with maybe a touch of tomato paste for counterpoint. I put the seat back up, threw my jacket in the back, and lit a cigarette.

"Do you have to do that?" she said.

"No, but I'm going to." If she had an aversion to smoke, I could find a way to accommodate that. But if she turned out to be a closet do-gooder and health nut, this was going to be a very short-lived partnership. I rolled my window partway down and tasted a bit more of my newfound waking state.

"You have any other nasty habits that I ought to know about?"

"Now's a hell of a time to ask."

"Well, we had other things on our minds, back in New Salem."

"Which you, of course, did nothing to cause."

"Why Herman, whatever are you accusing me of?"

"You seemed to have had a bag packed awfully conveniently."

"Oh, is that all that's bothering you? 'Packed' is the word, all right."

"What does that mean?"

"Have a look, if you want to. It's on the back seat."

I unscrewed two or three of my vertebrae from their sockets, twisting around in the seat, and popped the latches on the old fashioned overnight case. Inside was a leather purse, a lot of loose money, and the three other guns she had described to me back at the café. The revolver looked like a cannon with a handle. There was also something dark that could have been a ski mask. I didn't even want to think about that.

"Good grief," I said.

"I only took the important stuff," she said. "You can see, it really was a spur-of-the-moment thing. Well, mostly. A marriage of convenience, you could say."

"If that was convenience, I'll pass on the harder parts. And don't even think about using that other word."

"Have it your way. Anyway, I need to do some shopping."

That was one of the things she needed, all right. A good therapist also came to mind. "What's the smell?" I said.

"Dark coffee and pepperoni pizza-flavored egg rolls."

"Classy."

"BP Roadside Gourmet, the sign said. Not the chef's choice, though. He tried to sell me Ding Dongs. Says they don't mess up the steering wheel so much."

"Clean steering wheels are highly overrated. Especially if somebody else is driving." I threw the cigarette out the window and tried an egg roll. It actually wasn't bad. The coffee tasted more like Dow-Corning than Colombian, but it wasn't bad, either. I must have been ready to come back to life. Outside, the prairie was giving way to sodium floodlights and buildings. Better. The outskirts of Chicago, I decided, though it looked less like the threshold of a great metropolis than a compacted bunch of 1950s suburbs. One and two story businesses of no architectural style were jammed together with modest houses just as nondescript. The only way you could tell you were getting close to a major city was that the spaces between them kept getting smaller and the traffic denser and less polite. The chief industries seemed to be auto parts stores and unclaimed freight marts, with an occasional bowling alley or laundromat. If there were any libraries, parks, or public buildings, they were underground. Civilization, like prosperity, never really trickles down very far from its citadels. But there was an undeniable pulse to the streets that quickened as we got closer to the unseen lake and the famous skyline, and it was infectious.

We passed a small strip mall with a row of hotels across from it, and Rosie looked over at me and arched an eyebrow. I pointed at a Kinko's in the middle of the strip. We stopped, and I bought a couple hours on one of their PC terminals.

"Do you need any help with it?" The clerk was decked out in pimples and improbable studs.

"I just need to send and receive some email."

"Email or e-messaging?"

"Is that a trick question?"

"If you have a registered handle, you can do e-messaging, get an instant reply back."

"If I had a handle, I'd be using a CB."

"Gee, I don't know that technology. Sorry."

Sometimes I get very sick of being a dinosaur.

Rosie interrupted us to ask if she could go do some shopping and book us a room for the night.

"Sure," I said. "Where shall I find you?"

"I'll check back here once. If that doesn't work, look for me in the bar of that hotel." She pointed to the fanciest one of the row across the street, one that looked like it had maybe started its life as an Embassy Suites. I took her elbow and moved her aside, out of earshot of the gawking techie, and told her that if they asked her to write down the license number of the car, she should reverse the last two digits.

Her eyebrows tried to merge into a face-wide frown, but they didn't quite meet at the center. "Whatever for?"

"If somebody is checking to see if the car belongs in their parking lot, they'll just assume it was a mistake in writing it down. But if somebody is doing a computer search for the car, they'll come up empty."

The frown changed to a look of open admiration. "In the bar," she said. "Two hours, tops. You can pretend you're picking me up."

"I did that once. I think it was a mistake."

"I'll see what I can do about that." She gave me a kiss on the cheek which I had to admit was rather nice. The techie-type stared in obvious envy and possible astonishment.

"Show me about this e-mess business," I said.

He showed me, and also set me up with a "handle" for the chat sites, in case I felt chatty. I decided to be "Gypsy," but that turned out to be taken already. So was "Hermes," with or without an apostrophe. After several other tries, I settled for being "Numbersman." As if that weren't enough of an ordeal, I also needed an eight-digit or longer password. I picked MI5KG-BCIA. If you're going to play at cloak-and-dagger, you might as well go all the way. Besides, I thought I could remember it.

"Can I get messages here after I leave?"

The techie gave me a funny look. "How can you get anything here after you leave, man? That's like spooky. And you said *I* asked trick questions?"

"What I mean is, if I come back here tomorrow and buy some more time, will I be able to get any messages that came in the meantime?"

"Oh, like that. Well, of course. That's the whole point, isn't it? Anything else?"

"Show me where there's an outside public phone."

"What do you want a phone for, if you've got e-messaging?"

"I'm a renaissance man."

"Wow, I don't know that one, either. Is that a Microsoft program?"

I took the number off a pay phone at the end of the parking lot, in front of a bagel store, and then came back and sat down at the computer. I emailed Agnes first, remembering to add the cute little red envelope that seemed to be the key to all things urgent in her world. My return address, of course, was out of my control, but I could type in a subject title that she would see before she opened the message. I used "Detroit refugee calls home," and typed in the following message:

How's the heat there?

Forward the message to me, here, from the something-Cox address, the one about the valuable instrument. Then get hold of WTW and give him the number at the bottom of this message. Tell him to call me there every hour on the hour, starting at 9:00 tomorrow morning, until he gets me.

If the bond collateral is no good, tell me so at this address tomorrow at 8:00, when you come in for the day. I will check this site then and again around the middle of the day.

All best

Wandering Boy

I added the number from the pay phone and clicked the mouse on the phony picture of a SEND button. The "collateral" business, of course, referred to the possibility that somebody was looking over Agnes' shoulder when she opened my message, and the pay phone number was therefore compromised. If that happened, I was giving myself a couple hours to set up an alternate one and/or get the hell out of there, since we both knew that Agnes really got into the office at 6:00, not 8:00. Pretty clever, us spooks.

I thought about what to say in the reply to the message about the violin, but I really needed to see it again first. Like Agnes, I don't do video games or surf the web, and I was wondering what to do with the rest of my time on the terminal, when to my wondering eyes a message from Agnes appeared, complete with cute little red envelope. She was working late, apparently. I wondered why.

Hey, Wandering Boy, I've been worried about you.

Lots of heat earlier today, but it's cool and quiet now.

Collateral is good. WTW says he has news to report. I'll give him the phone # as soon as I finish this, plus forward the message you wanted.

Be careful out there. Strange things going on.

Stay away from dark alleys and loose women, ha ha.

I won't ask where you are,

Ag

I decided not to tell her that her advice about loose women was a bit late. I typed in a quick thank you and attaboy note and no sooner had it sent than the forwarded message popped up on my screen, again with the red envelope. Agnes really liked those red envelopes.

mr. jackson

i believe you are in possession of a certain valuable musical instrument that is the rightful property of my family.

i understand that you acquired it in good faith, and i am prepared to reward you handsomely for its return.

can we talk?

Can we talk, indeed. I decided to cut right to the chase.

Re: "certain valuable musical instrument:"

Just how handsomely, exactly?

I presume we're talking about the Amati violin. It is in my possession, but its legal ownership is somewhat unclear at the moment.

That was putting it mildly. If Jimmy Cox skipped

out on his next court appearance, it was mine, no question about it. But if he showed up and my bond was released, I was legally obliged to return the violin to a person who was no longer alive. And there was no use asking if she had a will, because she might not have been the real Amy Cox, if there even was a real Amy Cox. Jimmy Cox was supposed to have said he had no sister, but I only knew this from a phony cop who might also sometimes be a phony Jimmy Cox and who might or might not be the person who was arrested for careless Ludding. So whom did it revert to? The guy writing the email? The kid in jail, as I was sure he would be? I decided not to make any promises I might regret.

> *I might consider selling a Quit-claim deed for my interest in the Amati. Anything else would be premature at this time.*

Then, astonished that I hadn't thought of it earlier, I added:

> *Who the hell are you, anyway?*

> *H. Jackson*

Once again, I had nothing to do but wait for a reply that I wasn't likely to get very soon. I thought about what I had just sent to the mysterious person with the instrument-owning family and also about something my Uncle Fred had said to me back at

Redrock. Suddenly, I felt an irresistible urge to get to a phone. I called over to my friendly clerk-technician.

"I have to go make a call, okay?"

"You've got time left on the machine."

"That's why I'm telling you. I want it back."

"Oh, I get it. I won't let anybody else use it until you come back. Is that what you mean?"

"That's it." Maybe it has nothing to do with being a dinosaur.

I walked down the strip to a Snyder drug store and bought a phone card, then headed over to the booth by the bagel shop. Agnes tells me at least once a day that I ought to get a cell phone, of course. Since I don't want to hurt her feelings, I mostly pretend I don't hear her. The truth is, I would rather die than have one of those damned electronic leashes stuck on my ear like an alien parasite. That probably makes me some kind of techno-curmudgeon, and if I think about it, I might even like that title. In any case, I headed for the booth.

We must not have been very far into the Chicago metro area yet, because the phone was intact and working. I punched in a number I knew by heart.

Nickel Pete closes his pawn shop for the day anywhere from five to eleven, as the spirit moves him and depending on whether he's made any money yet. But he lives in an apartment above the place, and that's where I called him, letting the phone ring a dozen times before he finally picked up. I said hello, and he recognized my voice, which I found touching.

"You're a lot of damn trouble for the amount of business you bring me, Herman."

"It's nice to talk to you, too, Pete."

"Of course it's nice. That's because I'm not dragging you out of bed in the middle of the night."

"It's not exactly the middle of the night, for most people. Were you really in bed?"

"Would you believe with a hot little redhead who's trying to persuade me to give back her heirloom wedding rings?"

"No."

"No. Well, it was worth a try. With a bowl of popcorn and a dirty video, then. What the hell do you want?"

"You know the Amati violin I left with you?"

"Is this a memory test? Of course I know it. What do you want me to do with it?"

"I don't want you to do anything with it. Just go see if it's still there."

"Believe me, it's there. Fort Knox would kill for the alarm systems I got. If I was broke into, I'd know it."

"Would you take a look, as a favor? And take a flashlight with you. Shine it in the f-holes, see if there's a label."

"Now he not only wants a favor, he wants to tell me my business."

"Indulge me, will you? I'll owe you one."

"Damn right you will. You want to hold on, or should I call you back?"

"I'll hold." A lot of my profession consists of nothing more than waiting for a phone to ring, but I didn't seem to be wired for it just then. I waited through dim background noises of grunts and coughs, doors opening and slamming, and a soundtrack that really might have been from a dirty movie, at that. That, or Pete had a very large cat with serious hairball problems.

He was gone a long time, and I spent it looking around at the parking lot, memorizing the ways in and out and the possible places from which the booth could be watched. It wasn't a bad setup, for a random pick. Easy to spot somebody in the booth, but not so easy to trap him there. I wondered if the bagel shop had a back door. I would find out before I left. I also wondered if they had filet mignon with mushroom caps and bordelaise sauce. The pizza rolls were starting to feel a bit inadequate for the demands of the night.

Finally I heard the clunking sounds of the receiver being bounced off the floor and picked up again, and Pete's wheezing breath.

"I can't figure it out, Herman."

I felt a knot begin to form in my stomach. "What?"

"I swear, nobody's ever pulled anything like this

on me before. And mind you, they've tried."

"Will you please just spit it out? Is the violin there or isn't it?"

"Sort of."

"Well, that certainly clears it all up. Sort of. Are you having a senility attack, or are you capable of explaining that to me?" The knot in my stomach somehow got tighter and turned to ice, all at the same time.

"The case is there. The same case we both saw. I'm sure of it. And there's an old violin in it."

"But."

"But when I looked in the f-hole, like you told me?"

"You have to be coaxed for every damn word, don't you? What did you see, termites?"

"I saw a label that says Yamaha."

Pigeon drop.

Chapter Ten

You've Got Mail

I checked out the rear exit of the bagel shop, pretending to be looking for the restroom. I bought half a dozen bagels first, on the theory that regular customers are less likely to be remembered clearly than sneaky-looking idiots who just wander in and look for the back door. Behind the place was a wide gravel service drive and then a steep berm covered with untended weeds and brush. A chain link fence about half way up would be climbable, but a car couldn't get through it without major damage to itself.

I hiked up as far as the fence and looked over the ridge. Beyond it were several train tracks and then a clutter of warehouses and freight yards. There was an opening in the fence, opposite the end of the mall buildings, overgrown and hard to see from below. I went through it and up to the top, for a better look. In the black sky above, a big airliner suddenly switched on its landing lights and came screaming straight at me, like a fighter jet on a strafing run, only nose-high and with all its flaps and wheels hanging out. It passed over my head in a metallic storm of noise and flashing lights and then was suddenly gone, eager to flatten its tires on the tarmac at Midway or O'Hare.

A thousand yards farther ahead of me, a freeway passed by on elevated pylons, the lights of the cars giving an eerie internal illumination to a linear cloud of exhaust and aerated road grime. Service ladders went up some of the pylons, and twisted paths went away into dark places. All around, a thoroughly nasty landscape. It had complexity, distraction, and chaos. If I had to run, this would be the place to go.

I went back down the hill and walked around the outside of the bagel shop and back towards the main shopping center. The strip was laid out like a big horseshoe, with the bagels on one prong, a store selling dumpy shirts with the label sewn on the outside on the other, and the Kinko's down at the cleat in the middle. I imagined Rosie went someplace else altogether to do her shopping.

Rosie. I thought about what I had told her about the license number on the rented car. Did I really believe all that clandestine crap? If not, why did I make it up? *Because you wanted to impress her.* I did not. Where the hell was that coming from? *Denial is the surest indicator of a lie.* Sometimes I hate being so damn smart.

At least two thirds of the stores were closed for the night, and the parking lot was mostly deserted. A couple of semis were pulled up in the middle of it, the drivers taking a sleep break, and a squad car lazily cruising the perimeter didn't seem to care. I suppose the world always has a lot of cops in the background in public places. Somehow, I never noticed before. Now, I seemed to run into them constantly.

Maybe it was another example of what Uncle Fred used to call "The Green Volvo Syndrome." There isn't a single green Volvo in your neighborhood, the theory goes, until you go out and buy one. Then the whole world is instantly full of the stupid things. It's a morphing thing. Chevrolets and Fords morph into Volvos and ordinary citizens morph into cops. There's an automatic Nobel Prize in physics there, if I could just figure out where to publish my findings.

The short odds were that neither the morphed nor the regular cops would be looking for me here in Almost-Chicago, but I didn't want to count on that assumption. I decided a bold diagonal across the lot was a bit conspicuous, and I walked across the gap between the prongs of the horseshoe instead, where I could stay on the fringe of the light island. I wondered who I would be, if I got asked, and I realized I should have worked that out with Rosie before she went off. "Rosie's husband" didn't sound like a very convincing alias. James Stroud was probably even worse. Herman Jackson was still what most of the stuff in my wallet said, and I decided I had better do something about that. That was as far as my thinking went just then.

The squad car moved even more slowly than I walked, and I made it back to the Kinko's before he managed to get interested in me. But he did seem to be interested in the phone booth I had so recently occupied. He cruised over to it, then got out and had a look at the "instrument," as the former Ma Bell employees insist on calling it. That bothered the hell out of me.

"You got a message," said my friendly techie. He didn't know the half of it. I could hardly wait to see the one that he knew about.

"What's it say?" I said. I wanted to watch the cop a while longer before I went back to the terminal.

"Hey, I wouldn't open your mail. But it makes a little 'ding!' noise for 'Incoming.'"

"Better than a whoosh and then a big boom."

"Huh?"

Talking with young people is so refreshing.

The email message was longer than the first one. Apparently, my mystery man had found my reply stimulating.

mr. jackson

you talk like a lawyer or a confidence man. for your sake i hope you are neither. i do not take well to being toyed with. please do not waste my time with any talk about titles. i know that you have the amati. produce it and i will pay you $50,000, no questions asked. how you account for its disappearance is your problem. i can have cash ready in two business days.

where can we meet to make the exchange?

i am gerald cox.

Well. Not exactly a threatening letter, but close enough. And on the surface, at least, not part of the original scam. If this guy was the equivalent of the bogus "collector" in the classic hustle, he should have offered me more money, for one thing. Enough to be irresistible, but not enough to sound phony. Twenty years worth of inflation on a starting value of sixty thou was about a hundred and sixty or so, by my fast and dirty mental arithmetic. So someplace within about fifteen or twenty of that figure would be the right…

"Ding!" More incoming. Get your head down, soldier. This was from a different address, one I hadn't seen before:

The writer calling himself Gerald Cox is a fraud. Do not meet with him, if he suggests it. It could be dangerous.

For a price, I can tell you how to get the real Amati back.

A friend.

A friend, was it? Sounded awfully hostile to me. Also awfully convenient. Could the timing of the second message have been a coincidence? I didn't know anybody except the Proph who would think so. I looked out the glass storefront again and saw the cop still over by the pay phone. Then I went back to my newfound technical advisor.

"You seem to know a lot about computers, um"—I snuck a quick look at his employee name tag—"Brian." I lied. He didn't really seem to know what time of day it was, but I wanted some advice, and I figured it couldn't hurt to stroke him a little.

"It's like totally what I do, is all. My parents don't understand that, you know? They actually think I should go to college. They can't see that all the, you know, knowledge and stuff in the world is just right there on your keyboard, waiting to be downloaded."

"Maybe they want you to get some kind of knowledge that doesn't download." Parents get silly ideas like that sometimes.

"They want me to study law. Can you believe that?"

"No way." *You bet I can. They want you in a profession where being brain damaged is not a handicap.*

"I mean, the law is just so totally stupid," he said.

"I think Dickens said something like that, too."

"Is he a hacker?"

"Depends on who you ask." I wasn't going to go down that road.

"Listen," I said, "this stuff I've been getting and sending here is completely secure, right? I mean, nobody can trace it back to this site?"

"Well, yeah. I mean, duh-uuh. That's the whole point, you know?"

"They can trace it back to this place?"

"You said this site, not this place."

"Oh." Isn't semantics fun? "So what about this place?"

"No way."

"And nobody else can read it, either? I mean, without having access to the computer on one end of the message or the other?"

He shook his head. "Not unless they've got a sniffer."

I was afraid he was going to say something like that. I looked out the window and saw the cop leaving the phone booth and going back to his car.

"What's a sniffer?"

"It's like a wiretap, only for computers. But it has to have a dedicated phone line. Too many signals to sort out, otherwise."

"How comforting. And who would have one of these sniffers?"

"Them."

"Them."

"Yeah, you know. Men in Black, the Forces of Evil, aliens, the government, all like that. *Them.*"

"Oh, Them."

"You're making fun of me, aren't you?"

"Perish the thought, Brian. Who else could have a sniffer?"

"Rich people, I guess. And industrial spies. It's illegal for anybody, of course. Even the cops are supposed to get a court order first. But if you've got enough money, you can get any kind of hardware you want."

"And somebody like you to make it work."

He stood a little straighter and smiled around a stud.

"Sure, I could do that."

And if *he* could, the world was full of people who could. And one of them could have definitely asked the local fuzz to check out a phone number. I looked out the store window and saw the squad car leave the phone booth and head straight for us, though still in no hurry. Ahead of him, though, a brownish-red Pontiac stopped at the curb in front of the door.

At first I didn't recognize the blonde at the steering wheel. Rosie was wearing a low-cut white dress and lipstick, and she had her hair pulled back into some kind of roll. She looked five years younger than when we had last talked and a lot cuter, and her crooked smile told me she knew as much. She leaned over to look in the plate glass window, searching. I caught her eye and held up a hand that I hoped said, "Wait right there." Three seconds later, I was getting in the passenger door, ignoring the comments from young Brian that followed me out.

"Kiss me," I said.

"Why, Herman, I thought you'd never…"

"Kiss me like I'm your loving spouse, finally done copying the work he always takes home with him."

"Like this?"

"Mmph." I had been going to say, "Too passionate," but her tongue got in the way. She had a very talented tongue. Quite possibly electric, also, since it definitely activated things far removed from my mouth. I wasn't giving it the attention it deserved, though. Above her shoulder, I could see the squad car slow and hesitate, having to rethink the scenario he had just worked out. This was good. We held the kiss for a while longer, and then I got the rest of the way into the car and buckled my seat belt.

"Now cruise on out of here, nice and smooth and respectable. If that cop stares at you, give him a pretty smile and a wave."

But he didn't. He kept heading for the print shop. "Go out around the end of the mall by the shirt store, and watch your mirror."

"Hey, it was a great kiss for me, too, but you don't have to get all gushy about it."

"Is he following us?"

"No." She watched the mirror for a couple seconds. "Oops, yes, now he is. But not fast. Aren't you going to tell me I look stunning?"

"Actually, you do. How far back?"

"All the way to my irresistible round ass, what do you think?"

"How far back is the cop?"

"Oh, him. Half the length of the parking lot. Thanks for the compliment."

"My pleasure."

She turned by the trendy rag store, and by the time we got to the service drive entrance, the cop still hadn't made the corner behind us. "Turn in here," I said, pointing. "Put on a little speed, but don't spin your wheels. We don't want to leave a lot of dust."

We turned down the service road and accelerated,

and we were almost to the next corner, where we could turn again and be out of sight behind the main mall, when the cop swung in behind us and turned on his flashers.

"So much for finesse."

"You want me to lose him?"

"Are you serious?" I asked. "You know what you're doing?"

"Watch me."

"All right, I will."

"Really?"

"Punch it."

She stood on the brakes first, and when the I'm-smarter-than-you-are system wouldn't lock up the wheels, she hit the hand brake.

"Lots of dust," she said, by way of explanation.

"I noticed."

As soon as the brown cloud started to roll around us, she killed the lights and hit the gas, hard, taking the corner around the mall in a power slide and continuing to accelerate out of it. Halfway down the back service drive, the speedometer was passing sixty.

"I don't want to tell you your business," I said, "but for what it's worth, there's a break in that fence up there that a car could get through."

"Where?"

"Right by the back door of the bagel joint."

"Perfect. Hold tight. I think you'll like this."

We flew past the fence opening at seventy-plus. She spotted it and hit the hand brake again, throwing the car into a one-eighty half spin on the gravel.

"More dust," she said. I just nodded and hung on. We came out of our own cloud, slowly and smoothly now, turned up the berm, and went through the fence. Down at the far end of the mall, the way we had just come from, the cop's lights were just starting to emerge from the first dust cloud, slowly, tentatively. Before he was clear of it, we were gone, over the crest. In another world. Literally vanished in a cloud of dust. I was impressed.

The back side of the berm was less impressive. You wouldn't exactly call it a drivable surface, but the fact that it was downhill made it easier to jolt over the rocks and leap the chasms. The fact that it wasn't my own car whose undercarriage we were destroying didn't hurt my feelings any, either. I just hoped we didn't trip any air bags.

At the bottom was another service road, this one paved with cinders, that paralleled the railroad tracks. Rosie followed it for a quarter mile or so, until we came to a sort of crossing, and then we went over a bunch of tracks and down into the industrial backwaters. We were well out of sight of the mall now, even from the top of the berm, and she put the headlights back on and settled into an easy twenty-five. I toggled down my window and listened for sirens. Nothing. Just distant freeway noise and an occasional airplane.

"Slick," I said.

"Wow, an unsolicited compliment. Thank you. I had a lot of practice as a kid, chasing jackrabbits over plowed fields in a pickup."

"Ever catch any?"

"Of course not. Why would I want to catch a jackrabbit?"

Ask a silly question.

"If we want to get clear of this area in a hurry," she said, "we could go like a bat between two sets of train tracks." She obviously liked the idea a lot.

"Until we come to a bridge or a switch block."

"Fuss, fuss. What's a chase without risks?"

"A successful escape."

"You know, you really ought to learn to lighten up once in a while, Herman." Her shoulders slumped and she gave an exaggerated sigh. "Okay. So what's our plan?"

"Hide someplace in this area for a few hours, until our cop and all the friends he's calling right now get some other things to think about besides us."

"Pretty daring. You see a place you like?"

"Not yet. Cruise a bit." Another jetliner popped out of the sky with a full array of lights, and a block or so away, I saw a flash of what I wanted. "That way," I said, and she turned into the wake of the jet.

"Who are we, by the way?"

"I said I'd be your guide, not your shrink. If you're going to do identity crisis, you're on your own."

"I mean who are we if we get asked, like by a cop or a desk clerk, okay?"

"We don't talk to cops. Shoot the bastards on sight." She took both hands off the wheel and pantomimed mowing down the blue hordes with a machine gun.

"Will you please sober up?"

"Oh, all right. I don't know what to tell the cops, okay? As far as the hotel is concerned, I'm Ms. Rosemary Wapczech, and you're none of their damn business."

"Gee, for some reason, I thought it would be O'Grady."

"Nope, Rosie the Polack. Sorry. You want it to be O'Grady?"

"For the hotel, I want it to be whatever is on your plastic. But the none-of-their-damned business is no good. They might decide you're a hooker and toss you out for the sake of their fine reputation."

"Oh come on, Herman. Do I look like a hooker?"

"The classier ones are hard to tell from real women, you know."

"Based on your vast experience."

"Some of my best customers." Actually, my

experience was that the high-tone prostitutes—the society women who got their thrills with a little role-playing and a little walk on the wild side, or the spoiled college girls who didn't want to wait to cash in on the good life, or even the expensive call girls with their remarkable beauty and penthouse condos and silk-suited lawyers—were among my worst customers. They would stiff me, any chance they got. The real, hard-working street walkers, on the other hand, the ones with too much makeup and too little of everything else, including looks and brains, tended to be rock-solid reliable. I think it has something to do with honor and dignity being more valuable to the people who don't normally get any of the stuff. I don't have it all worked out yet. And I didn't try to tell Rosie about it.

"For the hotel staff, I'll be Herman—what is it, again?"

"Wapczech. It's easy to remember: just think, 'Italian bank draft.' But you don't have any ID."

"They won't ask, as long as we're using your credit cards. For the cops, though, we'll need something else. I have a sort of printing press in my briefcase. Maybe we'll cook something up when we get to settle down for a bit."

"Maybe, huh? Meanwhile, maybe we can just be who we are, and you can be taking me back home for jumping bail."

I thought about it for a minute. "You know, that's actually not bad. If they have a bulletin on me, we would have to reverse the roles, but it might still work. It would be even better if we had some handcuffs."

"I have some in my purse."

"You're kidding. Why would you…"

"Is that where you want to park?"

"That's it." *Handcuffs?*

We picked a spot in a steel recycling yard, where a lot of old cars were massed together, waiting to be crushed into bales and then fed into a blast furnace. I picked the padlock on the fence with a paper clip from Kinko's. After we were inside and re-locked, I took off our wheel covers and license plates and put them in the trunk, stuck a cardboard placard from another car on the windshield, and kicked a little extra dirt on the front end. Then we backed in between two other cars, so close on each side that our doors couldn't be opened. More to the point, it was also too close for anybody looking us over to walk up to the side of the car. It would do, if anything would.

"Snug," said Rosie.

"Inconspicuous, anyway. Tilt your seat back, so our heads don't stick up above the dash."

"Comfy. Can we call room service now?"

"I have to admit, that sounds good. I have some bagels, if you're starving."

"Hey, yeah? I have a bottle of champagne and some fancy chocolate-covered black cherries."

By now, I knew better than to ask if she was kidding, and I laughed instead. "You're just a bundle of surprises, Rosie."

"I am, aren't I? I want you to realize, by the way, that I booked us a deluxe suite at the Crown Regal Inn, with a Jacuzzi and a kitchenette."

"You want me to feel guilty?"

"Very, very guilty. Or disappointed, at the least."

"I can handle both of those."

"Anyway, I could see you were going to be a hard sell, so I picked up some goodies. I figured if I can't get laid, at least I can get high."

If I'd been eating a bagel, I'd have choked on it. Finally I managed to say, "You're going to get high on chocolate cherries?"

"You take your pleasure where you find it, Herman."

You do indeed, don't you? "Have a bagel, Rosie." I passed the bag over to her.

"Delighted, Herman. Have a swig of champagne. You have to open it, though. I'm terrible with those things. Also, I don't want to stain my new dress. That's okay, isn't it?"

"Why would you need my permission not to stain your dress?"

"Just thought I'd ask." With that, she leaned forward to undo her zipper, then slipped the dress over her head and placed it neatly in the back seat. "I didn't have time to shop for any underwear," she said.

I found myself recalling G. B. Feinstein's line about fine curves: *A subtle variation on a timeless theme.* Hers weren't all that subtle, maybe, but they were definitely fine.

"You are…"

"'Irrepressible' is the word that I always liked."

"'Sneaky,' is what I was going to say."

"That, too." She insinuated an arm around the back of my neck, and I didn't seem to do anything to stop her.

"You know, I never…" I began.

"No, you didn't. And you don't have to."

I was talking about promises. I hoped she was, too, since…

"You know why I never ran down any jackrabbits?"

"Um. Because you're too kindhearted?"

"Because I prefer the ambush."

She did good ambush. I have to say, though, handcuffs are not as much fun as people generally suppose. By the time we got around to the champagne, it was warm, and it exploded all over hell. But we didn't get any on our clothes.

Chapter Eleven

Love Among the Ruins

"Are you awake, Herman?"

"I am, but I'm in the middle of an intense intellectual exercise." I pulled my coat back up over her shoulder, where she had shaken it off in her sleep, and she snuggled a bit closer, making my left arm, if possible, even more numb. I did not look forward to the time when it quit being numb.

"Trying to figure out how you wound up sleeping in the middle of a junkyard with a strange woman?"

"No, I'm trying to decide which is more boring, the ceiling in a dentist's office or the head liner in this car."

"I thought a headliner was an overpaid performer."

"It's also the upholstery they put on the bottom of a car roof."

She rolled partway over and looked up. "You're right; that's pretty boring. Does it win?"

"It's a tough call. My dentist has artsy pictures on his ceiling, but the hygienist doesn't wrap her leg around my waist."

"That's why they need the pictures." She flexed the aforementioned limb a bit for emphasis and added an arm to the gesture, and the phrase *holding against the night* flashed into my mind. Maybe the holding thing is like the green Volvo: it only shows up when you're not looking for it. But my mind jumped just as quickly to a vision of a murderous black LTD, and the moment was suddenly gone.

"Do you have a watch, Rosie?"

"Don't you?"

"I do, but I no longer have the arm it was attached to."

She sat up, picked up my dead arm, squinted at the wrist, and let it flop back down. The arm woke up just enough to promise me a lifetime of agony.

"Three-thirty," she said. "You want to leave?"

"Give it another half hour. In a lot of towns, cops change their shifts at four. We'll slip out in the transition time."

She stretched and grimaced. "I'd suggest something very nifty to do with that half hour, but I think my back is broken."

"That's because you've been sleeping on top of a hand brake and a shifting lever."

"Tell me about it. Your arm helped some, though."

"I'm glad you feel that way. I'm thinking of having it amputated. Do we have any champagne left?"

She rolled back over to the driver's seat with a few appropriate groans, grabbed the bottle from under the brake pedal, and shook it.

"A little," she said. She took a swig and passed it over to me. "Also one bagel. You want?"

"Breakfast of champions," I said. "But I'll share."

She broke the bagel in two and handed me half, and we listened to our jaws work for a while.

"So, why are you on the run, Herman?"

"I bopped a cop."

"That doesn't sound so bad."

"Put that way, it doesn't, does it? I bopped a cop who was trying to abduct me. He's also trying to pin a murder on me."

"That sounds worse. So you gave him some more ammunition, by running."

"That I did. Seemed like the thing to do at the time. Still does, for that matter. Are there any more cherries?"

"If there are, they're all in the cracks between the seats." She made a "gimme" gesture, and I passed the bottle back to her.

"I thought I was the impulsive one here," she

said. "Why didn't you just stay where you were and rat this guy out?" She tipped back her head to drain the bottle, making a lovely line that started at her chin and swooped down, graceful and unbroken, all the way to the punctuation of her nipples. I made a heroic effort to return to my other train of thought.

"I can't do that, exactly."

"Then do it not exactly. Use a go-between. You want me to do it for you? While I'm at it, I'll accuse him of rape. You're staring, by the way."

"You don't have any evidence. And of course I'm staring. Don't you want me to?"

"Sure I do. I have plenty of evidence of sex. Beat me up some, and then I'll have a rape case, too."

"I wouldn't do that, Rosie."

"You're not supposed to enjoy it."

"Staring?"

"No, beating me up. It's okay to enjoy staring."

"You're crazy, you know that?" I gave her a very brotherly kiss on the end of her nose.

"That's me, all right."

"What happened to admiring good sense?"

"I admire that in you, not in me. Any time I completely quit being crazy, I feel dead."

"You definitely don't look dead."

"Well, I was. Very dead. People like you can be sane and logical and practical without being dead, but I'm not wired that way. That's why we're a natural pair."

"Oh, now we're a natural pair, no less. Where are you going with that?"

"Not where you think. Tell me why you can't rat out this cop, directly or indirectly."

"Because I can't have people looking into my business too deeply."

"Too many connections?"

"Too much history."

"That damn stuff." She tried to throw the empty bottle out the window, but it bounced off the junker next to us and came back. It bounced around the steering wheel for a while, until she caught it by the neck. "We all get that, don't we? But I thought a bail bondsman had to have a clean record."

"They do. And I do. But if you look back enough years, you'll come to a blank page. I can't have people trying to fill that page. Sooner or later they'll find an open arrest warrant. It doesn't have my name on it, but the file attached to it has my prints. That's why I can't ever go back to Detroit."

"Maybe the statute of limitations has run out."

"There is no statute of limitations on murder."

"Wow." She threw the bottle again, this time reaching an arm out the window to toss it backwards over the roof. It landed someplace behind us with a hollow "plonk" sound and stayed put. "You're wanted for a lot of murders, for such a sensible type. Some people would say you hang with the wrong crowd."

"Be careful whom you malign."

She laughed. I was starting to like that laugh. "Got me," she said. "I want you to know, though, that you were wrong about the abortion."

"What are you talking about?"

"Back at the café, you said I went away to Chicago for an abortion."

I had forgotten it almost as soon as I said it. It's a common enough reason for a young girl to go running off to the big city, especially if she's not otherwise stupid.

"It was a guess, that's all. But I didn't attach any…"

"You were wrong." The laugh and the smile were gone now, and she stared intently into my eyes.

"Okay," I said

"Don't humor me, Herman. I'm serious."

"I said, 'okay.'" I didn't back away from the stare.

She turned away first, and in the glow from the yard lights, I thought her cheek looked wet. "Tell me about the Gypsies," she said.

It seemed like a good idea to change the subject, so I told her the salient points, and I hardly lied about any of them. By the time I had finished, it was after four.

"You need to see my friendly bartender," she said.

"This time of night?"

"Trust me."

I did. We put our clothes on, put the car back together, and headed into the city.

Someplace south of the Loop, we parked at the curb on a narrow street where you wouldn't want to walk after dark alone and unarmed. Maybe not in the daylight, either. Rosie confirmed that impression by putting a nine-millimeter in her purse before we got out of the car, and I took the hint and pocketed my new three-eighty. We locked the car and headed out, and I felt like John Paul Jones, telling the Congress, "Give me a fast ship, for I intend to take her in harm's way." So of course, they gave him an under-gunned, worn out tub that steered like a lumber barge with the anchor dragging. He made history with it. I wasn't feeling that lucky.

"The street looks deserted," I said. "Are you sure this is going to work?"

"They shut off the lights and pretend they're closed at two," she said, "but the show goes on all day and all night. After hours, you just have to go in the back way and don't act like a cop or a social worker. It's actually the safest time. No rough crowds, just hardcore drunken oglers and the occasional pimp who's trying to recruit."

"Sounds wonderful."

"Nothing around here is wonderful. But if my Gypsy friend still works here, this would be his usual shift."

With the neon signs off, the street barely had enough light to navigate by. Marquees with names like *The Bronze Beaver*, *Sex City*, and *Hooter Heaven* were all totally dark, as were the smaller banner-panels with their understated headlines like, *"Real, Nude, Naked, Live Girls, On Stage!!!"* That about covered all the possibilities, I guessed. A few glassed-in stage pictures on the walls were still lit, like windows in the night. The photos looked ancient and yellowed, the girls in them, underaged and prematurely tough. They had names like Crystal Bryte, Ginger Snatch, and Betty Boobs. We walked past the front of a place called the New Lost City and turned into a narrow alley, by a picture of a blonde. It was a three-quarter rear shot, fully nude, with the poser looking over her shoulder at the camera. She had a splayed handprint painted on her ass in red. The name scrolled across the photo was "Third Hand Rose." I started to do a double take, but Rosie pulled me away, saying, "You'll never know."

Halfway down the alley, there was a door with a single lightbulb above it and a sign that said SERVICE. I bet.

"What now? Do we peek in a little door and say, 'Joe sent me'?"

"Nothing that fancy. We just walk in, and if we look like trouble, somebody throws us out again. If not, they collect a cover charge. Funny you should say that, though. Joe is the guy we're going to see."

The door was one of those metal-clad bombproof jobs that weighed about half a ton, but it swung away easily enough. We went into a blue-lit corridor, passed some restrooms and empty booze cases, and emerged into a large club room. If it had a decor, it was too dark to tell. Dark enough for the patrons to play with themselves or each other, I guessed, while somebody like Crystal Bryte did her best to inspire them. Mostly, what it had was space. It had a long, glossy bar on one wall that was lit, and a large stage with a runway and a couple of brass fire poles that were bathed in hot red and orange floods.

Some kind of grinding R&B tune was blaring on the PA system, while a young woman on the runway was doing some grinding of her own, getting a lot of mileage out of her ample hips. She was peeling off pieces of wispy costume and tossing them to three middle-aged business types at a front table. Even in the colored light, she looked ghostly pale, and I decided she used a lot of white body powder, accented by very dark eye makeup and lipstick, for a sort of vampire look. Her customers looked more like real vampires. Not pale, but definitely hungry, though a few of them looked barely conscious. Now and then, she would do a gyrating squat by a ringside table, and some of them would get up and stuff money into her g-string.

"She's running out of places to stick that stuff," I said.

"She'll make a pass around the far end of the runway and hand it off to somebody behind the curtain pretty soon," said Rosie. "Then she'll come back and give them a little reward. She'll toss the g-string and hump up to the brass pole a bit. If she likes them, she might even let one of them cop a pinch or a feel."

"Whaddaya, tourists? Out slumming?" The voice was sandpaper basso, and I turned around to see a figure that would have blotted out the sky, if there had been any sky. I thought of asking if his name was Joe, but I wasn't sure I wanted it to be.

Rosie took the lead. "My husband's bored, thinks I should learn some new moves."

"Yeah? Well, you wanna watch, you gotta sit down and pay, like everybody else. You gotta buy a drink, too."

"Okay," I said. "Anyplace? How about at the bar?"

"You too cheap to tip the waitress? Don't matter. You still gotta pay the cover. Twenty bucks."

I reached for my wallet.

"Apiece," said the monster. Rosie gave me a frown, but I couldn't tell if it meant the bouncer was lying or that I shouldn't make trouble.

"That's crap," I said, "and we both know it. Tell you what, though: how about if I give you fifty and I don't see you any more?"

"That'll work." It was hard to tell in that light and with his face so high up, but I think he smiled. "Don't be makin' no trouble for the artistes, though, or I'll be on you like holy on the Pope."

"Hey, you said it first—we're just out slumming."

"Yeah, whatever. Just don't say you wasn't told." He moved off into a dark cave somewhere, pausing on his way to whisper in my ear. Up on the stage, the writhing vampiress had ditched her wad of bills, just as Rosie had predicted, and she was working herself up to a finale. I pried my eyes away long enough to look over at the bar, which was being tended by a short, dark guy with a white shirt, black bow tie, and sleeve garters. He had a wedge-shaped face, sort of like Stroud, the phony detective, with a pencil moustache and slicked-back hair. His eyes seemed too big for the rest of his head, and he looked sort of fidgety, as if he were wired too tight for the job. Kevin Kline, trying to do a low-key role.

"Is that our man?"

"That's Joe, all right. I caught his eye when we came in. If we sit down, he'll come over. What did the bouncer say to you?"

"Tell you later." I fondled a chair in the dark to make sure it didn't already have anybody on it, then motioned to her to sit.

"Tell me now," she said.

I patted down another chair for myself and sat down opposite her. "Here comes our waitress."

The waitress looked young and out of place, not sexy enough to be up on the stage or tough enough to be down on the floor, and definitely not comfortable with the skimpy uniform of tight, shiny short-shorts and an abbreviated leather vest with no blouse under it. Susie Sorority, trying to work her way through Sociology 101 at some community college. She took our orders and fled.

"She didn't seem to recognize you," I said.

"She's not an old-timer."

"Doesn't look like she's about to become one, either."

"That's for sure. What did the bouncer say to you?"

"You won't like it."

"Tell me, already."

"He was warning me. He thinks you're a cop. Or a decoy."

"Why would he think that?"

"Because you accessorize your sexy cocktail dress with shoes that have rubber soles and arch supports."

"That asshole! I'll kill him."

"Hey, he's just giving a tip to another *guy*."

"If he'd shut up, you might not have noticed."

"You're right, I wouldn't have." And wouldn't have cared, if I had.

"I'll kill him, that's all." She drummed her fingers on the table and glowered.

I'll never understand what some people take seriously. While Rosie fumed, the bartender at the far wall put a couple of drinks on a tray, waved the nervous waitress away, and headed over to our table with them himself. When he got close, he started talking to Rosie's back.

"Looks like some people just don't know when they're well off. That *is* you, isn't it, Lisa?"

Lisa? Rosie turned in her chair and said, "Hey, Joe. How've you been?" Well, she did tell me she had used a lot of names.

"I've been here," he said. "What else do you have to know? Been down so long, it looks like up to me. Who's your friend?"

"He's good people, Joe. He rescued me from a fate worse than death. Joe Patello, this is Howard Jacobson."

God, it was a compulsion with her. I held out my hand and said I was happy to meet him.

"No offense, Mr. Jacobson, but I don't shake hands. It's a hygiene thing. It's also not a good idea if I look like

I'm getting too friendly with the customers. Believe me, you do not want to get thrown out of here."

"I heard that," I said, and took my hand back. Joe put the drinks down in front of us, collected another wad of money from me, and sat down next to Rosie. He did not exactly have the attitude of an old friend.

"What brings you back to the No Lost Titties, Lisa? I assume you're not here to audition."

"Howard here needs some information about Gypsies, and you're the only one I know."

"Does he now? Why? Is he a cop?"

"No," I said.

"A victim, then. Looking for some payback?"

"Why do you say that?"

"Because only cops and victims have any interest in Gypsies. And they have no interest at all in you."

"Are you sure?" I said. "Maybe I'm a writer. Maybe I'm about to make you rich and famous."

"If I believed that, which I do not for a minute, it would move you from uninteresting to unwelcome. We may be the only people left in America who don't want that."

"Getting rich?"

"Getting famous. Having our culture strip-mined for some half-assed book or movie."

"I'm not a writer. That was just a 'maybe.'"

"Maybe you should tell me what you really do for

a living, before I get totally pissed."

"I'm a bail bondsman."

He sat back for a moment, looking stunned, as if I had just changed the rules and he needed to think up a new game plan.

"I haven't needed a bondsman for a long time," he said, "but that could make you very interesting to the *familya* or the *kumpania*. Maybe even the *rom baro*. But I don't have their ear anymore, so I can't help you."

"Ro...I mean Lisa, said you were excommunicated, or something."

He smiled for the first time, showing a row of teeth that would make my dentist, the one with the ceiling-pictures, proud. "Is that what she called it? It should be so easy. I'm *marime*, is what I am. For your *Gadje* ears, that means unclean."

"*Gadje* just means us," said Rosie. "It's not an insult."

"Depends on your point of view," said Joe.

"Maybe I can help you." I had no idea how, but it seemed like a good thing to say.

"You?" He gave what could have been a laugh or a snort. "That would be like a coal miner offering to clean your linens. Nobody can help me. Our court, the *kris*, has found me *marime*, and there's no getting rid of that, ever. Are you from a farm background?"

"No," I said.

"Yes," said Rosie. "As far from it as I can get."

"I'll tell you a little rural humor. It's not the sort of thing a good Gypsy would tell, but since I'm unclean anyway, it can't matter much. You can stick a few bricks together with some mortar, the saying goes, but that doesn't make you a mason. And you can pound a few nails, but that doesn't make you a carpenter. But get caught in the barnyard with your pants down just once, and you're a pig fucker for the rest of your life."

"That's very colorful," I said. "I hadn't heard that before. Is that what happened to you?"

"Worse than that. The pig I got caught with—and all *Gadje* are pigs—was a man."

"Am I supposed to blush now? This is almost the end of the twentieth century, already."

"Not in the *familya*, it isn't. Probably never will be. Gypsy society has the most traditional, absolute moral code in the world."

I thought about it for a minute. Rosie was playing with her swizzle stick, looking bored. She had apparently heard it all before, but it was news to me.

"Nothing personal," I said, "but everybody I talk to says Gypsies are a bunch of..."

"Thieves, liars, con artists and cheats," he said. "All true. And we're very good at it. But that's all."

"Excuse me?" *Isn't that enough?*

"In all other things, we are the most moral people

who ever lived." I must have looked skeptical, because he went on. "I'll tell you a story, Mr. non-writer. It goes back to the year zero."

"As in the Garden of Eden?"

"Not such a nice place, and not that far back. Think 'Roman calendar.' Originally, the Gypsies were blacksmiths. One day some Roman soldiers came to a Gypsy blacksmith and ordered him to make four nails, for the crucifixion of Christ the next day. He didn't know who Christ was, but you can bet he made the nails. You didn't argue with the Romans back then." He leaned forward.

"But one of the nails kept glowing, long after it was out of the hot forge. That night, an angel came to the blacksmith and told him that the glowing nail was meant to be driven into the heart of Jesus. That was just too damn much of an atrocity, even for what was supposed to be an atrocity. So she told him to steal the nail and run away, which he did. Later, he was on the road, wondering what to do next, when the angel came to him again. From then on, the angel said, his people would always be nomads, without a land to call their own. But because of his service, they would always be free to steal whatever they wanted. And they would always be lucky at stealing."

"But in everything else, they were super-moral."

"Well, sure. I mean, what would you be like if one

of your ancestors had worked for an angel?"

I'd probably be shopping for an asylum. "That's quite a story."

"It's our touchstone: who we are and what we do."

"Do you also do murder?"

"Never. Weren't you paying attention to what I just said?"

"One of your people was murdered outside my place of business the day before yesterday. I'm trying to find out why."

"How do you know he was one of us?"

"She. Because she was working the 'old fiddle' scam."

"Anybody could do that. It's probably been around for longer than fiddles. Used to be the 'old lyre' scam. Greeks did it to Persians."

"She was using a phony identity. She also had a brother who has a dozen identities that he carries around in a briefcase, and a cop called him a Rom. Now he claims he never heard of her. And she switched the violins, smoother than I can believe."

He pulled at his chin and took a deep breath, pondering. "The identity shuffle would fit. The CIA doesn't have any secrets as well kept as the true, birth name of a Gypsy. But switching the fiddle is all wrong. The whole point of the con is to leave the pigeon with the object he thought he wanted. Otherwise, it's an egg without salt, if you get my meaning."

"It was a variation," I said. "She had to get the original back, because it really was very valuable. It was an old Amati."

Rosie still looked bored and restless, but Joe, if that was really his name here in the House of Aliases, was suddenly looking intensely alert.

"The Wolf Amati?" he said.

I'd never heard that name before, but candor didn't seem to be the order of the night.

"Yes," I said.

"Holy Mother of God. Could it really be?" He sat back on his chair and looked at the ceiling. "You wouldn't be trying to run a scam on me now, would you, Mr. J.?"

"Hey, I'm not the one whose ancestor stole a nail." As far as I knew.

He looked at the black ceiling for another moment, then jerked back forward, stood, and walked briskly away. "Wait here," he said over his shoulder.

"Sure," I said to his empty chair. To Rosie, I said, "Nice fellow."

"Believe it or not, he was being nice. His people take great pride in being rude." But she wasn't looking at me as she said it. She was now paying attention to the stage, where a new dancer had replaced Miss Blood Loss. This one was taller as well as curvier than the first, and she had short, thick black hair that she wore like a helmet. Prince Valiant's sister, maybe.

She did a slow, sinuous routine, and she shed her upper costume almost immediately, showing off the fact that her ample breasts did not need any external support. She kept her cavalier boots, g-string, and pasties, but they didn't matter much. She had one of those bodies that implies even more nudity than it shows. My Uncle Fred would have said, "She's got a lot of features, is the thing. And not all of them are shaped quite the way you expected, so you got to stare a lot."

So I did. And to my surprise, she stared back, completely ignoring the rest of the audience, which was now hooting and grunting for her attention. She did a series of torso thrusts that started at the ankles and rippled up through her whole body like a wave, all the while holding eye contact, then pulled off the pasties, one at a time. I thought I could hear a tearing sound, like a bandage being ripped off, and I wondered if that was a way of staging a nipple erection. I was going to ask Rosie, but when I looked over at her, she was positively radiating disapproval. Before I could ask her why, the dancer got our attention again by throwing the pasties on our table.

A drunk at another table yelled, "She wants your bod, guy."

"Wrong," shouted another one. "What she wants

is his bankroll."

"With her, same thing," said the first. "Trush me, I know."

"Why me?" I said to Rosie. "Why doesn't she play to the guy who yelled? Or somebody else who doesn't have a woman with him?"

The dancer was down on the edge of the apron now, nearly doing the splits on her knees, and thrusting her breasts at me as if I were a gravity well. Rosie picked up a pastie from the table and threw it on the floor, glaring at the stage.

"She thinks you're safe, figures I won't let you attack her. But that's just the cover reason. What she really wants..."

Joe was back suddenly, with a piece of paper that he stuck into my shirt pocket without waiting for me to reach for it.

"Go to that address tomorrow after ten," he said. "That's the *vista officia*, the check-in place for all the Yugoslav Rom. If you say you know where the Wolf Amati is—and don't tell me if you really do know or not—the *rom baro* might see you. He'll know I sent you, but don't say it. Don't say my name to him at all. And don't ask for him, either, just wait for him to appear. Pretend you're a customer."

"Do I tell him about the woman who was killed?"

"If he gives you coffee, look to see if the cup is

chipped. If it isn't, then he likes you and he'll talk to you for a while without any profit. You can tell him about the woman if you want to. If the cup is chipped, you're wasting your time, no matter what you say. If Lisa goes along, she should wear a long skirt. And she should keep absolutely quiet. If she doesn't, all you'll accomplish is dropping some money, which you should figure on doing in any case."

"I have to pay for information?"

"No, you have to pay for being a *Gadje*. No matter what, you do that. But if you act right, you might get beyond that."

"Sounds like a sucker game."

"It is what it is. And that's as much as I can do for you. I shouldn't be saying this to a *Gadje*, but Lisa's an old friend: Good luck to both of you." I stifled the impulse to shake his hand, and he left as abruptly as he had come.

Up on the stage, the curvaceous Dane was again writhing in our direction, making come-hither gestures at me. Rosie picked up the second pastie and threw it at her, which prompted a look of mock indignation and amusement.

"Let's get out of here," she said.

"Okay, but what were…"

"Now."

The dancer threw a pout at Rosie and a kiss at me.

I mouthed a silent "ciao" at her, waved, and followed Rosie back out into the night.

Walking back to the car, I said, "You were about to tell me something else about the dancer, when Joe interrupted."

"Was I? I forget."

"No, you don't."

"I was mad. You don't want to hear it."

"Yes, I do."

"I was going to say she was trying to take you away from me."

"Are you serious?"

"Believe it. She wanted it bad. As bad as she wanted to spite me."

"Why would she want that?"

"Because she's a mean, hateful little bitch."

"Nuh-uh. Not good enough."

She slowed her pace, finally, and looked down at her ratted-on, rubber-soled shoes.

"She was telling me I'm not the star anymore, okay? And as lousy as that life was, it still hurts to be told I'm a has-been. But you wouldn't know about that, would you?"

As a matter of fact, I would.

Chapter Twelve

A Death in the Familyia

"This location is compromised. I can't take a call here after this one." I didn't say hello or my name. I figured Wide Track Wilkie would know nobody else would be answering a pay phone at six in the morning. And by now, he would have taken the trouble to find out that it was a pay phone

"You want I should hang up now?"

"No," I said. "I don't know that we're being tapped, but a cop came by the booth last night and looked at the phone."

"Checking the number against the listed location?"

"That's the way I figure it. Checking on behalf of a fellow officer in another state, maybe. So I can't be seen here again. If he doesn't come back, somebody else will."

"Got you. Can you take down a number?"

"Shoot."

He gave me a number, and I wrote it on the piece of paper that Joe the Gypsy had stuffed in my pocket. "If you wind up ending this call in a hell of a hurry," he said, "I'll wait for you to call me there in ten minutes."

"Good." I tried to remember my underworld protocol for talk on open phone lines. "Ten minutes" either meant one hour, since it had a one and a zero, or it meant ten o'clock, for the same reason, or it meant the same time, one day from then. Maybe it meant all three. Hell, maybe it even meant ten minutes. Shit. I was out of practice at this fugitive stuff. And I had already violated the first rule: Never make contact with your old life.

I looked over the parking lot. The two semis were still parked where they had been the night before, their windshields glistening with heavy dew in the predawn light. Down by the other end of the mall, an old junker Toyota had the same covering, marking it for somebody's humble go-to-work vehicle that decided it had gone enough, thank you. In the center of the shopping strip, a step van was unloading something into the Kinko's, where the computer had found no new email for me that day. If my phone booth really was blown, Agnes didn't know it yet. At least, the receiver didn't have a bug in it, though. I checked, as well as I knew how. And the parking lot looked serene enough.

"What have you got for me?" I said.

"First off, I know you told me to strictly work on the woman, but you ought to know we could shift to her little brother now."

"You said you couldn't do PI work." Openly, anyway.

"Don't have to. He's a skip now."

"How can he be? His case won't come up for weeks yet."

"Yeah, and he won't be there for it. He's busy being dead. At least, if he's the same guy who was impersonating the detective, he is. Has a nice stainless steel drawer, right next to the sister he claims he never heard of."

"You saw him?"

"In the flesh. Which was not in very good shape, I might add. He's a John Doe at the moment. I didn't offer to identify him, figured the CIC will match his prints pretty soon."

"How the hell did you get into the morgue?"

"I pretended to be dead, okay?"

"Must have been a hell of an act."

"Hey, I don't ask about your trade secrets. You want to hear about the guy or not?"

"Yes." Did I ever.

"He's a hit-and-run victim, just like the woman. And just like her, he had his neck broken by somebody who was definitely not a motor vehicle. Your real cop/

phony cop pair were telling you the truth about that, it turns out."

"That's what the ME's people say?"

"Official and final. It's two homicides now."

"Holy shit. I don't suppose you found out what time they came to that conclusion about her?"

"Why do we care?"

"Because Evans told me about the broken neck when he 'fronted me in Lefty's. If that was before the examiners knew, that would mean he saw it happen."

"Aha. Or did it himself."

"There's that distinct possibility," I said.

"That's too bad."

"Why is that too bad?"

"Because I didn't find that out."

"Can't you do it now?"

"Hey, how many times you think I can play dead? People get suspicious, you do it twice."

"You're right: that's too bad."

The semi closest to me suddenly fired up its huge diesel, its twin stacks sending up black flumes that could probably be seen from the Sears Tower. The ground shook, and the plastic glazing in my phone booth rattled.

"So, what did you find out about the woman?" I said.

"What?"

I said it again, shouting this time, and Wilkie started to recite a list of aliases as long as that of little Jimmy-cum-Stroud. I couldn't hear them well enough to write them down, and I didn't see that it would help me any if I had. Eventually, he moved from aliases to a list of possible former addresses, none of which rang any bells for me.

As Wilkie talked, the semi driver decided he had played to an empty house for long enough, and he proceeded to put his show on the road. Either the engine was still pretty cold, or he had a hell of a load, because he pulled out really slowly, keeping it in super-low gear. I watched the pattern of the wheels with fascination. Four sets of four and one set of two, for a total of eighteen wheels, five of them facing towards me, all turning in perfect unison. I looked under the trailer frame and watched the outboard wheels, in deepest shadow, turning to the same rhythm, and beyond them, the dawn-lit wheels of the second truck, not turning at all. It all had a certain mechanical poetry to it. Until my eyes stopped on the farther wheels. There were too damn many wheels behind the moving truck. And four of them belonged to a low-slung, heavy car.

"...really did teach violin, in a little hole-in-the-wall studio over in the Macalister Groveland neighborhood, but she never played in the Chamber Orchestra, under any name, or..."

Wide Track went on with his recitation, but I wasn't listening. Why the hell does a car park between two semis, when there's four hundred open spaces in the rest of the lot? Sleeping off an all-nighter, maybe, someplace where he wouldn't be too conspicuous? Or getting set to stake out a phone booth, where there wasn't supposed to be anybody for another two hours? As inconspicuous a place as you could get, for that.

The front bumper of the car jerked upward slightly, from the torque of the motor starting up, and that decided it for me. A hung over party animal would not immediately move his car when the cover moved or got noisy. He'd just roll over and give God and the universe a piece of his blurry mind. I dropped the receiver without hanging up and headed for the bagel shop, before my cover, also, was gone.

The front door wasn't open yet, so I ran around the side, to the back service drive. The rented Pontiac was back at the hotel with Rosie, so I had exactly two options: go in the back door of the bagel shop, cover my face with flour and pretend to be the Pillsbury Doughboy, or go over the hill and into the area where Rosie and I had driven the night before. The big semi was rolling pretty good now, shifting up a gear, and I had no idea if he had screened the view of me for long enough. It occurred to me that I shouldn't have left the phone receiver dangling, but it was too late to go back and take care of it now. Over the roar of the diesel, I thought I could hear the chirp of smaller tires peeling off on the blacktop. I ran through the opening in the brush and didn't look back. Over the hill, as they say.

It had seemed smaller from behind the windshield, just a nice little berm that would make a good visual screen. It had grown since then, into one of the foothills of the Himalayas, and I scrambled frantically for the ridge, frequently stumbling on large rocks. A lot of rocks on that damn hill. I decided I would not look at the undercarriage of the rented Pontiac, assuming I ever got to see it again at all.

I finally made it over the crest, gasping for air and vowing to think again about that exercise program that I used to think about, I forget when. Or maybe not. The hill was probably just steeper and longer than I had remembered. What the hell, the Pontiac had needed 200 horsepower to get over it, and even with that, it wasn't happy about it. I stopped just over the crest, dove into a mass of low, tangly brush, and chanced a look back.

Below me, a big, dark gray Chevy was cruising around the corner of the strip mall, slowly. I couldn't see the driver's face, but the car damn sure looked familiar. I had almost taken the last ride of my life in a car just like that, and unlike the Proph, I did not believe in coincidence. The car stopped just around the corner, and I hunkered down lower, hoping the driver hadn't seen me. The sun was rising almost behind me now, so the odds were in my favor. I felt like Josey Wales with the rising sun behind me, about to waste the *Comancheros*, single-handed. *"Yup, it's always nice to have an edge."* I needed some tobacco juice to spit.

Behind the strip mall, one of the jolly bagel bakers, a young man of about my build, had just tossed a big plastic trash bag into a dented green dumpster and stopped to have a smoke, looking around furtively first, taking no apparent notice of the Chevy. He turned his back to the wind, to shelter his lighter, also turning away from the corner of the mall. Behind him, the car spun its wheels on the gravel, and its heavily muffled engine made a noise like a turbine winding up. Good God, he was going to run the kid down! *Déja vu*, all over again.

I stood up and yelled. The kid didn't seem to hear me, so I cupped my hands and did it again, as loud as I could.

"Get the hell out of there! *Anywhere!* Run!"

He wasn't back by the door to the bagel factory anymore, but he looked up in time to see the speeding car and to jump into the recess at a back door from some other shop. The car tore past him, sideswiping the wall and leaving paint on the concrete block. Then it swerved back away from the building, did a clumsy high speed U-turn, and stopped again. The driver's window wound slowly down.

Nice work, Jackson. You're still standing up, idiot.

"Oh, shit," I said aloud. The face in the car window, even from that distance and with a hand up to screen his eyes from the sun, was unmistakable: Evans. And there was no doubt that he had seen me.

I turned and ran down the back side of the berm, going straight across the road at the bottom, down through a small ditch, and up again, onto the black rock ballast of a railroad embankment. Behind me, I heard the blurbling turbine-like noise again and then the sound of the engine screaming, revving out of control. Off to my right, a freight train was highballing toward me, maybe a quarter of a mile away, and the engineer blew his horn. Maybe he saw me, or maybe he just liked to blow his horn. In any case, I relieved him of the awesome responsibility of running me down.

I crossed the tracks, went down another narrow ditch and up another embankment to more tracks. There was a train coming here, too, from my left, but not as fast and not as close. I could beat it, easily. Its engines were laboring hard, belching diesel smoke, hauling their load up a long grade. If the engineer saw me, he didn't bother to say so by blowing his horn. Behind me, the uncontrolled revving of the Chevy engine got louder, and I wondered if the car had rolled over.

I went back the way I had come, to where I could just see over the first tracks. Evans' car was hung up on the ridge of the berm, both wheels on the driver's side completely off the ground. He spun his wheels wildly for a bit longer, then threw open the door and piled out, breaking into a jerky, half-stumbling run, his loose coat flapping behind him. At the bottom of the slope, he stopped, looked around, then pulled out his sidearm. Good grief, was he seriously planning on shooting me? Hell, I was only "wanted for questioning in connection with." And we hadn't finished playing out the fiddle scam yet. And even if he was having a moment of pure lunacy, could he hit anything at this range and with the sun in his eyes? I hardly thought so.

Wrong. All wrong. He spotted me watching him, took a one-handed target stance, so he could use the other hand to shade his eyes, and methodically emptied his magazine. He walked the shots up the embankment like a machine-gunner finding his range, and just before the fast freight flashed in front of me, some rounds hit the rocks behind me and the rails off to either side. This guy was an obscenely good shot. I hunched down to look between the passing train wheels and saw him calmly eject the magazine and insert another, as he walked forward, closing the range. Time to move.

The second freight had caught up with me by then, and I was stuck in the space between the two trains. I tried to remember what I had heard about jumping a freight, from an old time hobo who had needed a bond for a breaking and entering charge once. "Take a ladder at the front of a car, not the back, so if you miss your handhold and fall off, the next set of wheels ain't so close to you." Maybe. Or maybe it was, "Take the one at the back end of a car, so…"

Oh, to hell with it. I picked a flatcar full of packaged lumber on the slower train, ran alongside until I was almost up to his speed, found a rung and a handhold, and pulled myself up, even as more bullets ricocheted off steel wheels and machinery. My grip held, and I became one with the rattling freight. The distance to the other train closed down rapidly, the space between them getting noisy and claustrophobic.

At some level, my mind knew that the two trains wouldn't actually hit each other, but my instincts didn't believe it. I worked my way across a machinery platform, to the opposite side of the car. Then I swung myself around to the side of a lumber cube and looked back. By the time the fast freight had quit blocking my view, the shopping center, Evans, and his bullets were long gone. Once again, I had fled into another world. I wondered how many times I could keep doing that.

The train snaked its way through the industrial back-yard of greater Chicago, passing new and abandoned factories, slums, switchyards, and grown-over land that looked as if the city had simply forgotten it. Far off to my right, in the east, I could see glimpses of the famous skyline, but it didn't seem to have anything to do with the back-alley world I was moving through. We never picked up very much speed, but sometimes we passed other trains that were going even slower. At one of them, I decided to make a change. I read a newspaper article once about a young man who wanted to try his luck at being a hobo and wound up getting crushed to death by a shifting load of lumber, on the first freight he ever hopped. So the next time we slowed for a long grade with another train alongside us, I jumped down and changed to an empty flatcar. It was just behind a boxcar with the five-pointed star of anarchy spray-painted on it, along with "RACINE IS A MEAN CHICKENSHIT JERKWATER TOWN," in big, three-colored shadow letters. Wow. A lot of paint in that statement. It must have carried some heavy passion. Since that was pretty much what I thought of Racine, too, I took it as an invitation. The flatcar was fairly clean and had a big center frame for securing some kind of freight. I leaned up against it, made a pillow out of my rolled-up jacket, and settled down for a long haul to I knew not where.

We seemed to be going north, which was as good as anything else I could think of. I didn't know where

I was going, but I damn sure knew what I was going from. Evans was a complicated character, I thought, and his actions up to now could be interpreted in a lot of ways. But there was only one way to interpret the bullets by the railroad tracks: He wanted to kill me.

Why? That wouldn't get him a violin or a wad of money, or even a big fat promotion with the cops. It was simply irrational. I thought back to what my Uncle Fred had said about murder by motor vehicle being a crime of rage. Was Evans full of rage? And if so, how in hell did it get directed towards me? I didn't think the answers were anywhere ahead of me on the tracks, but I didn't know where else to go at the moment.

I faced forward and amused myself by waving at people in tenement yards and reading the black and white signs that occasionally passed by, written in railroad gibberish. I had almost stopped trying to make sense of them when I passed the one that said SKOKIE.

I mentally took back all the sarcastic things I had thought about the Proph and his ideas. This absolutely had to be karma. The train was going faster now, but there were patches of tall grass along the tracks that looked fairly soft. I picked one and jumped. It may have been soft, but my body didn't think so. It promised to remind me of this silly stunt for a good long time. But I didn't break or seriously wrench anything, so I got up to look for something that might be the center of town.

I found a C-store not far from the tracks, and I bought a throwaway shaving kit, some moist towelettes, cigarettes, a cup of coffee, and a couple of stale doughnuts.

"Restroom's back in that corner," said the clerk, a dumpling-shaped, frizzy redhead who looked as if she probably drove a Harley to work.

"Thanks," I said. I didn't ask how she knew I needed one.

"You don't look like a regular 'bo," she said. I think she may have been trying to give me a come-hither look, but it was hard to tell on her.

"Thanks again, I think."

"Yeah, you do that," she said. "You think."

I beat a hasty retreat to the room she had pointed to, where I shaved, cleaned my clothes up a bit, and generally tried to make myself look like a candidate for humanity. I tried some coffee, which wasn't bad, and a doughnut, which was awful. I would have thrown it in the toilet, but I didn't want to plug the poor thing up. On the way out, I asked the clerk if there was a good restaurant anywhere close.

"Them doughnuts ain't much, are they?" she said.

"Oh, I wouldn't say that." They were much, all right.

"I make a lot better ones myself, but they don't let me sell 'em here. The company says we gotta sell the ones off the big truck, which ain't here on time, mostly."

"Well, that's a big company for you. No respect for individual talent."

"Ain't that the truth?" I think she batted an eyelash at me. When I appeared to be immune to it, she gave me directions to a 24-hour pancake house. "Comb your hair," she said.

Then I showed her the paper with the address that Joe the Gypsy had given me. "Where would that be?" I said.

Her expression couldn't have changed faster if I'd tried to rifle the cash drawer. "Aw, shit," she said. "You one of them?"

"Not exactly."

"What's that supposed to mean?"

"It's a long story."

"I just bet. Get out of here and tell it to somebody else."

I didn't wait for her to add an "or else." Fifteen minutes later, I found the pancake house. It was pushing nine o'clock by then. Instead of showing the waitress the address in my pocket, I asked her where I could find a city map, which turned out to be a much better strategy. She gave me more coffee than I asked for, heated up my apple pie, and let me look at a map in the front of a phone book, though she didn't let me tear it out. Then she told me about the local city bus schedule and where to catch one. So much for not looking like a regular 'bo.

A little after ten, I was getting off a bus and walking up to a heavily curtained storefront. The sign said "Spiritual Consultations," and in smaller print, "Madam Vadoma, Seeress." There was also a picture of a hand with a lot of numbers and lines and an eyeball in the middle of the palm. If that was a sign I should have recognized, I flunked out. I might as well have been playing Scrabble in a foreign language. But in the time-honored phrase, it was the only game in town. A bell just like the one at Rosie's café announced my arrival, and I stepped into a world of dark drapes and dim candlelight.

"*Droboy tume Romale*," said a voice in the shadows.

"I'm sorry, I don't understand."

"Of course, you do not. You are *Gadje*, then."

"Yes."

"Shut the door." The voice was soft and feminine and a touch breathless, but it carried authority. It also carried some kind of eastern European accent, but I couldn't identify it any more exactly than that. I stepped the rest of the way into the tiny shop and closed the door behind me. This time, it didn't jingle.

"Sit." Again, the velvet-covered command. I sat.

The woman who sat behind the small table was neither young nor old. She had high cheeks, a hawk-like nose, and eyes too wild for the rest of her manner and too big for the rest of her face. She also had silky black hair that seemed to flow everywhere. And while I wouldn't have said she was either sexy or beautiful, she had a definite *presence*. If I were the sort of person who goes to a spiritual consultant, I would have said she had a strong aura. Of course, that could have been the lighting. With the sunlight streaming in through the open door, the place had been merely a tired old office, with threadbare carpet, a lot of dark drapery on the walls, and a round table covered with dark red felt. With the door shut, it was a place of mystery, even possible magic. Exotic incense hung in the air, the corners disappeared, and the woman's dramatic features were highlighted by candlelight and carefully placed pin spots. And the crystal ball.

I have to admit, I was impressed by the crystal ball. I had always thought they were a mere cartoon cliché, and I never expected to actually see one. This one was maybe six inches across, lit from within or below with a blue-white glow, and it seemed to have tiny wisps of smoke slowly curling around inside it. The woman cupped her hands over the ball without touching the glass, then opened them, slowly, sinuously, like an exotic flower unfolding dark petals. She may have been as phony as a politician's promises, but she definitely had style. In spite of myself, I decided I was going to like this game. She looked up.

"The crystal is clouded," she said. "You see?"

"It's not always like that?"

"It reacts to your troubles."

"Oh. Well it would, wouldn't it?"

"You mock me? That would be a great mistake. I have the gift of the evil eye. I can make you wish for the rest of your life that you had never walked into this place."

I didn't know which eye was evil, but I looked at both of them, and I believed her. "I'm not mocking you," I said.

"Then you are wise, to that extent. Now you make a gesture of good faith."

I didn't have to be told what that might be. Fifty seemed to be the minimal unit of trade here in greater Chi-town, and I laid my last one on the table. She didn't lay either eye on me, so I guessed I picked the right amount. She passed her hand over the table without touching it, and the bill vanished. A simple enough trick for a practiced conjurer, but still impressive. Then she asked for my hand.

She held my hand in hers, palm up, and studied it. Her touch felt hot and slightly electric.

"I see you have much strength of character."

"How nice for me."

"Not always. You are a man with a troubled past."

Well, who the hell wasn't?

"You acquire fine things, then you lose them."

"I don't know what you mean." *The keys to my safe deposit box? My life back in Detroit? My wife? Or merely the Amati?*

"Yes," she said. "All of those." Cute. I began to see how the fortune-telling game worked.

"But there is one object, in particular, that troubles you. A recent one. You must get it and bring it to me."

"It troubles me less than the people who died over it."

She looked up abruptly. Her eyes got even bigger, and her mouth made a round "o". Then she peered intently at my hand again. "Death?" she said. "I see no blood here."

"No. Not on my hands."

"Then it is the object that is the evil. To be free of it, you must get it and…"

"Understand something very clearly, Madam Vadoma: I can bear to part with the violin, maybe even be cheated out of it, but not without finding out who did the killing. If you can't help me with that, then I've come a long way for nothing."

"It is a violin, then?" she said.

"Of course, it's a violin. Weren't you told?"

"I was only told that a *Gadje* would come, a man in a great deal of trouble, who…"

I was thinking that she must use the same prompt book as the Proph, when she was interrupted by another voice, a deep bass belonging to a man who had come up behind her without either of us noticing.

"I will talk to this gentleman now."

"But I was…"

"It is all right, Vadoma. Go and bring us some coffee."

She looked as if she were suppressing a passionate desire to either punch him out or stomp on his instep, but she gathered herself up in a flurry of skirts and hair and rushed out, taking her crystal ball with her. I was surprised to see that there was not a hole in the table with a light coming through it. The crystal must have had its own illumination. But then, I was supposed to think that, wasn't I?

"I am Stefan Yonkos," he said. "I am the *Rom Baro*. And you are Howard Jacobson."

Good thing he told me. I wasn't sure I could remember the name Rosie had used for me in the strip joint.

When he came farther into the light, I could see why he would be accustomed to moving around in the dark without bumping into anything. His eyes had no pupils at all, just rolled up whites, making him look like a fugitive from a zombie movie. And though he had to be as blind as a mob lawyer, I felt as though he were staring at me, right into my soul.

Unlike the other Gypsies I had met up to then, he was square and solid, with features that looked as if they were carved out of ancient oak with a chain saw, then left unfinished. He had thick, wavy hair and a Stalin moustache, both of them salt-and-pepper now gone almost entirely to white. And though his neck had shrunk a bit and his jowls sagged, they, too, looked solid. Only his posture looked like that of a younger man. He carried himself like ex-military, and when he sat at the table, there was no doubt that he took charge of it. If the seeress had a strong aura, his was thermonuclear.

"I apologize for the woman," he said, spreading his hands.

"Why? I thought she was very good."

"She rushed you. That cannot be allowed, ever. The game has a rhythm that must be respected. But she has not so much experience yet. She will learn."

"And if I didn't come here to play a game?"

"No? Why then, you would be a fool. And an easy mark. But I do not think you are a fool. I do not think a fool would have a priceless violin, for one thing."

"Even a blind squirrel finds a nut once in a while. No offense."

He chuckled at that, and pointed at me in a gesture that said I had scored the first point in our strange game. But not the last. "Very good, Mr. Jacobson. You talk like me. We shall have a fine time lying to each other. No offense. Vadoma! Where is that coffee?"

The woman came back in as if she had been waiting for her cue, just offstage. She put a tray on the table, took a cup from it for Stefan, and poured steaming liquid from an ornate, antique pot. As she was reaching for a second cup, he said, "Make sure you take a good cup for Mr. Jacobson. We would not want to offend him."

And just like that, I was in. An audience with the big kahuna, an unchipped cup, and everything. Or I was the biggest pigeon on the north side of Chicago, neatly set up by a bartender who chose his words just as carefully as the man in front of me. And the only way to find out was to play out the hand. I waited until the woman left, then took a sip of coffee and made appreciative noises.

"You know about the violin?" I said.

"I am told you have the Wolf Amati."

"Possibly, maybe not." *What the hell is the "Wolf" part, anyway?*

"Explain this to me."

"I wish I could," I said. "A woman calling herself Amy Cox gave me an old violin as security on a bond for her brother. Then she was killed in front of my place of business. Now the brother has been killed, too, and another man calling himself Cox wants me to give him the violin, for a lot of money. I have reason to think they are, or were, all Gypsies. I came here hoping to find out enough about them to help me figure it all out, but all anybody wants to talk about is the damn fiddle. If the thing you call the Wolf Amati has something to do with a family called Cox, and if the family is one of yours, then maybe we can help each other. If not, we may both be wasting our time."

"You come straight to the point, don't you? Very artless, but it moves me to believe you, I must say."

"Well, we're here to move each other, aren't we?"

"So we are," he said, nodding solemnly. "But I am supposed to be better at it than you."

"Then I'll do my best to let you think you are."

He laughed heartily this time, slapping the table and making it bounce. Something about the laugh seemed hollow, though, a stage laugh for an audience of one.

"By God, I like you more and more!" he said. "Will you take some brandy in your coffee?"

"Will you?"

"Alas, I cannot. A stomach condition." He patted his midsection, which looked about as fragile as a boiler plate.

"What a coincidence. Me, too."

He smiled out of one side of his mouth. "Perhaps it is something contagious."

"Quite possibly."

"What about some pastry, then?"

"That would be fine."

This time Vadoma came in without being called, bringing a carved wooden tray of little date and nut-filled tarts that tasted like pecan pie without the Southern accent. I was tempted to put a few in my pockets. After all, who knew what kind of transport I would be taking out of here, or in what direction?

"So you are a bondsman, Mr. Jacobson?"

"Yes, but not in Illinois, I'm afraid."

"A pity. We might have done some business. It is good to have a bondsman in one's, um…"

"Pocket?" *And an occasional policeman, too, I suspect.*

"How very original. I was going to say 'acquaintance.'"

"Of course. But we might yet do some business, Mr. Yonkos. Tell me about the Coxs."

"Again, you come straight to the point, and so shall I. Amy Cox and her brother, or the people who were using those names, were my people, yes. And their deaths leave a great hollow place in my heart that can never be filled."

This time, I believed him completely. As craggy as his face was, it was capable of registering deep pain.

"But this is my burden," he went on. "For your part, do you truly not care about the collateral?"

"I never said I didn't care about it. I said I care about the dead people more."

He chewed on a tart, and I was positive he was staring into my eyes again.

"We have a saying," he said. "With one rump, you cannot ride two horses. Which horse do you ride, Mr. Unkempt Bondsman?"

"The one that takes me to a killer."

"Why? So the dead can get what street people nowadays call 'their propers?' Their propers are a hole in the ground and a place in heaven, both far from here. It is a very bad business, involving oneself with the dead. And in any case, it would be my business, not yours."

"You have no desire to set things right at all?"

"Now you speak of revenge."

"Maybe just simple justice," I said.

"There are things that can never be forgiven, Mr. Jacobson, debts that can only be repaid in kind. But not blood. The blood feud can never be our way. It would be the death of the *familyia*, and that is unthinkable. There are many luxuries one can have in this world, but vengeance is too expensive for anyone. For us, anyway.

The grief will be with us forever, but there will be no payback."

"But the violin is another matter."

"Not exactly. It is the one member of the *familyia* that may actually come back home." He smiled. "And you have it, you say?"

"I didn't actually say that."

"Not quite, but close enough, I think. This violin is very bad for you. If you don't know that already, you will find it out soon enough. The woman, Vadoma, was not deceiving you when she said it is evil. You would be better off rid of it."

"And I just bet I know somebody who will help me in that regard, don't I?"

His smile could have charmed birds out of an empty sky, and again I had the feeling that the blank eyes were watching me. "I think perhaps we both know such a person," he said.

"If it's really so evil, why do you want it? Why not let it work its ways on a worthless *Gadje* and let it go at that?"

"Neither money nor the devil, they say, can ever stay at peace. But a Gypsy can keep a devil in a bottle, because he knows how and when to let it out to play. A *Gadje* can only get hurt by it. Especially a demon as powerful as the one in the Wolf."

"You still haven't told me why you think I have

that exact one. Why is that, I wonder? It makes me wonder what else you aren't telling me."

"Again, you go straight to the heart of the matter, don't you? But first things first, I think. You claim to have come all the way here to find a killer. You are not the police. Why would you do such a thing, go to so much trouble?"

"Well, there is also the small matter of clearing my name."

"Aha." He paused to pour himself more coffee, never spilling a drop, then gestured to me to do the same. I assumed we were respecting the rhythm of the game again, and I obliged him.

"Now I see," he said. "Names are so important to you who have only one of them. Yes. And I think Howard Jacobson is not quite the one you are concerned about, yes?"

"Maybe not."

"Well, maybe mine is not quite Stefan Yonkos, either. Fair enough. And for the sake of your fine name, which you do not care to tell to me, you would be willing to part with this violin?"

"In principle, yes."

"Again, the two horses. One cannot do business 'in principle.'"

"No, one can only have an understanding."

"Just so. In the interest of understanding, then, I

will tell you a story."

"Does it begin in the year zero? I heard that one already."

"It does not. It begins a little over fifty years ago, in what my father and grandfathers liked to call 'the old country.' I think you will like it."

Chapter Thirteen

The Fox in the Forest

March 15, 1945
The Ardenne Forest

Mist rose silently from the forest floor and filled the ravines that ran through the dense black-green stands of fir and spruce. It could have been snow evaporating in the warmth of the coming dawn, or new fog, or just lingering smoke. Against the lightening sky, the silhouettes of the trees were fractured and bent at frequent intervals, and the mist smelled faintly of cordite and high explosive. There had been heavy fighting here, with armor and artillery, but it had all moved south now, as the invading armies closed in on Berlin, faster and faster, smelling its blood, thirsting for the kill shot.

It would all be over soon enough, but the man

who threaded his way through the trees couldn't wait. He had escaped from a death camp, with no money and no papers and a damning tattoo on his arm, and he knew he would be hunted. People were not allowed to escape, ever, and the fact of it had to be eradicated. He had to be eradicated. Better to give up the last bridge over the Rhine than to admit that a single, wretched Rom had escaped from the world's most adept jailers, history's most airtight prisons.

It was hard navigating in the dense woods, especially with no stars and the frequent stumbles over hazards of corpses and abandoned hardware, hidden by the indifferent snow. But it was a traditional skill among his people, an inherited instinct, and he was confident that he was still headed north, into the low country. There would be a lot of confusion there, and a careful man, a resourceful one, could make his way to a neutral country, or even a liberated one. Maybe even one where his skills and his people's reputation were unknown.

He pushed on, ignoring his wet feet and chilled body, wanting to get as far as possible before the daylight forced him to hide and creep. The floor of the forest pitched up uniformly, coming to a roadbed, and he quickened his pace, driving himself up the embankment. His foot broke a fallen tree branch, making a sharp crack in the cold air, and he cursed silently and slowed a bit, straining to see into the mist.

"Halt!"

The word was the same in German and English, he knew, but the accent made it unmistakably a Hun. One of Little Adolph's rear echelons, pretending the world wasn't crumbling around him. The Rom stopped in his tracks and scanned the dim landscape intently. It was too dark to see colors yet, but the silhouette showed the unmistakable coattails of a winter greatcoat. This was good. It meant Wermacht, not SS or Gestapo. The fact that the figure was hunched over was also good. It meant that he had a rifle, not a Schmeisser machine gun. If the Rom ran, the man would have to aim, not merely spray. It also meant that he was probably rearguard, a reservist, too young or too old or just too unfit to be a regular combat soldier. And that was best of all. It meant that he could probably be bribed. And if he could be bribed, he could also be cheated.

"Don't shoot," he said in German. "I'm only a civilian."

"Come out where I can see you. Now!"

"Ya, ya, I come. Only, don't shoot." He reached in his improvised backpack and took out the violin case, holding it aloft as he advanced, now making plenty of noise on the forest floor.

"What is that in your hand?"

"It is not a weapon, sir, I swear. Only my violin that I don't want to damage. It is very old, you see." He stopped again. *"I will put it down, if you want me to. See, here I am, putting it down."*

"Bring it here."

Bribable, yes, indeed. A man who takes himself very seriously, though. He would probably prefer to think that he had stolen something. Well, the Rom knew how to arrange that. Or rather, he didn't know it yet, but it would come to him. It always did. He walked up the roadway embankment and stopped when the German told him to.

"Let me see it."

"Of course, your honor." He bent down on one knee, took off the work cap he had stolen at a farmhouse the day before, and placed it on the ground. Then he put the violin on top of it, enhancing the image of value without being too blatant about it, and opened it towards the soldier. Inside its case, the instrument gleamed dully in

the dim light.

"This is a good fiddle?"

"The best, your excellency. It is 350 years old, made by a famous luthier named Amati."

"You stole it." Not a question. By this time of the war, anybody who had anything valuable must have stolen it. Unless, of course, he were a Nazi, in which case he had confiscated it from some subhuman scum. This was not stealing, merely restoring the natural order of things.

"It is mine. A family heirloom. I play it in the Berlin Symphony. Or I did, before they told us all to leave."

Never tell a lie that doesn't have at least a crumb of truth, he told himself for the thousandth time. Complete fabrications are hard to remember, and they will come back to trip you up. He truly had played in an orchestra for a while, but it wasn't the Berlin, it was the forced ensemble of the Treblinka death camp. And the instrument really was a family heirloom. It had been used by his family in scams of one kind or another for more generations than they could easily count. It was not truly his yet, though. Not because he had not inherited it, nor even because his hand had not modified it, but because he had not yet used it to cheat anybody. With any kind of luck, that was about to change.

"The Symphony has gone? Why would they do such a thing?"

"I hesitate to tell a brave man like yourself, it's so…"

"You had better tell me, and be quick about it, too."

"Everyone is fleeing Berlin, sir. The end is near, and nobody wants to be captured by the Russians. But we did our duty, all the same, playing every Sunday, until some officers came and told us to leave. They told us to go north or west, to look for the Americans or the British."

This was also essentially true, if only by coincidence. The Rom had surmised it from bits of rumors that came in with the trainloads of the doomed, adding a heavy dose of his own wishful thinking. He didn't really have any facts, but his account made sense, and he told it haltingly, for the fullest possible effect on the soldier in front of him.

"I don't believe you. I think you are a thief and a liar, and probably a Jew, to boot. I don't even believe you are a musician. You look like a peasant." He raised his rifle again, menacing, working

himself up to do the unthinkable.

"*If I were a peasant, I would be wearing the feldgrau now, just like you. I was deferred to play in the great symphony, which is now, alas, scattered to the winds. As for being a Jew, do you want me to drop my trousers and show you the proof?*"

"*What do you take me for, a pervert?*"

"*Perhaps you would prefer that I play something, then, to prove that I am a musician.*"

"*Now you think you can bluff me. Play, peasant. And it had better sound good. Don't think for a moment that I don't know real music, just because I'm only a foot soldier. Make a fool of me, and you will not live to gloat about it.*"

We'll see about that, thought the Rom. He put a bit of rosin on his bow, took the instrument from the case, and began to play, a popularized version of Tales From the Vienna Woods. *It was complicated enough to sound like a serious work, but simple enough for the Rom to play it well, even exceptionally. He had no formal training, but he was good, a natural talent with a perfect ear and instinctive phrasing. He let the instrument run the gamut, from sweet to coarse, subtle to insistent, but always returning to mellow, heart-rending richness. And it was, indeed, a fine instrument.*

As he played, he watched the soldier relax, then slump, until he looked as if he were about to cry. The Rom wished the soldier would interrupt him, since he couldn't remember how the piece was supposed to end, but the man gestured him to play on. He improvised an ending, based on the dominant theme of the opening stanzas, and before he could be challenged on it, he slipped into a lively Strauss waltz. At least, he thought it was Strauss. It seemed to suffice, whatever it was.

The German sat down on a fallen tree trunk, his rifle upright between his knees and a faraway look in his eyes. Putty.

"I heard the Symphony once," he said. "Before the war. We went to Berlin, my parents and I, to see the city and to take my father to a famous hospital there. He had been in the Great War, you see, had his lungs burned out. They were going to try some new treatment, we were told. I think they lied, just to get him off the pension rolls. My mother and I left him at the hospital and never saw him alive again."

"I thought only we Germans had the poison gas in the last war."

"*That's what they tell you, isn't it? But you know what? The wind doesn't give a pfennig who released the terrible stuff. Unlike my poor father, it doesn't always go where it's told.*"

"*A great tragedy for you.*" He touched the strings lightly again, slipping into a slow, high version of Lilli Marlene. He spoke while he played, watching the soldier with great care. "*They don't care about the little people, do they? About the ones who just follow orders?*"

"*Ya, ya,*" he said, now rocking back and forth slightly. "*This is so true.*"

"*They left the orchestra to fend for itself and now they leave you to be captured by Russians. They hate us, you know.*" He didn't say if he meant the Russians or the high German leaders.

"*That's what you say. I think this is a safe enough place. I think I will be here when the war is over. Then I will just put on some woodsman's clothes and melt into the landscape. Maybe I will have a violin to keep me company, hey?*" His eyes lost their faraway look and began to turn menacing again.

"*Or the Russians will.*"

"*They will not come here. My lieutenant told me so.*"

"And where is he now? Eating hot soup in some prisoner camp, fifty kilometers west of here, out of harm's way? I passed an advance Russian patrol the day before yesterday. Wild, crazy men with submachine guns, looking for anything to shoot or burn. I hid from them, but there will be more. And they will come this way, soon enough."

"You lie."

"Kill me and take my violin, and you can only find out the hard way." He shifted to playing *Deutschland Über Alles,* slowly and transposed into a minor key, as if it were a dirge.

"Where were they, exactly?"

"Why should I tell you?"

"So I don't shoot you?"

"Much good it would do you."

"Then what do you propose, herr musician-peasant?"

"You wish to survive the war?" Suddenly the plan that he had been looking for became crystal clear, laid out before him like a multicolor battle map. All his best schemes came to him that way, quite unbidden and unforeseen.

"Ya, I wish to survive the war. Who does not?"

"Then follow me. I will take you past the patrols, to a safe place. Along the way, we will look for a dead American with a uniform that will fit me, and I will coach you in a most wonderful charade that we are going to play."

"Why do we need to play at anything?"

"Because when we run into another Russian patrol, then I am an American GI, and you are my prisoner. They won't like it, but they won't interfere with us."

"I hope you know what you are doing."

That made two of them. The Rom repacked the violin, crossed over the road, and continued to walk north, the rising sun on his right now illuminating the forest floor, displaying the litter of battle. There was a tense moment or two when he thought he could feel the German aiming his rifle at the center of his back, but finally he heard the man shoulder his gear and trudge after him. The man made more noise than a Tiger tank, which was what the Rom had really hidden from two days earlier. Then, after dark, he had garroted the watch stander on the turret and stolen the man's field rations. He could have killed the private who now followed him, too, any of several times in the last few minutes, but he had faith in his own ruse, and he needed the man for a shill. And he was tired of both the killing and the hiding. Killing is not the Gypsy way. He was ready for a more honorable and interesting game, one more suited to his talents. He was ready to perpetrate the biggest fraud of his career.

Six days later, a gaunt and disheveled U.S. Army corporal wearing the insignia of the 101st Airborne walked into an advance camp of a combined U.S.-British task force in Belgium. The man had lost his weapon, but he carried a Mauser rifle and a violin case. He had also apparently lost his memory and was suffering from what was then called "battle fatigue." He was sent to England for treatment and evaluation, and then home to an early discharge, a modest pension, and a family who didn't seem to know him. His dog tags said his name was Gerald Cox.

Chapter Fourteen

...and the Fox in the Town

The coffee had cooled to tepid by the time he had finished, but the woman, Vadoma, brought in a new tray, with fresh coffee and different pastries, and we again attended to the rhythm of the game. Or maybe we were doing something else. This time, Vadoma didn't leave. She stood off in a corner of the room, behind me, with her arms folded, as if she were waiting for orders of some kind. Or acting as a guard. I began to think I was being deliberately detained.

"You're right," I said. "I like your story. How much of it is true?"

"Truth, you want, also? Sometimes truth is more eel than fish, my friend. It is a story. I was not there when it happened, nor was the man who told it to me, nor, I'm sure, the man who told it to him. But for us, it is always a question of how much needs to be true, to be useful."

"And how much of this needs to be true?"

"Only the bones. It accounts for many things. There was a violin, famous among our people, that disappeared about that time. There is no doubt about that. And it was valuable, so it should have turned up in a market somewhere, sooner or later, but it did not. Believe me, we would have known.

"There was also a young Gypsy man who vanished, but that is less in need of explanation. Many, many were lost in that terrible time. The Jews like to think the Holocaust is their own personal horror, but there were many other groups targeted, as well. The only difference is that some of the others were better at running away. We Rom have been running for a long time. Our instinct for it is well developed. Still, many were killed."

"But some were not."

"Just so. And those who were not, but were scattered across the earth, told their stories to anybody who would listen. That's important to us, always. Stories travel, just like people. And if a man's story makes its way back to the *Natsia*, they will know to look for him."

"And put a light in the window?" I said.

"Something like that, yes."

"But nobody came to the light."

"Many came, after the war, but not a young man with a violin. There has been no epilogue to the story until you came here." He spread his hands out on the table, as if it were my turn to speak. While I debated what to say, the woman stepped forward and whispered something short and urgent into Yonkos' ear. He nodded and gestured to her to be calm.

"If I'm supposed to come to a conclusion from all that," I said, "I don't know what it is."

"Then, maybe it's your turn to tell a story, to match mine. I have already heard one other, you see, about a man named Jackson who killed a poor Gypsy woman and stole her violin."

And as suddenly as it had begun, the party was over.

"From a bent cop named Evans? It's a lie," I said.

"Of course it is." He spread his hands again, smiling. "All stories are lies, at some level. The question, Mr. Jackson, is whose story is more useful, yours or his? And which one will get the famous violin back where it belongs? If I were you, I would be making this simple Gypsy an offer right now."

"The violin for Amy Cox's murderer?"

"That would be fair, wouldn't it? But I do not have that to offer, I'm afraid. You will have to settle for the violin for your freedom. You see, I've already been offered the violin for your head. Or some part of your anatomy, anyway. But I don't think the man, Evans, has the object to offer yet. In fact, I'm not even sure he knows where it is. He may have the foolish notion that if he hurts, maims, and threatens to kill you, you will then take him to it."

"And then he will kill me, anyway."

"He does seem to want that very badly, yes. And it is a sad fact that policemen don't seem to be capable of a small amount of innocent corruption. Once they step over the line, they lose their way completely, and there is nothing they won't stoop to. A delicate thing, dealing with them."

And with you, I thought, and I casually let my right hand settle onto my lap, to reassure myself that the .380 was still in my pocket.

"But you are a different animal, aren't you?" said Stefan.

Now where the hell is he going? "I don't think I've heard it put quite that way before. I take it that's a compliment?"

"In a way, yes. As I said, I like you. And fool that I am, I'm sentimental about who I do business with."

It was my turn to laugh, but I wasn't sure if he had really been joking. "And if you indulge your foolishness and deal with me," I said, "how would you be sure of delivery?"

"That is a problem," he said. "Yes. With you or him. It comes down to trust. I think I do not trust Evans. Can I trust you?"

"Trust me to deliver the violin in return for no more than a dash out into Main Street at high noon, with a trigger-happy posse in hot pursuit? No. Hell, no. Without my name, I have no freedom."

"And what if I can resolve that little problem for you?"

I thought about it for a minute, and about the many ways the game could play from there, and Uncle Fred's advice that it could get bloody before it was done. For the moment, at least, Stefan seemed like the best option I had.

"Do that," I said, "and you have yourself a deal."

"A deal, you say. And a violin?"

"That's the deal."

"This I like. It is more difficult, but it will work." His hands went palms-down on the table, and he nodded with his whole upper body. "I will make a call to our people in St. Paul, set something in motion. Mind you, we may not be able to find your killer..."

"It could be Evans himself, you know."

"Or it could not. No matter. We can get you clear of the whole business without resolving that. We are good at getting clear, Mr. Jackson. Will this do?"

"Yes," I said.

"Yes. Then it shall be so. But I have one last problem. I cannot look into your eyes to judge your sincerity." Funny, but I'd have sworn he was doing exactly that.

"What am I supposed to do about that?"

"Shake my hand, Mr. Jackson."

"Really? I thought Gypsies didn't do that."

"It is only a hand. It can be cleansed. Do it now. We do not have much time."

We stood up and shook hands, and I wondered if he crushed croquet balls for idle amusement, or merely walnuts. I gave him what I hoped was a reassuringly firm grip in return, thinking I could find a physical therapist for my hand later. From her spot near the wall, Vadoma said, "*Ove yilo isi?*" Or something like it.

"Yes," said Stefan.

"I think so, too," she said.

"Then it's unanimous," I said. At least, I hoped that's what it was.

"Push your chair away," said Stefan.

"I don't understand."

"You understand 'chair?'"

"Yes, but…"

"Then put it behind you, as the saying goes."

I pushed my chair back with my heel, keeping my eyes on the man and woman. As I did so, he added, "It has been a pleasure, Mr. Jackson, I assure you. Now, prepare to have your horizons expanded."

Then the lights went out.

I felt the breath go out of me with a violent whoosh

and my knees buckle, and I was suddenly sitting down on something not quite soft. Sand, I decided, when I felt it with my hands. I had been dropped through a trap door, just like a stage magician, and I was sitting under the Rom office, on a dirt floor. Above me, I could hear muffled shouts and some frantic steps on the floor. I think the woman shouted, "No, don't go that way! The police are out in front!" Then there were quick steps in that direction and the sound of a door being slammed, complete with the jingle bells.

The rest was not so clear. A heavier set of steps entered from the back, and there was a lot of angry shouting that I couldn't quite make out. Evans' voice was clear enough, though, screaming "Bullshit!" several times. Whether he was refusing to believe that I had fled through the front door or that the two Gypsies had tried to stop me, I couldn't tell. The volume increased, but the clarity didn't get any better. There was some scuffling, and the woman shrieked a couple times and somebody fell to the floor once, hard. If my newfound allies were doing a bit of street theater, they were very good at it. It was also possible that Evans was part of the show, as well, the three of them doing an elaborate shadow play for an audience that couldn't peek through the curtain.

I sat tight and waited for my eyes to become accustomed to the darkness. It didn't help. There wasn't one candle's worth of light in the whole damn place. The trap door above me was defined by a thin, faint yellow outline of light, but that was all, and it wasn't much. Then the bullets punched some holes in the floor, and light came through them like tiny spotlight beams sprinkled with dust motes. In another life, I would have said they were pretty.

There were two shots at first, in rapid succession, then more shouting and then a third. The argument still continued after that, though, so I assumed Evans was just trying to intimidate people. By shooting through the floor, where he couldn't hurt anybody, that is. Right. Swell. I hoped he had made his point.

Without really knowing what I was going to do with it, I reached in my pocket and pulled out the .380. It was a good thing I hadn't had to draw it in a hurry, because after all the bouncing around of my recent travels, it came out pointing backwards, at me. I carefully corrected the error of its ways and held it in one of the light beams, to check whether there was a shell in the chamber. There wasn't, but I couldn't think of a silent way to put one there, so I left it for the moment. I didn't check to see how many rounds I had in the magazine, either. Whatever the number was, it would have to be enough. I had no spares. I reached in another pocket and took out my lighter.

I could make out a pull chain in the gloom now,

hanging from a bare light bulb, but I didn't yank it. If Evans was restaging the Saint Valentine's Day Massacre upstairs, it probably wouldn't be too good for him to see his bullet holes suddenly lighting up. But I figured I could risk the flame of the lighter.

I moved away from the sparkly light beams, to an outside wall of rough stone, and used my lighter and my considerable groping skills to work my way around to a doorway and into a narrow passageway beyond it. I wasn't sure if I owed Stefan Yonkos anything else for that handshake, or even if he needed any help, but there was little enough I could do for him and Vadoma, in any case. I had a loaded gun, but the Marines don't attack from the low ground, and neither would I. I stumbled through the moldy-smelling tunnel until I came to a dead end with a crude wooden ladder fastened to the wall, and I went up. The rungs were irregular and rotten, and it was slow going.

Behind me, the sounds were more muffled than before, but I clearly heard another shot and another thud on the floor. After that, the arguing voices were all male. Oh, shit. That stupid bastard, Evans, had shot the woman. *Shit, shit, shit. Goddamn him to hell!* I stopped on the ladder for a moment, then felt my feet going back down. Then they were on the floor and going back down the tunnel, the way I had come. I still had no idea what I was going to do, but somehow, now I couldn't leave. I had done nothing but run and hide since this whole, sorry business started, and I just couldn't do it any more. And at some level, I knew that just sticking around to be a through-the-floor witness wasn't going to work, either. Maybe it was time to die, I wasn't sure. *What the hell, everybody's got to die of something.* It was damn sure somebody's time.

My stomach was a solid knot when I got back to the area under the trap door, and I had to work hard at breathing. I was sweating heavily, too, and I did not imagine that it had anything to do with the temperature in the cellar. I swallowed the taste of tarnished pennies, decided that was just too damn bad, and looked up.

Above me, there were now only two holes letting light through the floor. I thought I could dimly see the third hole dripping some kind of liquid, but that was probably just my hyped-up imagination. The next two shots were real enough, though. The first was followed by a low, guttural cry, which could have been a Gypsy curse or just an involuntary grunt. After the second one, there was nothing. I jacked a shell into the magazine of the .380 and tried to find a place with enough light to let me see the sights. I think I heard myself snarl.

Evans must have heard me, too. I heard some confused muttering above, then a distinct shout.

"Jackson, you asshole, is that you? Are you hiding under this floor like the fucking rat you are? Answer me, or I'll ventilate this place!"

One of the last two light-bearing holes went dark, and I assumed Evans was bending down to get a look or a better shouting spot.

This is it, kid. He's a better shot than you are, he has the high ground, and he probably has more ammunition than you do. This is as good a chance as you get.

I pointed the gun up, held it in both hands, and emptied it into the floor around the darkened hole. Splinters of wood flew back in my face and the world was full of noise and fire. I found it strangely fascinating that I could hear the empty shells being ejected and clinking against each other on the floor, but I didn't seem to hear the shots. Four of the rounds made new light-holes. The rest did not. Evans let out something that could have been either a scream or a shout or both. There were some more rapid shots, but this time, none of them came through the floor. Then everything fell deathly silent.

I found the pull chain again and jerked it, squinting at the sudden glare. I didn't know what Evans' state was, but there was no more point in being secretive. There was also no point in sticking around. Another ladder stood by the hinge side of the trap door, but I couldn't see any way to trip the hatch from down here, so I headed back to the tunnel I had found before.

I was still drenched in sweat, but my breathing was easier now, and I took my time. Time went back to normal, and relief flooded through me like a cool tide. I seemed to be preoccupied with the monumental question of which I wanted more, a hot shower, a stiff drink, or a long, long nap.

Do it in the right order, and you can have it all.

True enough, but first, I had to…

Behind me, I heard the sound of the trap door opening again, and I turned around to see Evans hit the dirt in a heap. He rolled over, groaned loudly, looked around, and propped himself up on one elbow. With his other hand, he slowly extended his huge semiauto in my direction. His shirtfront and one side of his face were covered with blood, drool was coming out of his mouth, and one of his legs was twitching oddly. But there was no doubt that he had me squarely in his sights. And at this range, he couldn't miss. Hell, in that narrow little passage, he could have bounced the bullets off the walls and still been sure of hitting me. From the shop above, I thought there was the sound of the jingle bells again, but it was hard to imagine them doing me any good.

"Out of bullets, are we?" he said. "What a fucking shame."

We both looked at my right hand, where I still held the .380, the open chamber clearly advertising that it was empty.

"Why don't you hop a freight train again, asshole?"

"That's a good idea," I said. "Know where I can find one?"

"I just happen to have one, pointed straight at you. And you are standing on the tracks, right where I want you. I'd rather run you down with a car, of course, but we don't…"

"Why, for crying out loud?"

"Huh? The hell you mean, 'why?'"

"Why means why, is all. Why a car, why me, why Amy Cox, why any of it? If you're going to waste me anyway, you could at least tell me."

"You trying to confuse me now?"

Do I have that option? Damn right. "What do you mean?"

"What do you mean, what do I mean? You think I'm half gone, you can play with my mind? I ain't that far gone. Tell you what, though: you tell me where the violin is, and I'll let you off with a nice, clean, pain-less head shot. Or better yet, don't tell me, and I'll just shoot both your kneecaps off and let you bleed out. I'd like that a lot."

"Or maybe you ought to just drop the gun now, while you still can." The voice came from above, through the still-open trap door. Rosie, bless her rabbit-hunting, free-spirited little heart. I could only see her in backlit silhouette, but she had never looked so good to me.

"Who the fuck are you?" said Evans, and without

waiting for an answer, he rolled over, pointed his gun up, and started to squeeze the trigger. Or at least, he looked like he was going to squeeze it, and that was enough. Rosie let fly with three shots that pounded him into the dirt floor as if a building had dropped on him. His gun arm flopped to the dirt beside him, and he didn't move after that.

"Herman?" Rosie came partway down the ladder and squinted into the cellar. "Are you down there, Herman? God, I hope you are, because otherwise, I just killed a man for some complete stranger."

"Relax, Rosie."

"Are you all right, Herman?"

"I am now." I laughed, first a giggle and then a roar. I couldn't help it. After what seemed like ages, I sobered up, kicked the gun away from Evans' inert hand, just to be safe, and climbed the ladder by the trap door. "Let's get out of here, my love," I said.

"What did you call me?"

People say the damnedest things under stress.

Chapter Fifteen

Aftershock

"Praise Yah!" said the voice on the phone.

"I absolutely do not believe this. Prophet?"

"Himself. The disembodied voice in the wilderness, the unobserved of all observers. How goes the sojourn, Pilgrim?"

"I've had better trips. What the hell are you doing on Wilkie's phone?"

"As usual, the pilgrim sees but does not comprehend. It is the big man who is at my phone, not the other way around. Except that at the moment, he's at my laptop, probing the dark secrets of the cosmos. You wish me to interrupt him?"

"I wish." *Your laptop? Dark secrets of the cosmos?*

I waited and listened to some predictable background noises, while outside the plastic half-egg canopy of the public phone I was using, a thousand seagulls kept up a running argument with the waves that exploded against the breakwaters in front of Chicago's old Navy Pier. The place had been converted since I was last there into a sort of combination upscale flea market and fast food emporium. It was a good place to get lost in a crowd. Lots of young families there, with loud, badly-behaved little kids. People like that only pay attention to themselves and their own little broods. It was better, Rosie said, than Grant Park, which had a lot of old people on benches, people who watched and remembered everything and everybody.

Rosie was out by the rocks, throwing popcorn at the gulls and looking fresh and smart in some new slacks and a pullover and jacket from Marshall Fields. She had been shopping again, while I took a tourists' boat ride up the Chicago river, complete with running commentary by an architecture student from the University of Illinois. Along the way, I dropped the disassembled pieces from my .380 and Rosie's nine-millimeter over the stern, in six different places. I dropped one of the receiver assemblies within sight of the old Jewelers Building, which, according to our guide, used to be one of the operations centers for Al Capone. It seemed like a fitting thing to do. Not a tribute so much as an addition. The last two pieces, the actual gun barrels, Rosie now tossed into Lake Michigan, along with more popcorn. If anybody noticed the large, dark lumps flying off among the smaller white ones, they damn sure were not going to jump into that kind of surf to check things out. The gulls didn't seem to care, one way or the other.

Rosie's sharp new outfit also included a pair of stylish unlined driving gloves. Neither of us knew if latent fingerprints could survive being underwater, so we had wiped down all the metal and handled it literally with kid gloves after that. If somebody else's prints were on the shells left in the magazine, that was their problem. All in all, the events of the late morning were already starting to seem like another lifetime.

I pretended not to have survivor's euphoria, mainly because I didn't want Rosie to think I was celebrating the fact that she had been forced to kill a man. The fact that I would have gleefully killed him myself if I hadn't been out of bullets was beside the point. Killing is never a trivial event, and I wasn't sure how it would hit her when it finally soaked in. Hell, I wasn't sure how it would hit me. The only thing that will affect your psyche more profoundly than killing is being killed yourself, and we're not even sure about that. So Rosie romped with the gulls, and I took that as a good thing, while I privately drifted between elation at still being alive and sorrow over what we had left.

Stefan Yonkos had still been alive when we left him, though his odds for staying that way did not look good at all. We made some crude but effective compress bandages for him from the fotune-telling table cloth, then put his feet up a bit and covered him with a drape to help with the shock. That was as much as we knew how to do. Vadoma was beyond help. Evans had shot her in the head, and she was probably dead before she hit the floor. The sight of her had made me want to kill him all over again. *Easy, there, Herman. You're just a minor referee in the big league justice game, remember?* Like hell. I calmed myself with a major force of will and remembered to wipe down the coffee cup that had been the token of my acceptance, way back when. Then we split.

When we left, there were still no sounds of sirens. Apparently Gypsies only call the cops if they are *their* cops. And if there was a doctor on the way, he must have been riding one of those horses that Yonkos said requires a whole rump. Rosie and I casually slipped into the rented Pontiac and cruised away without meeting a single emergency vehicle. We stopped at the first gas station, used a pay phone to call 911, and left again without giving the operator any unnecessary chitchat, like who we were. A clean exit, but a sorry business to leave behind.

Not that I expected anybody to be sorry about Evans. If there was a Mrs. Evans, we could probably have hit her up for a service fee. But there I go, taking people at face value again, which is exactly what bondsmen, cops and judges do, and exactly what human beings should not. Shaky Bill said it best: one man in his time plays many parts, and the people who sometimes act like assholes are not always evil from the ground up.

We have an entire industry devoted to judging people for specific acts, not basic worth, and for better or worse, I'm part of it. Most of the time, I play the part with professional detachment. I think of myself as being like the croupier at a craps table. It's none of my business that most of the people who bet too much shouldn't even be playing, or that I can see when they're going to lose even before the dice start to turn on them, or that I can spot the cheats from across the room. I just collect the fees and make sure everybody plays by the rules and gets the same, pathetic chances. As much as anybody, I have a right to be cynical about it. But it's hard to see things that way when it's personal.

Personal or not, I thought I had learned as much as I could here on the sparkling shores of Lake Michigan. True or false, Evans and Yonkos had told me all they were going to. And one thing Evans had told me, whether he meant to or not, was that, rotten as he might have been, he did not kill Amy Cox. I still hadn't figured out why he wanted to kill me, but I did not think his confusion, when I had asked him about Amy, had been faked. So the truth, whatever it was, lay somewhere along the road that had brought me here. Time to go back. If I could.

"Herman, my man! You remembered the code."

I did? I looked at my watch and saw that it was just after one o'clock. God, was that possible? Three hours since I had first stepped into the world of the crystal ball? A lifetime and a blink. *How time flies when you're halving guns.* I chuckled at my own horrible joke, realizing that I had been strung much too tight for much too long.

"Good to hear your voice, Wide. What are you doing with the Proph?"

"Would you believe it's his cell phone you're calling?"

"No. What would he be doing with a cell phone?" *Not to mention a laptop.*

"Just because you're a holy man doesn't mean you have to be a techno-dumbshit, he says. That's not how he said it, but…"

"I'm hip."

"Yeah, that's what he says, too. You're hip. Personally, I never know what the hell he's talking about. Anyway, I'm out doing a little poking around here and there yesterday, earning your money and all, and he keeps popping up in my shadow. Says he has a holy mission to find you again, and some kind of Carmen bullshit, and I should give you his cell phone number, in case you need an untraceable contact point."

"Oh, really? You think he actually knows if it's untraceable or not?"

"Beats me, but he knows a whole shitload more stuff than I would have guessed. He's got a laptop that's wired into more damn secure databases than you can shake holy water at, and he knows how to massage them all. Would you believe I checked out the Amy Cox ME report that way? It doesn't give a time of discovery, by the way, only a time of death and the time of the autopsy. I flunked out there. I suppose I could try to schmooze one of the lab staff. There's a really ugly broad there who thinks I'm kind of…"

"Forget it. It's not an issue anymore."

"It's not? Why's that?"

"Tell you later. I don't suppose the Proph does all this high-powered computer searching just for the good of his and your souls?"

"No damn way. He may be goofier than a clock going backwards, but he's not stupid. I'm into him for a yard and a half already, and more getting added up right now. You did say it was all right to run up some expenses, didn't you?"

"I didn't say, but it is. In fact, it might be more than all right. With all those high-powered illegal entry portals, can he get into military records?"

"You mean like where the Pentagon hides the ICBMs and the good booze?"

"No, I mean like Army personnel records. Discharges, duty stations, stuff like that."

"Hell, is that all? He can probably get *Cuban* army personnel records, with CIA footnotes on them. You want I should ask?"

"Ask." There was some more background noise while I waited again and watched Rosie frolic around the waterfront like a little kid. I found myself staring at her shoes. This time around, she had managed to include shoes in her shopping, and the ones she was wearing now were white, with a sort of squashed, compromise high heel that gave her foot a very nice line. *And so what?* So what, indeed? Since when did I become a fancier of shoes? They must have reminded me of something else, something back at the scene I didn't much want to remember, back in the cellar and the dark, when…

"The Proph says if you've got the bread, he's definitely got the meat."

"What the hell does that mean?" I said.

"It means tell me what kind of records you want to see, and he can get them, but the meter is running."

"Remind him that I gave him a Chevy and a holy mission, will you? You got something to write on there?"

"Fire away."

"Okay, I want the service record of one Gerald Cox, Gerald with a 'G,' who served with the 101st Airborne in World War Two."

"Jesus, Herman, why don't you give me a toughie? The Army never heard of computers back then."

"The Proph says he can get it, so let's give it a try. I'm especially interested in his mustering-out physical exam. Get a print of that if you can. If there's anything on what happened to him after the war, that would be good, too. In fact, that would be better."

"I can see the dollar signs rolling up in his big, spaced-out eyes now."

"If he comes through, it'll be worth it. Tell him if he doesn't, you won't pay him at all."

"No starter's purse, huh?"

"None. My money, my rules."

"That ought to do it. Anything else?"

"Two things. Go see Agnes and find out if the check we got from Amy Cox was any good. If it was, find out where the funds came from. I want to know a person, if possible, not just an account number."

"That ought to be an easy one. What's the other?"

"Have Agnes show you a couple of emails I got from somebody claiming to be Gerald Cox. He wanted to set up a meeting, to buy the Amati violin. Send him a reply telling him you accept, or I do. Have Aggie draft it. She knows how I write. But don't send a final confirmation until you and I get a chance to talk about the place for the meet. I want someplace where you can cover my back."

"Hey, I know how to do that. Does this mean you're on your way back? Is the heat off?"

"Good question. You really believe this is a secure phone?"

"No."

"Me neither. Look into it a little, okay? I'll call you tomorrow, same time."

"I'll be here. The Proph says to keep the faith, by the way. Am I supposed to know what that means?"

"If you figure it out, let me know."

"Not likely. Tomorrow, my man."

"Talk at you, Wide."

I hung up just in time to turn and get an open-mouthed kiss from Rosie, who was apparently out of popcorn but not energy. And either I felt the same way or it was infectious.

"You were staring at me again," she said.

"Again?" She couldn't possibly have seen me looking at her shoes.

"The last time, I didn't have any clothes on, remember?"

"Oh, that time. Well, that'll do it."

"Maybe it's time to do it again, see what happens when there's no brake lever to get in the way."

"I do seem to remember something about a hotel room," I said.

"You figure it's safe now?"

"Since when do you use words like 'safe?'"

"Since I started hanging around with this guy who

needs an armed escort."

"You ought to dump him. He's going to get you seriously killed one of these days."

"Uh huh. Well, in the meantime, he better be ready to make it all worth my while. What temperature do you like the Jacuzzi?" So much for the question of how the events of the morning were going to hit us.

Much later, we sat at a table by the window of a Hungarian restaurant Rosie knew called Csardas, back on the near-north side, in the middle of a Hispanic-looking neighborhood. The streets there had more people on them than cars, all in a high state of animation and noise, and it was another good place to get lost.

It had turned out to be quite a day. A little pursuit, a little intrigue, a little adrenaline, a lot of blood, a bit of prudent track-covering, and finally some celebratory sex and coma-like sleep. All that activity tends to make one hungry. We had gorged ourselves on food with unpronounceable names like *halászlé* and *gulyás*, which was about half paprika and totally delicious. Now we were drinking a sparkling wine called *Törley* and seriously working at the business of doing nothing. It was dark outside by then, and the waiters were going around lighting the candles on the tables, while the yellowish overhead lights bumped up a notch, accenting the stamped metal ceiling panels. Fans lazily turned below them, rustling the plastic leaves on some phony grape arbors. In the back of the place, a troupe of Gypsy musicians were getting their gear out and warming up.

"You didn't tell me this place had live music," I said.

"I didn't remember that. You want to leave?"

"When they start, maybe. Somehow, I don't feel like hearing a Gypsy violin just now."

"Gee, I can't imagine why you'd feel that way. Did you at least find out what you needed to, back in Skokie?"

"Is that where we were? I thought it was Tombstone. Or Dodge City. How did you find the place, by the way?"

"Well, I heard Joe tell you the time, back at the club, but not the place. When you didn't come back from your phone call, I figured either you had walked out on me or something had gone very wrong."

"That would be a fair description of it, yes."

"Either way, I thought you'd try to make the appointment if you could. So I went to downtown Skokie and looked for a fortune-teller's sign that was different from all the others."

"Different, how?"

"I didn't know how, at first. But finally I found the one with that gross picture of the eyeball on the hand. The others didn't have that. I figured that made it either the secret inner sanctum or a Gypsy optometrist. It took me a while to find it, though. And even after I found it, I wasn't sure if I should go in. For all I knew, you were about to wrap up the deal of a lifetime. Then I heard the shots, and I decided I not only better go in, I better go in ready to shoot."

"That's the way a gangster or a cop thinks," I said. "Why didn't you just drive away?"

"Hey, if I did that, I'd never know if you really meant to dump me, would I?"

"Are you serious?"

"What do you think?"

"Tell you what, Rosie: if I decide to sneak out on you, I'll tell you about it first, okay?"

"I'll hold you to that, Herman."

In the rear, the musicians were starting to stroll and perform. I beckoned the waiter over to our table, ordered another bottle of bubbly, and gave him a twenty to give to the band, with the request that they leave us alone.

"You are sure?" he said. "Is very nice music, make the lady feel very romantic."

"We need some quiet time to talk," I said. "We're working out the terms of the divorce."

"Aw," he said. "So sad. And she is so beautiful. I will tell them." After he turned his back, I think he said, "Bullshit" under his breath. Rosie was obviously having a hard time keeping a straight face.

"So, ratface," she said, in a voice louder than necessary, "how did it go with the lawyers today?"

I pretended to slam my fist on the table and said, "You'll never get a damn penny!" Then I lowered my voice and talked about what was really on my mind. The adrenaline and the glee were long gone by then, the wine was starting to do its work, and I badly needed to unload. I told her everything I could remember from my meeting with Stefan and Vadoma, elaborating when she asked questions, trying to set it all firmly in my own mind. I didn't know what points would be important later on, so I worked hard at being able to recite them all. Somewhere in there was more information than I knew I had, of that much I was sure.

"So this Evans guy was the same cop you bopped, back home?" said Rosie.

"That's the one," I said. "He also had a phony partner named Stroud, who turned out to be the maybe-brother of the also maybe-phony Amy Cox, the woman who was killed in front of my place. Before I had to run this morning, I found out that Stroud has been killed, too. Should I draw you a score card for all this?"

"It probably wouldn't help. With or without it, though, aren't your problems over now? If Evans killed the Cox woman and tried to pin it on you…"

"He didn't kill her."

"Excuse me? Are you hanging that on the fact that he was a little confused when you asked him about it? He was a mess, Herman. He'd have had trouble if you'd asked him how high was up."

"That's what gave me the first suspicion, but you're right: it's hardly state's evidence. But then I remembered the violin. Evans wanted me to tell him where the violin is. It's the only reason he didn't shoot me when he had the chance."

"So? It's worth a lot of money, you said."

"Yes it is, and whoever broke Amy Cox's neck has it."

"Oh."

"Oh, it is."

The waiter interrupted us then with our new bottle of wine and wouldn't leave until I had admired the cork, sipped the wine, and praised it all lavishly. As he was leaving, he said very quietly but firmly, "Is very good music." I still didn't want the musicians hanging around our table, but he had managed to make me feel guilty about it.

"Where were we?" I said.

"Talking about what Evans didn't know. Mostly, it seems to me that he got here awfully fast."

I nodded and sipped some more wine. "I thought about that, too. No way I believe my car has a bug in it. I figure he must have tapped my email or my phone back in St. Paul, and he hit the road as soon as he got the location of the phone booth by the Kinko's. That probably also means he was traveling when the maybe-brother got hit."

"Let's put that aside for a minute. It seems to me he had already done a lot of wheeling and dealing with Yonkos before you ever got there."

"Dead on." God, I love a smart woman. "I think they knew each other long before Amy Cox ever walked into my office. I think Yonkos was a bigger boss than I thought, had his fingers in Gypsy doings and their dealings with crooked cops as far away as my humble little town."

"Or if he didn't play an active part, he at least knew about them."

"That's more likely, I agree. Either way, when Evans lost me at the shopping center, he probably went to see his old buddy Stefan for some advice. He must have been blown away by his own good luck when he found out I was on my way there, too."

"Or horrified at it," she said.

"How's that?"

"Well, Evans was a cop. If he was trying to keep his ties to the Gypsies a secret, he had to know that game was going to come apart when you came here. Maybe that's why he wanted to kill you."

"That would fit, all right, but that wasn't his reason."

"How do you know?"

And suddenly, I did know. "Because of his shoes," I said.

"Huh?" She made a cradle out of her folded fingers and dropped her chin into it with a look of wide-eyed bewilderment. "Maybe I need that score card, after all. I thought I was doing great, up to then."

"Think back on the scene in the basement, Rosie."

"Must I?"

"Well, maybe not all of it. But try to picture Evans' shoes."

She closed her eyes for a moment.

"Sorry," she said. "It's a pretty ordinary pair of shoes."

"Expensive?"

"Are you kidding? Discount store. Plastic soles. Not even a good big-brand knockoff. His suit, the same thing."

"That's what I think, too. It's not just a matter of taste. This was a guy who never bought anything that wasn't cheap to start with, and on sale besides."

"What I said. So?"

"So how do you get to be a plainclothes cop?"

"Is this a test? Do I get a prize if I guess right?"

"You already got your prize."

"Oh, dreadful macho vanity there. What's your point, slick?"

"My point is that you get to be a detective by putting

in your time in a uniform first. And uniformed cops, just like you when you were waiting tables, get to appreciate good shoes. So this detective goes on the take to a bunch of con artists, risks his badge and his pension, even. I'm saying that even if he is too smart to make a big splash with his ill-gotten extra money anyplace else, he at least buys himself a really good pair of shoes."

She thought it over for a minute. "Okay," she said. "So he wasn't on the take, had to scrape by on a mere fifty-five thou a year, or whatever cops make, poor baby."

"But he was definitely in cahoots with the Rom on the fiddle scam, all the way. He even accused the young guy, Jimmy, of screwing it up."

"You're arguing with yourself, Herman. People pay therapists a lot of money to deal with that, you know."

"No, I'm not. I'm saying Evans was in on the con, and probably others as well, up to his badge, okay? But not for the money."

"What else is there?"

"I'm surprised at you, Rosie. You of all people, to ask such a question."

"Are you telling me that he was Amy Cox's lover?"

"Bingo. It makes everything else fit, doesn't it?"

"I guess. And he wanted to kill you because…"

"Because he really did think I had murdered her. That was where all the rage came from."

"Good grief," she said. "So he wound up almost killing you and getting killed himself, all because he wasn't a very smart detective."

"That's about the size of it."

"And we're right back at square one."

"No, we're not," I said. "But that's where we're going."

Chapter Sixteen

Looking Backwards

Even in a real war, they don't campaign every day. Sometimes they have to wait for the Lost Patrol to find itself or the supply lines to catch up with the advance columns, and sometimes they just have to stop and figure out what the hell is going on. I needed a day for Wide Track to sniff around and find out if I could come back to St. Paul without a lawyer at my side. And to be honest, I still didn't know where I would go when I got there.

We went to a different hotel that night, a huge new highrise down by the Chicago River, either because I don't like leaving an easy trail or because Rosie just liked the looks of it. Maybe both reasons, plus the fact that she was still working at running up such a huge tab on her plastic that she wouldn't ever be tempted to go back to the diner in New Salem.

She had noticed the place from down on the

lakefront, and she wondered if the rooms right under the massive lit-up sign would be bathed in flashing red light, just like in an old cheap-detective movie. They weren't, as it turned out, and the desk clerk said he got really tired of people asking him about it. But we booked a top-floor room anyway, with another Jacuzzi and a view of the lake and the city skyline. In the morning, we had eggs benedict and fresh fruit brought up by room service and watched the morning sun burn off picture-postcard layers of orange and magenta clouds over a lake that looked like lead glass.

"Is this how it feels to be rich?" said Rosie.

"No, this is how rich people thought it was going to feel. By the time they get there, they can't remember the feeling or the reason anymore. Then they get a little deranged."

"That's pretty cynical," she said. "Are you speaking from experience again? You have millions stashed away that you haven't told me about?"

I smiled and poured myself some more coffee. The thin, crisp-edged porcelain cups with the hotel logo on them reminded me of the ones Yonkos and I had used, and I thought of the way his sightless eyes had seemed to light up when we talked about the Amati. It was his only display of weakness.

"There was a time," I said, "when I chased the big bucks as hard as any other idiot. But I've made and lost enough money since then to say that of all the phony dreams they sell you in this country, the joy of being rich is the phoniest."

"Yeah, huh? Well let me tell you, being poor isn't so hot, either."

I smiled again. I've been there, too. Bought the tee shirt, rode the tour bus, did the whole scene. She was right: It sucked.

"Too true," I said. "Either poverty or wealth can own you. The trick is to stay in the middle, where you might actually find out what's important."

"And that is…?"

"Did I say I knew?"

"You know more than you think, Herman."

I certainly hope so.

To kill some time until I could call Wilkie again, we went out and acted like typical tourists for a while, strolling through the downtown parks and shopping in the Loop for things we didn't need. Rosie bought me a watch, with more fancy dials than anybody could read and a lot of extra buttons. I've owned cars that cost less.

"I don't need that," I said.

"Your old one looks like a dime store Timex."

"It is a dime store Timex. What's wrong with that?"

"You're a successful businessman," she said. "You should look like it."

"Back in the real world, what I am is an officer of the court. A coat and tie are my work clothes, but it's actually better if they're not too flashy. Successful businessmen these days dress like wannabe bums, except that they have designer labels sewn on the wrong side of their rags and cell phones grafted to the sides of their heads. I wouldn't look like that if you threatened me. I was proud, the first time I could afford a real suit."

"Be proud again. Wear a nice watch."

What do you say to something like that? I decided to be proud. I should have also drawn a conclusion, but I didn't.

We went to a yuppie coffee bar downtown, and I used one of their public PCs to check in with Agnes again. The coffee there was three to five dollars a pop, even in a paper cup, and their pastries were so expensive they kept them in a locked case, like fine jewelry. But the Internet time was free. I'm not sure how it all balanced out.

I sent Agnes a short message, telling her I was all right and would be talking to Wilkie later in the day. She gave me a cheery little acknowledgment and added that nobody had been around looking for me recently, except for Wilkie with the chores I'd given him, plus a deranged, babbling street preacher, whom she had thrown out. Served him right. Holy mission or not, the Proph shouldn't be bothering my secretary.

There wasn't any other incoming traffic right then, which made me wonder if Evans had been the author of some or all of my earlier e-mails, and hence there would be no more of them. I had Agnes forward me a copy of the sales offer I had told Wilkie to send under my name.

Re: Amati violin

Your offer is accepted in principle, but the minimum price is $75k.

If this is acceptable, where and when do we meet to conduct the sale?

H J

I had been right: Agnes knew exactly how to write it. I wouldn't have changed a word. There was no printer in the coffee shop, but I also had her forward me the earlier messages again, and I reread them, making a few notes. The one that was signed "a friend" did not offer to sell me back the Amati, I noticed, merely to sell me some information on how to get it. So the writer didn't have it but claimed to know where it was. He or she also told me Gerald Cox was very bad news and much to be avoided. Interesting. A falling out among thieves, maybe?

The writer claiming to be Gerald Cox, on the other hand, flatly stated that he *knew* I had the violin, which suggested to me that whoever he was, he was not

Amy Cox's killer. Or did it? Maybe he was just upping the ante for the anonymous "friend."

I tried to think of another scenario, one in which the same person had sent both messages, to see which one I would bite at, but I couldn't quite make it all hold together. While I was busy knitting my brows over it, the reply came back to Wilkie's message, and Agnes dutifully forwarded it to me at once.

mr. jackson again

you should have accepted my offer when i made it. now there is blood involved, and what you have to offer is worth much less on the open market. i suggest that i would be doing you a favor by simply taking it off your hands, but i will be magnanimous and give you the fitting sum of $18,000.

time and place to follow.

how do you like beautiful downtown skokie, by the way?

g c

Oh shit flashed into my mind, but that didn't begin to cover it. Somebody—probably somebody very bad—not only knew how to reach out and touch me here on the road, he also knew just way too damn much about my affairs. I wondered if it was even safe to go back to the hotel. The cold feeling in the pit of my stomach was starting to feel like a familiar but unwanted guest. I grabbed a notepad off the counter and copied down the message verbatim. Then I looked at my fancy new watch. Still almost two hours until it was time for my call, and not a single useful thing I could do before then. I collected Rosie from where she was ogling the pastry case, and we went off for another casual stroll. If we talked, I have no idea about what.

We had a junk food lunch, Chicago-style hot dogs and fries from a street vendor. The hot dogs had about a pound of veggies and onions on them and dripped with sauce, and I wondered if they sold the same kind at the baseball games there. If so, they must hose down the bleachers after every game. After we ate, we washed our hands in a public drinking fountain, while a couple of monumental bronze statues frowned down on us in disapproval. Then we went back to the hotel to pick up the car and drove until we found another pay phone.

"Praise Yah, okay?" Wilkie's voice carried a distinct lack of enthusiasm.

"He's got you saying it, too?" I said.

"He wouldn't let me answer the phone unless I promised to. You believe that?"

"I don't believe you actually did it. You got anything for me?"

"I got a lot, but not all of it exactly in my hot little hand. The military records you wanted are all paper.

We could get some PFC clerk to fax them, if we had a fax number that would stand up to a hard look, but that's as high tech as they can go. We can't use the Internet for it."

I thought for a moment and got one of my rare inspirations. "Go over to the County Sheriff's office, across from the Courthouse," I said. "See a deputy named Janice Whitney and tell her I need a favor. She'll probably give you their fax number and even pick up the stuff for you, if you ask her nice. She owes me one."

"Is she cute?"

"What difference does that make?"

"I seem to make out better with broads who aren't cute."

"You're not supposed to make out, you're just supposed to get a fax number. And yes, she's cute."

"That's too bad."

"Would I hire you for something easy? What else have you got?"

"Well, the big news is, our good buddy the shady detective has got himself dead, no less, in some 'burb outside Chicago. Shot."

"I'm shocked."

"I figured."

"How'd you find out?" I said.

"Hey, I called his work number. Thought I'd say I got a postcard from you from Ixtapa or some such shit, ask him did he want the address or wasn't he interested anymore? And somebody told me he checked out."

"They tell you if they're looking for anybody special for it?"

"They're not looking for you, at least not yet. Not much being given out, but it sounds like a hell of a complicated mess. I took one of the lower-downs in the department there out to lunch, a very much not-cute gal named…"

"Spare me."

"Okay then, this *person* I know says we got three people dead, all with some kind of bad history or other. Some major turf war going on between cops, too. The locals think our boy was bent, so how can his own people be trusted to investigate his killing? But our people think *all* the cops over there in Illinois are bent, so how can they be trusted to investigate the price of free doughnuts? They'll probably never get it all straightened out. You don't know a thing about any of it, right?"

"A check of my credit card records will show that I was on a train to Seattle," I said. "And the ticket clerk should remember me, too."

"Good deal. How is it in Seattle these days?"

"Windy. I'm thinking of coming back."

"I would say that's not a problem. According to the Prophet's computer, you're not on any wanted lists."

"I was," I said, "but maybe they were all put out on

the personal authority of our one guy. When he died, so did they."

"Yeah, could be. And as far as the thing in Chicago goes, there's not enough of you to make a good suspect."

"Excuse me?"

"Well, it's just the guy was shot by at least three different people. I guess I didn't mention that before. I mean, he really knew how to piss off a lot of very bad actors."

"Are you sure about that, Wide? You're absolutely sure it was three, not two?"

"Hey, that's one of the few things everybody agrees on in this case. Three shooters: one with a three-eighty, one with a nine, and one with a seven millimeter. The seven is why everybody remembers it. You don't see a lot of them."

"No, you don't," I said. I had that strange feeling again, as if that should tell me something really important. I think I hung up without saying goodbye.

I went back to where Rosie was sitting behind the wheel of the Pontiac, ready to do another fast getaway should the phone suddenly turn into a monster or a cop. I slid into the passenger seat and tried to make some sense of what I had just heard.

"Rosie," I said, "back when you found me at the fortune-telling parlor…"

"Rescued, Herman. The operative word is definitely 'rescued.'"

"Okay. Back when you were the cavalry and I was up to my ass in bloodthirsty Indians…"

"Oh, much better. Yes, back then, what?"

"How did you open the trap door?"

"Huh?"

"That's not the reassuring reply I had been hoping for."

"What are you talking about?" she said. "It was already open. It was a hole in the floor, with your voice coming out of it and some goon all covered with blood at the bottom of it. I didn't open anything. How would I?"

"Good question. So who did, I wonder?"

"What difference does it make? It was open, okay? I mean, it had to be…" She stopped and turned to look at my face.

"No, Herman. Damn it all to hell, no."

"No what?" I gave her what I hoped was an innocent look.

"You've got that look, like a doctor about to give out one of those awful good-news-bad-news things. Don't tell me what I can see you're about to tell me." I switched to faking a reassuring smile, but that obviously didn't work, either.

"It's crazy and it won't accomplish anything," she said.

"Then just drop me off, okay?"

"You know about how likely I am to do that?"

"Yes," I said. "So let's go."

"We are talking about the same thing here, right? For some utterly insane and self-destructive reason, you want to go back to the Gypsy *officia*?"

"That's the plan, yes."

"The plan sucks."

"It does, doesn't it? Hit it."

"Shit." She peeled away from the curb without looking, and a cabbie she had cut off blew his horn. She did as elegant a job as I have ever seen of flipping him the bird.

"You know, I'm supposed to be the crazy one," she said.

"Isn't it interesting, how roles sometimes reverse?"

"No."

◇◇◇

The storefront had yellow crime scene tape over it, but all the action had long since gone elsewhere. There were no cars and no activity anywhere on the block.

"Cruise on past it," I said. "Keep your head pointed forward, just watching the road like any other slightly lost driver." While she did, I tried to scan the windows and roof parapets across the street without making a show of craning my neck.

"Anything?" said Rosie.

I nodded. "Second floor, two thirds of the way down the block. Either somebody with the biggest eyeglasses ever made likes to sit in the dark, or there's a goon in there with a pair of binoculars."

"A cop, you think?"

"That would be my guess, yes. They deliberately cleared the street to keep from scaring anybody off. Now they're waiting to see who shows up, if anybody. They must not have any real leads to follow at all."

"So that's it, right? As in, 'We're out of here?'"

"Wrong. It's just harder now. But there's still something I've got to find out here. Go straight until we're out of sight of him, then look for a big drugstore."

"You need some antidepressants? I do."

"Tools," I said.

We found a Walgreens half a mile away, and I went in and got disposable latex gloves, a pair of needle-nosed pliers, some paper clips and hairpins, a spray can of penetrating oil, and two good, big flashlights. Wonderful places, these modern pharmacies. Just on principle, I added a roll of duct tape, too. Remembering the unpredictability of some of my recent meals, I also stocked up on mixed nuts, beef jerky, potato chips and pop. And some chocolate-covered cherries for Rosie. Never let it be said that I'm an inconsiderate date.

I got back in the car and we headed back the general way we had come, but on a parallel street a block over from the one with the Gypsy building. While Rosie drove, I set about converting the paper clips and hairpins into a set of lock picks. If the Gypsy community had gone all electronic, then the picks wouldn't help me, but I was betting that people whose ancestors talked to angels were even lower-tech than I. We passed a second hand clothing store along the way, and while I hadn't given any thought to trying to disguise ourselves, it seemed like a good idea to at least get something that would make our features hard to make out. We went in and got some nondescript, oversized shirts and jackets, plus hats with big, floppy brims.

"You go to a costume party?" said the withered woman at the cash register.

"Something like that."

"*Ashlen Devlese, Romale.*"

"*Ashlen Devlese,*" I said, nodding solemnly. I must have said it right, because she smiled through about a thousand wrinkles and gave me a wink.

"What was all that?" said Rosie after we got back outside.

"Beats the hell out of me, but I have a good ear for accents, don't you think?"

She giggled. "And you said we weren't a natural pair."

We parked three blocks away from the *officia*, put on our makeshift disguises, and walked through the alleys to the back of the row of connected stores. If there was another watcher in the shadows somewhere, I couldn't spot him.

"You think the back door won't be flagged off, too?"

"I'm sure it is," I said. "But we're not going in the back door. That cellar I was in had a tunnel going out of it, maybe thirty feet long. We're looking for the building where it comes out."

"It's the middle of the day, Herman. Don't you think anybody will notice?"

"It's also an official crime scene in the middle of Gypsy home turf. I figure the locals are all off on urgent, unexpected visits to their relatives in Pago Pago."

"And if they're not?"

"Hey, I'm a homeboy. I speak Rom. Didn't you notice?"

"God help us."

Two stores down from the fortune-telling parlor was a carpet store that looked as if its last customer had been Aladdin. I strode up the steps of the loading dock as if I had every right in the world to do so, went up to the small door at one side, slipped on a pair of latex gloves, and proceeded to work the lock. Rosie stood behind me with her hands on her hips, so her elbows stuck out and gave me some visual screening. If I ever decided to turn to a life of crime, she would definitely be my first choice for an accomplice.

"Yes?" she said.

"Ka-lunk," said the lock. We were in.

We went through the door casually, making little gestures with our hands, as if we were in the middle of an animated conversation. Once inside, we relocked the door and got away from the glass as fast as possible. Then we pulled out the flashlights and looked the place over. The interior held several rolls of carpet, piled in no observable order, an old desk with scattered papers on it, some trash cans, and the kind of serious dust and cobwebs that only come with long neglect. But the dust on the floor had tracks in it, so the place wasn't completely abandoned. We traced the paths of the tracks with our beams. Most of them went to a door that must have led to the front of the store, where I was hoping I wouldn't have to go. Some wandered around aimlessly, and a few led to a crudely framed closet that poked out from a side wall. We followed that set.

The closet was also locked, with a heavy-duty Schlage cylinder that looked even more ancient than the one outside the dock. I gave it a shot of spray oil first, then went to work on it with the picks. For something that looked like late pre-Industrial Revolution, it slipped open with amazing ease and smoothness. And the door opened without a sound. A perfectly built fallback exit, if I had ever seen one.

Inside, the tiny room was lined with electrical panels and telephone switch gear that looked as ancient as the lock. A lot of it had no wires left, just empty metal fuse boxes and knobby terminals. I looked for one that had signs of being handled recently, and found a main disconnect with a tattered decal remnant that now said "DANG…HI….AGE." I rather liked that. So did somebody else. When I threw the big switch arm on the side of the box, a piece of the floor sprang up to greet me. A sigh of clammy air came with it, laced with the scent of damp limestone and old secrets, and the familiar chill settled into my lower guts again. If somebody else had tried to make me go down there, I'd have told them to take a hike. Inside and below was the shaky ladder that I had last seen from the bottom end only. I tested the top rung to see if it would hold me and, unable to think of any excuse not to, descended. The floor below was soft and gritty, just as I had remembered it.

"Are you going to leave me here, Herman?"

"Only if you don't come along."

"I was afraid you'd say something like that."

I stepped to one side of the ladder and shone my flashlight on the floor below it while Rosie came after me.

"Did you close the door after yourself?" I said.

"What are you, my mom?"

"No, I'm your paranoid partner." I went back up the ladder. At the top, I looked through the closet door and back to the one where we had first come in, the one with the small window in it that I hadn't paid any attention to. Something was definitely obscuring the light in the dirty glass panel. I tried to remember if there was a big dirt smear on the glass. If not, then there was a person trying to peer in. Swell. And I had to make a joke about being paranoid. But if it was a person, it wasn't doing anything but looking. No door rattling, no flashlight, no automatic weapons, no concussion grenade. Whatever was out there, we could deal with it later. I closed the closet door quietly and ever so slowly, relocked it, and went back down the ladder. At the bottom of the shaft, the blackness closed around us like Methodist gloom.

Chapter Seventeen

Flashbacks

"Whoever was here last was either very fastidious or really cheap," I said. "When you and I left the place, there was a light on."

"I just hope there aren't any tiger traps or land mines. Are these the biggest flashlights you could get?"

"The biggest ones you could hope to hide under a jacket, anyway." I had to admit, they seemed like a couple of candles in a coal mine. When I played the beam of mine across the ceiling, I heard a soft rustling sound, which I took to be the resident cockroaches, running away from the light. A lot of them. I decided not to mention that to Rosie, nor the rather evil smells that had been added to the general decay and must since I was last here. I switched to sweeping the light over the dirt floor ahead of us.

"Lots of footprints," I said. "The forensic crew had a real party down here. That should mean we don't have to worry about wiping out our own tracks when we leave. There are already so many, they'd never sort them out."

"How nice. It probably also means there's nothing left for us to find. What did you see at the top of the ladder, by the way?"

"Did I say I saw anything?"

"Stop it, Herman, okay? I saw how careful you were when you closed the closet door."

"If you absolutely must know, I think there may be somebody outside, on the loading dock."

"You *think* there *may* be."

"Yup, that's about the size of it. See? You should have let me lie about it. Keep your voice down, by the way."

"You think they might add disturbing the peace to the charges of breaking and entering and murder?" But she was whispering now.

"Only if they catch us," I said.

"Well if they do, don't blame it on me. Did you bring a gun?"

"I didn't have to. I travel with this woman who always has a bagful of the things."

"You take a lot for granted, you know that?" She shoved a semiautomatic nine into my free hand. "How are you fixed for socks and underwear?" she said.

"You should know."

"Yeah, huh? I guess my focus was somewhere else when I could have checked."

I led the way through the narrow tunnel and into the cellar where Evans body had been, being careful not to step in any of the stains. The trap door was shut again, preserving the total blackness. This time, I did not pull the chain to turn on the overhead light.

"So what is it that we're looking for, again?"

"This." I went over to the free standing ladder by the door and shone my beam up. On the bottom side of the lid, there was a lot of odd looking hardware that all connected to some device by the hinge. And coming out of the nameless gizmo were several skinny wires. Some of them went to a switch box by the top of the ladder and the others led to a small hole in the floor, further back, by the far wall. I went up the ladder a bit and touched the box, which turned out to have not one, but two toggle switches. I picked one at random, took a deep breath, and put my finger on it.

"Lights out," I said, switching off my own beam.

"You're going to open that thing? Seriously?"

"As seriously as I know how."

"Wait one sec." She took a half-stride stance and extended both arms up, towards the trap door, one holding her pistol and the other the flashlight. She shut off the light with her thumb, and we were in blackout again. "Okay, do it," she said.

I threw the toggle and the trap door snapped open with incredible speed, then immediately slammed shut again. It was a good thing I wasn't directly in its path, or it would have knocked me into next week. I mean, that thing *moved*. I returned the toggle to its original position, flipped it again, and the door repeated its performance. Open, shut. Wham, bam, thank you ma'am. A guillotine should be so fast. The brief strobe view of the room above was poorly lit, except compared to where we were. It looked as if the place was abandoned. I flipped the switch once more to be sure, then returned it to the neutral position. Then I tried the other switch. This time the door flew open and stayed that way.

"Is this a good thing?" Rosie's body said otherwise. She still had her gun pointed up, and she was doing a good impression of a big bomb with a very short fuse.

"Tell you in a bit, when I see where the other wires go." I climbed up the ladder and into the fortune-telling, shootout room, keeping low and checking sight lines to the outside world as I went. The heavy floor-length drapes in the front were barely cracked open, too little for our silent watcher across the street to see anything. The back door out of the room opened into a short hallway that ended at a high window with frilly, once-white curtains over it. It gave the place enough light to move around by, but not much more than that. So far, so good. I called quietly for Rosie to come up.

"Can I use my flashlight?"

I nodded. "Just be careful not to point it outside. And don't put the gun away just yet."

"I heard that." She came up quicker than necessary, and it occurred to me that she knew perfectly well what the rustling sounds had been.

"What am I trying to find?"

"The upstairs duplicates of the switches I just used on the trap door. They have to be in this room somewhere."

The round, velvet-covered table was still in the middle of the room, though it looked as if it had been knocked around a bit. We checked there first, looking and feeling all around the edge and bottom for something that somebody seated at the table could have reached. Nothing. I chanced using my flashlight a bit then, exploring first the floor and then the walls, unintentionally lingering on the area where we had last left Stefan Yonkos. More nothing. Bullet holes all over the damn place, though. Also a lot more bloodstains than I had remembered. Hadn't we done the compress bandage right? Or had Yonkos been shot yet again, after we left?

Finally, I peeled back a drape on the back wall and hit pay dirt. A pair of toggles just like the ones in the cellar were mounted into the plaster, just under a regular light switch. Painted the same dirty yellow-cream as the walls, they would be almost unnoticeable if you weren't looking for them.

"Are you clear of the trap door?" I said.

"If there's only one of them, then I'm clear of it."

I worked the wall switches and got the same result as with the first set. One switch had an open and a closed position, and the other one triggered a quick open-shut action. So back when I had been unceremoniously dropped into the cellar, the switch had not been tripped by Yonkos, who was still seated at the table, hands clearly visible. It had to have been done by the woman, Vadoma. That was why she had been standing back by the wall, looking like a sentinel or a bodyguard. But later, when the trap door opened again and stayed open, dumping the wounded Evans down into my world, it couldn't have been tripped by her. She was already dead. Nor was it tripped by Yonkos, who would have been slumped against the adjacent wall by then, oozing his essential fluids, nor by Evans himself. There was no way the same person could stand on the trap door and also reach the switch.

Rosie continued to use her flashlight to look at bullet holes and bloodstains, not paying much attention to what I was doing or to the expression on my face. "What do we know now that we didn't?" she said.

"We know there was another person in this room, just before you came in."

"What? You mean like another shooter?"

"Just like that."

"Then why are you and I still alive?"

"When you started to open the front door, he couldn't have known who it was. He must have assumed it was the cops and split by the back exit."

She knitted her brows a bit and shook her head. "No way. I'd have heard the door."

"Maybe he didn't go all the way out."

"Oh, that's a cheery thought."

"Isn't it, though? Let's see what's back there."

"Must we?"

"In for a penny, and all that." I led the way into the back corridor, gun ahead of me, flashlight ready to use as a light or a club.

Directly behind the parlor was a small kitchen and pantry, and a toilet beyond that. At the back, the short hallway split into a T, with a back door to the alley on one end and a narrow stairway going up on the other. Neither the little window nor the glass in the back door showed us anybody lurking outside, but we didn't linger there anyway. I went up the stairs quickly, leading Rosie by the hand behind me.

Upstairs were two tiny bedrooms, furnished in garage sale decor with the occasional genuine antique thrown in. The floors were all covered with ornate throw rugs, rather than carpet. *The mark of a perpetually transient people?* There was also another bathroom, several closets, and a steep staircase leading up to the roof. The whole place, and the kitchen below as well, hadn't exactly been trashed, but it had been searched more crudely than the crime lab team would have done it. Pillows and mattresses were cut open but not disemboweled, and most of the furniture was still upright, though all the drawers and doors were open, all the contents dumped. The lid of the tank on the toilet was off, also.

"They didn't rip the backer paper off the pictures," said Rosie, "or smash the glass in the mirrors."

"No," I said. "They wouldn't."

"Oh?"

"They weren't looking for anything that you could hide in the back of a picture or a mirror. They were looking for the violin."

"That fits what we're seeing," she said. "But you said Yonkos made a deal with you, for you to go get it. Why would it already be here?"

"It wouldn't. But somebody didn't know that, or they thought I might have brought it to him." *Some-body. Somebody didn't know it wasn't here. Evans didn't know where the hell it was and Yonkos didn't know either, but he had faith in me finding it. One emailer says he knows I have it, but Nickel Pete says it's been swapped. So Amy Cox had to have it with her when she was killed, but if her killer was also the secret gunman here in Skokie, why didn't he already know where it was? In fact, why*

didn't he already have it? Another emailer says he can tell me
where to find it. As if it were lost. So who lost it? Amy's killer,
maybe? Or somebody from the Ardennes Forest, with an old,
old score to settle? Was that possible, after all these years?

"A man I know named G. B. Feinstein says great
violins have dark stories attached to them," I said.
"He also thinks they have souls, and I guess the souls
could be dark, too. Stefan Yonkos said this one is evil,
a demon, something that destroys people."

"You believe that?"

"I don't know if I really believe in evil, but I definitely believe in luck. And that stupid fiddle is bad luck,
if I've ever seen the stuff. Everybody wants the damn
thing, everybody who has anything to do with it seems
to wind up dead, and everybody, I mean absolutely
everybody, thinks I have it."

Rosie shrugged. "Maybe you do."

I gave that a moment's thought. "Maybe I do at
that," I said. "If that were true, it could be the real
reason why we are still alive."

"I'm not sure I like that reason," she said. "It sounds
to me like one that could be canceled at any moment."

"There is that," I said. "But somehow, I don't think
this is the moment."

I went over to the side of a window that faced the
street and risked a peek out the edge of a tattered curtain. The window down the block where I had seen the

watcher with the binoculars was still dark, unreadable. A quick look out the back window into the alley was just as inconclusive at first, but then something made me do a double take. I didn't have a good enough view of the loading dock, where we had come in, to see if anybody was hanging around down there. But on the other side of the alley, further down, in deep shadow between two buildings, was something that definitely didn't belong with the rest of the general clutter. Dark, massive, and almost out of view was the unmistakable front end of a shiny black LTD.

"Time for us to get the hell out of here," I said.

"A man after my own heart," said Rosie.

"Quiet and smooth."

"You forgot 'quick.'"

"No, I didn't." But I took two steps down the stairs and froze. This time there was no question about it. There was somebody standing outside the back door, possibly also working on the lock.

Rosie bumped into me from behind, nearly knocking us both down the rest of the steps. "What happened to the quick part?" she said.

"It got a little more complicated. Go check out the door to the roof."

She left and I backed slowly up, the way I had come.

"It's locked," she said from behind me.

"Does it open onto the alley side or the street side?"

"Damfino. Let's see, north is where the little dipper points to the big hand on your watch, if there's any moss on it, and…"

"Will you please cut that out?"

"I'm nervous, okay? Street side, I think. What are you going to do, pick the lock, pop out and drop a water balloon?"

"No, I'm going to go enlist the aid of our spy across the street," I said. "Stay where you are a minute."

I went to the front of the flat and deliberately shone my flashlight out the window, ruffling the curtains a bit for good measure. Then I thought, *what the hell, why fool around being subtle?* and I cracked one of the panes with my elbow, adding a little noise to the bait. Down the street, on the dark second floor, the shiny twin discs of the binoculars flashed as they swung around towards me, then disappeared into the shadows again. The guy was alert for having had such a long, dull wait, I had to give him that. I let him see another bit of flashlight beam, just so he'd know he hadn't been imagining things, and then I pulled the window shade down, fast. Then I did the same with the other one in the second bedroom. I looked at my fancy new watch. It probably had a stopwatch function, but I didn't know how to work it yet, so I settled for watching the sweep second hand. If the Skokie cops were any good at all, I figured three minutes, maybe three and a half, tops.

"What are you doing down there, Herman? You're starting to make me very nervous."

"Stay put, Rosie. We're about to set the wolves to devouring each other." *Unless, of course, they are all from the same pack, which would not be good at all.*

When my watch rolled up two minutes and fifty seconds, I looked out the back window and saw squad cars converging on both ends of the alley. A large man in a dark coat saw them, too, and headed for the black LTD, running hard. That was as good a diversion as we were likely to get. I ran up the stairs, brushed past a tense-looking Rosie, and went to work on the lock to the roof door. Which didn't budge.

From the alley below came the tinny, rasping sound of a voice on the speaker from one of the prowl cars, saying, "You there by the dumpster! Stop where you are and put your hands where I can see them! Now!" Since nothing around us looked anything like a dumpster, I assumed the cops were talking to somebody else. Poor fellow. I sprayed some oil in the lock and went back to work.

"I said stop!" said the mechanical voice below.

I said open! I thought at the lock. But it remained frozen solid. I hadn't found a single tumbler slot yet.

Then I heard the sound I'd been dreading. At the back door downstairs, there was a crash of broken glass and the clicks and clunks of a lockset being hastily jangled open, then the door slamming again. Whoever was down there was inside the building now. And I did not think he was a cop, who just wanted the facts, ma'am.

"Give me a little room," I said. "And cover our backs." She went part way down the stairs and pointed her automatic back at the hallway, taking a braced stance against one wall of the stair shaft. I took a half step back from the roof door and cocked my foot for what I hoped was the kick of a lifetime.

"Whatever you're going to do," said Rosie, "you'd better do it now. I think he's coming up the stairs."

Amen to that. The first kick merely made my foot hurt. On the second one, though, I got my weight behind it better and kept my foot flat to the panel. The door shrieked, splintered, made a sound like a ruptured oil drum, and then flew outward. We ran through and slammed it behind us.

We both blinked at the return of daylight. Crouching low to avoid being seen above the parapet walls, I scrounged up a scrap of wood from the roof and wedged it into the door jamb, then looked around and took stock of our surroundings. Half a block of low roofs stretched out in both directions, all interconnected but set apart by low, fence-like fire walls of dirty red brick. Between each set of walls was another slope-backed little shed with a door in it, like the one we had just come out of.

"I take it we aren't going back down in the tunnel," said Rosie. "Not that I'm complaining, mind you."

I shook my head. "This is better," I said. "Lots better." I could see she wasn't buying a word of it. "We can get further away than the carpet store before we have to go back out in the open."

"Like this isn't out in the open?"

She had a point. "Well, back in plain sight, then. Which direction do you like?"

"You seem to be running on pure luck today. You choose."

I did at that, didn't I? I picked the direction away from the end of the block with Mr. Binoculars, and we scuttled off, hunched down like soldiers under fire. The commotion in the flat below got louder, then more remote.

We went over four more buildings without slowing down to try the doors. On the fifth one, at the end of the block, we stopped and I tried the lock. This time, I oiled it up first and took my time, doing it right. I had two tumblers locked in neatly and was reaching for another pick when the door flew open in my face, nearly smashing my hands. Framed in the dark opening was a very short, dark-complected young man with a very large sawed-off shotgun in his hands. If he'd had a pointy hat, he could have been Chico Marx with a vaudeville prop, sly grin included.

"Um, *Ashlen Devlese, Romale,*" I said. Did I mention that I have a good memory, as well as a good ear for dialect?

"Yeah, sure," he said. "Who are you trying to con, *Gadje?*"

But not good enough.

"Anybody I can," I said. *That alone should make me one of your brothers.* "But maybe we should have this conversation someplace a little less conspicuous?"

"Come," he said, backing down the steps but keeping the gun trained on us. "Get off the roof before the *jawndari* see you, and we'll see how much that insult to our language is going to cost you."

Behind me, I knew, Rosie had her gun held inside her purse. She shut the door behind us and we regrouped in an upstairs hall just like the one we had left down the block.

"Look," I said, "I didn't mean any disrespect back there."

"I think you didn't mean to be on the roof, either, did you? But you will pay for both."

"You know Stefan Yonkos?"

"Knew, you mean."

"Yes," I said.

"A great tragedy," said Rosie.

"Women should be silent when the men talk business," he said. "But she shows more respect than you do."

So we were talking business, were we? Things were looking up.

"Of course, I knew Stefan," he said. "Everyone knew Stefan. A great man, a great loss. What do you think that will buy you?"

"The man we are running from is his killer."

"Is that so? The same one who ran away in the alley?"

"The same."

"That might buy you something, after all. How do I know it's true?"

Good question. I wasn't even sure how *I* knew it was true, apart from having seen the black LTD again.

"My name is Herman Jackson," I said. "I had an understanding with Stefan Yonkos. He was going to help me find a killer and clear my name with the police, and I was going to deliver a violin called the Wolf Amati to him." That wasn't quite the deal, of course, but I figured if I got caught in the lie I could always feign confusion. There was damn sure plenty of the stuff to go around.

"That's a good story, Mr. Jackson. But now he is dead."

"Now he is dead." I nodded gravely. "But as far as I'm concerned, it was a good deal when I made it and it still is. And somehow, I'm inclined to believe there's at least one other Rom who still thinks so, too."

"Mmm. You could be right. Let's get someplace further away from the *jawndari* and find out."

"How about putting away the gun?"

"The woman, first," he said. Damn, he didn't miss a trick.

Rosie took her hand out of her purse, the young Rom made the shotgun miraculously vanish under his coat, and I suddenly knew what it felt like to walk away from the brink of Armageddon. We went down the stairs and around a corner, to a back room, where our new guide touched a button on the wall.

"Oh shit, no!" said Rosie. "Not another damn tunnel."

Chapter Eighteen

Revelations

Rosie dozed on the seat beside me while I snacked on beef jerky and salted cashews and watched the dashed white centerline of Illinois Fourteen feed into my headlight beams. In the cracked rearview mirror, Des Plaines, Mount Prospect, and then Arlington Heights suggested themselves one last time and then faded into dim memory. Past Palatine, the countryside opened up into featureless dark prairie, which was fine by me. It looked like a blank slate. Or maybe a threshold.

The battered pickup wasn't as nice as the Pontiac, to say the least, but the engine ran okay, if a bit feebly. The brakes and lights worked, and the steering only wandered if there was a wind from the side. I decided not to take it on the freeway. At anything over sixty miles an hour, the question was not whether a wheel would fall off, but how many of them would stay on. But it would do for the one trip it had to make. If somewhere else, not too far away, there was a black LTD on the Interstate racing us back to the fair city of St. Paul and winning, that was all right, too. In fact, that was better than all right. That would work.

I had needed to give the Rom council, or whatever it was they called the surviving bunch of *kumpania* leaders, something besides my good word and winning smile to get them to reinstate Yonkos' deal, and the rented car was the logical choice. We debated and postured and traded lies for a long time, doing what Yonkos had called "respecting the rhythm of the game," but we all knew where we were going in the end. The junker that they traded me for the Pontiac probably had a thousand miles left in it, max, but that would be enough. The trade was a damned high price to pay for the mere one-time use of an emergency exit, of course, but I had a fairly limited selection and no time to shop.

The other deal, the bigger one, with the promise of the violin, was another matter. I could have done without that, quite possibly didn't even need the help of the Rom anymore. But part of the game wasn't played out yet, and part of me said that wouldn't do. The game had started with Amy Cox, and the Rom were definitely her people. It had to end with them, too. They would never be my allies, but if I left them as happy customers, that would work, too.

Someplace in the middle of Illinois, a state trooper

tailed me for a while, but when I didn't break the speed limit, he lost interest and peeled off on a side road. The Gypsies had told me the plates on the pickup were good, not forged or stolen, and that seemed to be the acid test. I thought again about Stefan Yonkos and what he had said about names being so important to those of us who have only one. Good license plates are a sort of face-value proof of identity. *Names and labels, Stefan. Too damn right. Names and labels and identities are everything. That's what this whole chaotic business has been about from the get-go, but I couldn't see it before. First, I needed to get in a junker pickup that even Pud and Ditto, from New Salem, wouldn't be caught dead driving.* I chuckled at the thought of the two hayseeds, and Rosie stirred, sat up, and looked over the dash with one bleary eye.

"Where are we?" she said.

"In the middle of nowhere."

"That's a good place."

"The best."

"For a while, I thought we weren't going to make it."

"Me, too," I said.

"If we ever get to the middle of somewhere, wake me up, will you?"

"That's a promise."

She curled back up, popped a chocolate cherry in

her mouth, and chewed it with her eyes closed. The clunker steadily chewed up the miles.

The sun was well up by the time we rendezvoused with Wide Track Wilkie at a truck stop about twenty miles south of St. Paul on old Highway 55. Rosie and I had anemic-looking fruit plates with yogurt and bran muffins, while Wilkie worked on maintaining his monolithic figure by ordering one item each from the breakfast, dinner, and dessert menus. He was obviously a little embarrassed about it, though. Funny how I had never noticed that in him before: he really didn't function well at all in the presence of a pretty woman. For a while, we sipped black coffee and soaked up the smell of fresh toast and orange juice, and made small talk. I didn't know if Rosie was really interested or just being friendly, but she asked Wilkie a lot about his trade.

"So you're a bounty hunter?" she said. "That's what you do?"

"Sometimes. I do other stuff, too. Whatever comes up that lets me still be my own man. I'm a pretty decent pool hustler. Maybe Herman told you that?"

"No," I said.

"Thanks a lot."

"Tell me about the other thing," said Rosie. "You like it?"

"It's nice, I guess. No health plan or vacation, you

know, but no time clock, either. Lots of action, which I personally like, and nobody's ass to kiss. And the work is as steady as you want. There's never any shortage of assholes who think they can run away from their own stupidity. No offense, Herman."

"None taken," I said.

"What do you need?" said Rosie. "To be a bounty hunter."

"You mean like license and bond and that kind of stuff?"

"Well, and..."

"Clean criminal record?"

"Yeah, that one," she said.

"None of that's a problem. Mostly, you just have to be a mean motherfucker and look like it. Um, I mean..."

"I've heard the expression once or twice before," said Rosie. "Is it something I could do?"

"You? Get serious. I mean, you seem like, well..."

"Only seem like? If you mean a woman, Mr. Wilkie, I definitely am. Tell him, Herman."

"I've never known her otherwise," I said. She squeezed my knee under the table.

"It's not that, exactly," said Wilkie. "I once knew a bounty hunter who was a midget, no less, but he gave off menace like a pit bull with rabies. Looked like he'd bite off your kneecap just for arguing with him. So nobody did. You seem too nice. That won't get you very far in the bounty business. If you're nice, you might wind up having to be deadly, too."

"Maybe I am. Herman, tell him…"

"Maybe it's time we did some work," I said. Or anything else that changed the subject. I turned to Wilkie and said, "What have you got for me, Wide?"

He looked relieved. What he had was the full file on one Corporal Gerald Cox, US Army, and it was interesting reading, even in bastardized military non-English.

"Looks like our boy missed all the fun of V-E Day," I said.

"Yeah, they shipped him home just before then, certified him not-quite-sane-but-what-the-hell, or something like that."

"'Battle fatigue with indeterminate prognosis,'" I quoted.

"What I said."

"Where was home?" said Rosie.

"Short Straw, Texas, or some such shithole, but when you muster out, the Army will send you damn near wherever you want to go, if you've got a good reason. Especially back then. They did everything for the vets after that war."

"Not after your war, I take it?"

"Don't get me started, hey?"

"So where did our damaged corporal decide to go?"

"He told them he wanted to go to Chicago, where there was a better VA hospital."

"Or a better something," said Rosie.

"The Gypsy Promised Land," I said. "Did they give him a pension, to boot?"

"Just a little one, 'cause he was only a little crazy. Three hundred bucks and change, every month."

"That was a lot of money back then. He was maybe crazier than we think. Does he still collect it?"

"Would you believe he does? Never did get sane, I guess. Also never died. Or never admitted to it."

"Probably never will, either. Want me to guess where the pension gets sent to?"

"General Delivery, Skokie, Illinois."

"Bingo," said Rosie.

"More bingo than you know," said Wilkie. "That's also where the money for the eighteen hundred dollar check from Amy Cox came from. First Bank of Skokie, Illinois."

"Did we get his mustering-out medicals?" I said.

"I already told you, he was absolutely sort of crazy is all. Everything else was just your normal used-soldier stuff."

"Let's see."

Wilkie pulled the appropriate part of the file, and I looked at the grainy faxes of the even grainier old mimeo forms and found the section headed

"Distinguishing Scars or Marks."

"Seems our man Cox had a nasty scar from a burn on his left forearm," I said. "And fairly new, back then."

"This is important?"

"This is the clincher," said Rosie, and I nodded in agreement.

Wilkie gave us a perplexed look and I gave him a short version of the story about the Ardennes Forest. "He had to burn himself to cover the tattoo from the concentration camp," I said. "I thought at the time Yonkos told me the story, he was lying about something, but I couldn't tell what. All that poetic stuff about not knowing where the story came from originally? Hell, he *was* the story."

"Well, part of it," said Rosie.

"Exactly half," I said. "Now the question is…"

"Who was the German?" said Wilkie.

"That's the question, all right."

"I don't think even the Prophet can run that one down for us."

"He doesn't have to. The man will come to us."

"Yeah, I'm so damn sure he wants to," said Wilkie.

"He will?" said Rosie.

"You bet. In a shiny black LTD with a bag of money in it. We're going to accept the last offer from Mr. G. Cox."

"I don't trust him," said Rosie.

"I don't trust him twice as much," said Wilkie. "And when I don't trust people, that's not a good thing. Especially for them."

"Hold onto that thought, both of you," I said. "Hold it really well."

Wide Track went back to my office to send the email to Cox accepting his offer, and to wait for a reply. Rosie and I took the limping pickup into town and to the Amtrak depot, to pick up my BMW. It had evolved into a much nicer machine in my absence. Or maybe it just profited by comparison with the 1968 International Harvester pickup. Rosie went inside the terminal to get a schedule, so I would know what train to claim I had come back to town on. I wiped down the pickup, checked it one last time, and left it with the keys in the ignition. It was a sort of feeble, blind payback gesture. The naive but sincere young woman who had rented me the Pontiac might or might not get in trouble when I didn't bring it back. Not a damn thing I could do about that. But some poor bastard fresh off a freight train from North Bumjungle might just get a shot of unexpected good fortune by finding the clunker. It wouldn't really balance the cosmic scales, but it was the best I could do.

Rosie brought me a printed schedule that showed a train arriving from Seattle in about an hour, which meant any time in the next half day, and I made a mental note to come back and hassle the ticket clerk again at the appropriate time. If I had time, that is. But first, we got in the BMW and went to see my friendly pawnbroker.

Nickel Pete was sitting on his regular perch and, as usual, took his hands from under the counter and smiled when he saw me.

"Herman, my friend! And with a brand new blonde, too. Is this maybe a new feature of the bonding business I didn't know about? I renew my offer to partner with you."

Rosie gave me a raised eyebrow and I told her the last time I had been there was with Amy Cox.

"I hope that time didn't set a precedent," said Rosie.

"Don't give it a thought, young lady." Pete waved a hand dismissively. "Nobody will ever do that to me again, I promise you. But I still got good instruments to show, if you want."

Rosie looked more puzzled than ever at that, with a look that asked, "do *what* to him?" I didn't bother to explain for Pete. He was a big boy; he could extract his own foot from his mouth. Or choke on it. I took the pawn ticket for the Amati out of my wallet and laid it on the counter. "Let's have a look at this one," I said.

"Ah, Herman, what can I say?" He put his hands against the sides of his head, as if it needed to be kept from exploding. "Forget about paying off the ticket. Forget about the vig, even. I owe you way more than that for my stupidity. I don't know how I'm ever going to make it up to you." Apparently simply paying for the lost violin never occurred to him.

"Let's just see it, first," I said.

He went in the back room and returned with the battered black case, which he put down on the counter and opened. I couldn't remember the original one Amy Cox had shown me all that well, but this seemed like a plausible likeness.

"Have you looked at it since we talked on the phone?" I said.

"Why would I do that? To remind myself what a dope I was? This I do not need. I'd be happy if nobody ever looked at it again."

Once again, I had a tiny flash of insight into why some con games work so well. Once the mark decides something is a disaster or a triumph, he never looks at it again.

"It looks old, anyway," I said.

"Sure it looks old. You think I'm going to get taken in by a shiny new plastic one? The broad was slick, Herman. The slickest. She must have made the switch right after she asked if she could kiss her old violin, just for sentimental reasons."

"She did? I didn't see that."

"You were busy scribbling numbers on your little pad or something. It was just so damned corny that I thought I'd be polite and ignore it. And it was a really short time, anyway. Ten seconds, tops. Well, maybe fifteen. But I swear, she never had both cases within easy reach at the same time."

"But she held the Amati up to her face for a little while, with the bottom towards you, hiding what she was doing?"

"Well that would be how you'd kiss the stupid thing, wouldn't it?"

"Maybe. But in this case, I think it was how she changed the label."

"You're a nice guy, Herman, but you're nuts."

"That's a different topic. You got a dentist's mirror and a little flashlight? A long tweezers with a kink or two in the prongs would be good, too. I had a professional lecture about violin labels a while back. I want to see if it was true."

"You mean like, 'labels come and labels go'?"

"Mostly, they accumulate, is what I was told. Get the stuff, will you?"

He went in the back again and returned with an enameled steel box full of tools. I picked a little maglight, shone it in one f-hole, and peeked in the other one. I didn't need a mirror or a magnifying glass to read the name Yamaha.

"This label is oval-shaped and sort of big," I said. "Is that what a Yamaha label should look like?"

"Who the hell knows? The logo is right. Sometimes companies change the shape of the rest of it over the years. And they have been making Yamahas for a while, you know. I don't know them all."

"Uh huh. Give me the tweezers, will you?"

"Sure." He handed me something that looked like a surgical tool. "What are you going to do with it?"

"Peel the label off."

"Excuse me for saying so, Herman, but now you're talking like the amateur you are. Those things aren't meant just to be peeled off. They're stuck on with some damned good glue that has to be steamed or scraped or…"

"It's coming."

"It can't be."

But it did. First one small arc of an edge, then a bigger and bigger blister, and finally the whole thing. The label paper wasn't exactly happy about it, but it didn't pull apart, either, and soon I had it hanging from the jaws of my tool like the skin of a tiny molting reptile. I carefully pulled it out through the f-hole and held it up.

"Looks like stickyback," said Rosie. "Sort of yellowy-colored, but definitely new."

But Pete wasn't looking at the newly peeled label. He was peering intently into the f-hole again, where the faded black script on a crackled paper label could still be clearly seen to say, "Nicolò Amati, A.D. 1643."

"Holy shit," he said.

"No, just an old violin," said Rosie. But she took a look, too.

"Of some kind," I said. "Have you got anything here that will make a small, directable jet of steam?"

"I got a thingy I use to clean complicated jewelry sometimes. What do you want it for?"

"Now we're going to see what's under the Amati label."

Chapter Nineteen

Fiddle Game

Considering that the mighty Mississippi was once the very highway of commerce for St. Paul, it's amazing how much of the present-day waterfront is either undeveloped or abandoned. On the flats below limestone bluffs that hold up downtown are some railroad tracks, an empty warehouse that used to hold huge rolls of paper for the *Pioneer Press*, the back door of the jail, and at the bottom of the appropriately named Steep Street, the County Morgue.

Farther upstream, I'm told there used to be an Italian neighborhood called, not too surprisingly, Little Italy. But it couldn't survive the triple plagues of flood, fire, and the Zoning Board, and by the time I came to St. Paul the area had reverted to a wasteland of weeds, scrubby trees, and surreptitiously dumped junk. There was also a scrapyard and two power plants, one abandoned and one working, but the dominant landscape was urban wilderness. They shot a really awful movie there once, with Keanu Reeves and Cameron Diaz, about small-time crooks. I think the former Little Italy was where they went to bump people off.

Next to the river, there's a couple miles of paved walkway. Nobody ever uses it because it doesn't go anywhere, it's exposed to traffic on the area's only road, and you can't park within half a mile of either end. Also, the police don't patrol it much. And that's where Gerald Cox, which was not his name, chose to trade me eighteen thousand dollars for my violin, which was not really mine. And I didn't even consider refusing. Was the spell of the thing getting to me, too?

Wilkie didn't like the setup, but then, he wouldn't. When he covers my back, he likes to do it from close range, where his sheer physical presence and strength are big advantages, and his lack of speed doesn't matter. He also likes to hear what is going on, and in the time we had to get ready, there was no way we could get a hidden radio rigged up. Somehow, I didn't think the hastily scrounged cell phone in my pocket, even with an open connection, was going to be much help. I had slightly more faith in the nine-millimeter semi-auto tucked into the belt clip at the small of my back. Slightly. I didn't have a whole lot of faith in anything just then. But if we quibbled about the setup, we were liable to get another one just as bad, besides making our man more wary and less likely to go through with the deal at all. I didn't want that. I wanted some kind of conclusion. It was time to quit being sneaky and clever and make something happen.

The offer was simple enough:

mr. jackson

bring the violin to the pedestrian walk along shepard road, across from the metal scrapyard, at midnight and walk from the upstream end to the downstream one. You will be given eighteen thousand dollars cash for your violin, and our business will then be at an end. You will not need any assistants or observers.

tonight.

g. cox

And wasn't that just too, too fearsomely cloak and daggerish? Some bored bureaucrat, dying for a bit of drama and intrigue? Wilkie bitched and said it was the perfect setup for a hit. Rosie just rolled her eyes and shook her head sadly. I accepted the offer. Then I went off to the Amtrak depot to wait for the train. After all, it wouldn't do for me to get killed down by the river if I hadn't yet come back from Seattle.

There weren't a lot of streetlights along Shepard Road to

begin with, and several had lamps that needed replacing. The ones that worked made a ragged line from the black parking lot of the abandoned power plant to the illuminated arches of the Robert Street Bridge, some three or more miles distant. The walkway itself wasn't lit at all. It was not as dark as the cellar in Skokie had been, but it damn sure wasn't the Great White Way, either. On my right was a line of concrete freeway barriers about three feet high, which are used to hold sandbags during floods. I touched the tops now and then to keep my spatial orientation. Beyond them, the river rushed and gurgled, occasionally showing a glint of reflected light on its dark, undulating surface. It looked fast, powerful, and very close, and it occurred to me that I would not care to find myself trying to swim in it. No wonder Wilkie hadn't liked the setup. But I had agreed to be there, I reminded myself, and it was too late to back out now. The streetlights beckoned and I went.

Off to my left, the expanse of scrubby brush got wider as I went east, downstream, finally flaring out to a full quarter of a mile. Rosie was out there somewhere, shadowing me as well as she could without being too obvious about it. Our thinking was that if she got spotted, our mystery man, assuming he was local, was not so likely to associate her with me, though the new all-black catburglar outfit she insisted on wearing probably made her more, rather than less, conspicuous. Wilkie, on the other hand, would stand out like Wilkie, no matter what he wore. I didn't know where he was. He had told me I didn't want to know and I had believed him. But wherever my people were, I definitely felt alone. Alone and vulnerable.

I started down the walk exactly at midnight, using one of the flashlights I had bought in Skokie for occasional guidance and moral support, carrying the violin case in my left hand. I walked steadily but not in any hurry, and I stopped from time to time to listen to the river. There was nothing else to listen to. No footsteps, no cocking of guns, no banshees or werewolves.

A thousand yards down the walkway, as I was about to pass under High Bridge, I came upon a leather briefcase sitting on top of one of the flood barriers. It had a tiny flashlight on it which was turned on, presumably so I wouldn't miss the case in the dark. I stopped and played my own flashlight beam over it, and I saw something glint on the side, under the handle. When I went closer, I could see it was a shiny brass plate. Closer still, and I saw my name engraved on it. *Nice touch. A personalized booby trap.* But I didn't think so. I put the violin down on the sidewalk.

From inside my jacket pocket, I could hear a small, tinny version of Wilkie's voice. I think he was trying to whisper and scream at the same time.

"Don't open that thing, Herman! Don't even touch it!"

I popped the latches.

"Goddamn it, Herman, I know you can hear me!"

I opened the lid.

"Get away from that thing, now!"

I looked. Inside the case were several stacks of bundled bills and a note. The bills were all used twenties, and I didn't try to count them, but it seemed like about the right amount of bulk for eighteen grand. The note was not as elegant as the brass plate. Done in magic marker on a plain sheet of typing paper, it simply said:

LEAVE THE VIOLIN WHERE YOU FOUND THE CASE
TAKE THE CASE
GO

Simple enough. I saw no reason to argue with any of those instructions, other than the fact that I had really come there to meet their author. I snapped the case shut, picked it up, placed the violin in the same spot, and stepped back. But I didn't leave right away. I had no urge to kiss the fiddle, or even shake hands with it, but it didn't seem right simply to turn away and never look at it again. Maybe I thought it owed me an apology.

In my pocket, the mechanized Wilkie shouted, "Will you please get the hell out of there?" His voice had less conviction than before, but I knew he was right. As I was about to oblige him, I heard the crack of doom from the jungle to my left. It was loud and high-pitched, and it had that kind of lingering reverberation that comes only from very high-powered, heavy caliber rifles. A deer rifle, I thought. Definitely not one of Rosie's handguns. Not a seven-millimeter, either. I hit the dirt, or rather the sidewalk, and put the briefcase over my head.

The first shot hit the concrete bumper, close to the center, making a distressingly large crater and showering me with shards and powder. *One shot to find the range. The next one will be for real.* The second one hit the violin. It hit it squarely and explosively, smashing both case and instrument into splinters and dust and sending all the pieces spinning off into space. Or rather, into the black river, which swept them away forever. I tipped the briefcase up on edge, making an inadequate wall out of it, and I braced myself for the heavy slug that I was sure would find me next. After a second, I also drew my knees up in front of my torso, thinking it was better to have a shattered leg than a bullet in the gut. Then I drew the nine millimeter from under my jacket, and I waited. And waited. Where the hell were my partners?

There was no third shot.

After what seemed like forever, Rosie came running at me from the bushes, her big revolver at high port, eyes scanning all directions.

"Herman? Herman, if you're dead, I am going to be so damn pissed at you, I'll never let you forget it."

"I'm flattered."

"*Flattered?* What about shot?"

"No." I rose to a more dignified position and started to stand all the way up.

"Well, maybe you ought to be. I mean, walking into a setup like that, with…"

"Herman? You okay, my man? You catch one?" Wilkie, this time, breaking out of the bushes like a small herd of mammoths. He had some kind of an assault rifle with a night scope, but having no target for it, he didn't quite seem to know what to do with the thing.

"I already had this conversation, Wide. I mean, if you can't come in at the beginning, you could at least…"

"You sure you're not shot?"

"I'm sure. I'd have noticed, you know? Are you sure you didn't catch anybody?"

"Um," said Rosie.

"Well, see…" said Wilkie

I put the nine back in its holster and dusted off my

clothes. It definitely wasn't the way I had expected the scene to play out, but I was fairly certain it was over. At least as far as our mysterious Mr. Cox was concerned, it was. He had given us money, bullets, and excitement, but no interview, thank you.

"Anybody see anything?"

"Muzzle flashes off that way," said Wilkie, pointing to a wall of vegetation that looked like the rain forest on the banks of the Amazon, black and impenetrable.

"Let's have a look." I picked up the flashlight from where I had dropped it and headed that way.

"Are you nuts?" said Wilkie.

"He could still be there," said Rosie.

"I don't think so. If he wanted me dead, I'd already be that way. I think he's gone."

"So what did he want?" said Rosie.

"Obviously, he wanted to destroy the violin. And he likes rivers better than bonfires, I guess."

"That's crazy," she said.

"No, but I think it may be tragic, in the classic sense."

"Same thing," said Wilkie. He went ahead for a bit, to beat a trail into the brush. We could smell the cordite now, as sweet as lingering lilacs on the cool night air.

"What's in the case?" he said. "The one that you picked up in spite of all my good advice."

"Money."

"Real money?"

"It sure looks real, anyway. And I'd be willing to bet it's exactly the right amount."

"I don't get it," said Wilkie.

"Me either," said Rosie.

"I think I do. I think in his own way, our Mr. Cox is an honorable man. That's why he offered me eighteen thousand, the exact value of my bond. He was buying the violin back and giving me a chance to get clear of it. Not to get rich or even to make a profit, mind you, just to get clear. And if I took the money, that would show him I was honorable, too, and he would settle for that."

"But why…?"

"It was the final con, the one that got him clear, too. He not only had to destroy the violin, he had to be sure I saw it destroyed. That was the whole point."

"But it's not…"

"Here," said Wilkie, shining his own flashlight on a small clearing in the bushes. The brush was trampled down a bit there, and on the ground lay a very old, heavy rifle. It fit. In fact, everything finally fit.

"Mauser?" I said.

"The man knows his guns."

"No I don't, but I know my history. Sometimes I even know my modern myth. The gun is a throwback to another age, and so is our shooter. Also a romantic. I think he left it here to show us that the affair is over, that he's done with it."

I picked up the rifle and looked at the oiled metal and polished wood, lovingly cared for by professional hands. Hands I had seen. Big, strong hands that could push a carving chisel through a block of hard maple, without using a mallet. Hands that could also break somebody's neck.

"I can't believe how long it took me to figure it out," I said. "I know this man."

"It's the German?" said Wilkie.

"Yes." I nodded. "The German from the Ardennes Forest. Only, now he makes fine violins and even better coffee. He also tells great stories. His name is G. B. Feinstein."

◇◇◇

"I don't sell..." he began, not looking up from his work.

"Out of the shop," I finished for him. "I knew that already."

I held up a package of rolls and a bottle. "Actually, I came here hoping for some coffee."

He put down the chisel, stood up, and laughed, the only time I ever saw him do so.

"Ah, coffee," he said. "Well, that would be a different matter altogether. Come in, *mein herr.*"

The cinnamon rolls weren't quite as fresh this time, but they weren't bad. I figured the delivery man from the bakery wouldn't buy my phony cop routine a second time, so I followed his truck to an all-night convenience store and bought the rolls, legit. I also stopped at Lefty's bar and got the bottle, not quite so legit. Lefty's license technically doesn't allow him to sell liquor for consumption off the premises, but he indulged me, for future times' sake. He does enough things outside the law that, while he might not always accommodate a cop or even a wise guy, he won't risk offending his bondsman. Every profession has its perks, they say.

Feinstein brewed the coffee in the same freestyle way as he had when we first met, and as the aroma began to fill his shop and we smeared butter on the warm rolls, it was tempting to think that nothing had happened since that first time. But of course, it had, and we both knew this was as much a farewell as a reunion.

"I didn't expect to see you again, *Herr* Herman."

"A lot of people have had that prejudice, over the years. But I'm not as easy to get rid of as they generally suppose."

"Are you again on the run?"

"I don't think so. It's hard to tell for sure, but the cop who wanted me is dead now, and I think that's the end of it." *But then, you already know that.*

"The coffee is ready, I think."

I held out my cup and he poured steaming black liquid in it, leaving room for the obligatory spike. As he did so, I watched his hands and again saw the steady power and control. No wonder I hadn't noticed his age. I could see it now, easily enough. The shoulders were stooped a bit, even when he wasn't bent over his work, and the slicked back hair was obviously dyed. And he had strong facial bone lines, but like my Uncle Fred, he flashed intelligence and energy from eyes that were nevertheless trapped in a matrix of wrinkles. He poured coffee for himself after serving me, then put the pot down and added booze to both cups, taking a swig directly from the bottle first.

"This is excellent brandy," he said.

"Technically, it's five-star cognac, but I have to admit the distinction is somewhat lost on me. Brandy is brandy. The only difference is who you drink it with."

"I think I like that." He clinked his cup to mine. "To present company."

"To old friends," I said.

"You think so?" He smiled and took a large drink. "I like to think we might have been, in another world. But our history did not go that way, yes? It is a terrible burden, history."

"It can be," I said, meaning it more deeply than he would ever know. I took a gulp of the steaming brew and savored the familiar hot rush. "But are you talking about you and me, or about the history of a place called the Ardennes Forest?"

"You know this story, then? I am impressed."

"I know a version of it, anyway. Shall I tell you?"

He nodded and took a bite of roll, settling down on a corner of a workbench. I retold Stefan Yonkos' story for him, including where and how I came to hear it. As I did so, he alternately shook and nodded his head, smiling sadly the whole time. At one point, he may have blinked back a tear. He waited until I was done before he said anything.

"Well, that's the way he would tell it, wouldn't he? And he's had a long time to polish it up. But he left out the most important part."

"Which was?"

"When he killed the real Gerald Cox."

Chapter Twenty

End Game

March 17, 1945

The American was on the road when they first saw him, walking with his head down and his rifle at sling-arms. They spotted him in the mist before he was aware of them, and they immediately ducked behind a tree.

"Give me your rifle," the Gypsy whispered in German.

"But he is not a Russian. We do not need the charade that you planned."

"We need another one, if we want to be treated well."

"But we..."

"Trust me, this will be better. I will say that I am

a partisan, a resistance soldier, and that I have captured you. Then he will take us both to his superiors, not just to a prison camp, and the war will be over for us."

"You think you can convince him of such a story?"

"I speak enough English, and he looks stupid enough. And he will want to believe it."

"If you are sure..."

"I'm sure. Quickly now!"

The German handed over his Mauser and felt the power of it pass to the other man as well. He immediately wondered if he had done a foolish thing, and he felt in his coat pocket for the reassuring bulk of the 7 mm Luger he had taken from a dead SS officer. But he didn't know if he could bring himself to use it, even to save his own life. A gangly youth with a hooked nose and dark hair, trying to be a grown up soldier in an army that worshipped tall, square-featured blond goons, he had never had any confidence in anything. He let the Gypsy push him out onto the road, hands aloft, rifle poking in his spine.

"Hey, GI! I have a prize for you. I make you a hero, okay?"

The American, probably ashamed at being caught off guard, snapped his rifle up to his shoulder and went down on one knee and into a firing position.

"Who the hell are y'all? I mean, who goes there? Halt, is what I mean."

"Okay, Joe. It is okay," the Gypsy crooned, and his voice became progressively lower and more rhythmic. "I am partisan, okay? I capture Nazi bad guy for you. Here he is, you see? He is halt already."

The American got up and advanced warily, keeping his rifle trained on both of them, but mainly pointed at the German.

"He don't look like much of a soldier to me."

"He is a boy, is all. The Nazis are all out of men. Now they send children to fight. You take him for a prisoner, yes?"

"He's all disarmed and all? He ain't got no knife or nothing?"

"I have his rifle," said the Gypsy. "Is all he had."

The German continued to hold his hands up, looking fearful, understanding small bits of the conversation but mostly wondering if both he and the Gypsy were about to be shot. The GI came up close to him, stared into his eyes, spat on the ground, and finally lowered his weapon. The moment he stepped back, the Gypsy raised the Mauser and pressed it to the side of the American's head. "Now you give us your weapon," he said.

"What are you doing?" said the German. "He wasn't going to shoot us. I'm sure of it."

"Take his gun."

"Have you gone mad?"

"Take it, or I'll shoot both of you."

The German lowered his arms and took the US Army carbine, holding it uncertainly. And he noticed the man's name, stenciled on his fatigue jacket: G. B. Cox.

"Do you think this American will give me his clothes now?" said the Gypsy. "Will he give me his identity?"

"Of course not. Why would he do that?"

"I don't think so, either." The Mauser was still at the American's head, and he pulled the trigger, sending the man's helmet flying off into the trees, along with large pieces of his skull and brains.

*The German soldier didn't wait to see what would
happen next. He fled into the forest as fast as he
could run. More shots from his own gun slammed
into the trees around him, but he never slowed
down and never looked back. Finally, miles later,
when he could run no further, he fell to his hands
and knees and retched uncontrollably onto the
carpet of pine needles. And he wept. He wept the
tears of a boy who has realized his own fear and
a man who has witnessed an obscene atrocity and
was utterly unable to do anything about it. He
judged himself and found himself lacking, and
he wept and trembled and vomited until he was
empty and spent.*

*He slept then, on the rough forest floor, through
the day and into the darkness. When he finally
rose again and left that place, he vowed that he
would never weep or tremble again.*

He may have never trembled again, but he had
tears running down his cheeks as he finished the story.
He turned his back to me and busied himself with
making a fresh pot of coffee.

"Good lord," I said. "You were right about Yonkos
leaving out the most important part. What happened
after that? Did you also vow to kill the Gypsy?"

"No. That did not happen until much, much
later. The rest of my war story is not so interesting,

I'm afraid. I went back to the place where Cox had been shot. The Gypsy had left his own clothes there, and I took them. I threw my own uniform away and I became what he had said he was going to pretend to be, a partisan living off the land. I also threw away the American gun, which I didn't know how to use, and found another Mauser. It was a hard life for a while, but I didn't care any more. I found my way to an American army camp, a staging area, and they kept me around, like a mascot. That was when I took the name of Feinstein. I thought they would be more likely to believe I wasn't a Nazi if I had a Jewish-sounding name. And I added the G. B. so I would always remember the name of the dead American."

I poured myself some more coffee and thought of Rosie and her many aliases. *Doesn't anybody or anything in this damn world go by its real name anymore?* Then I remembered my own past and bit my tongue. Feinstein, for that was now his only name, continued.

"I worked on their trucks and did menial jobs, and they taught me bits of English. You wouldn't believe how long it was before I learned that 'fuckin' A' was not the correct way to say 'I agree.' And when the unit was sent back to the United States, I stowed away on the transport ship."

"Along with the Mauser?"

"Yes. And the Luger. There were many, many

souvenir guns being taken back. A few more didn't matter. I never got a visa or any citizenship papers, and I never will. Your wonderful government gave me a Social Security card anyway. After you have that, you can get anything."

"Under your assumed name."

"Of course. I got a job cleaning up and doing general labor in a guitar factory, and I decided to teach myself luthiery. It seemed like a way of coming to terms with my great downfall, you see. A calling, if you will. The rest is pretty much what you would expect."

"How old were you, back when you met the Gypsy in the forest?"

"I was born in 1931."

"Jesus, Mary, and Joseph. You really were just a kid."

"Not after that, I was not. After that, I was never young again."

"No. You wouldn't be, would you?" I stopped for a moment, took a deep breath, and braced myself. Sooner or later, somebody had to say the obvious, and I decided it might as well be then.

"So you killed Stefan Yonkos, finally…" I began.

"And his daughter and son, don't forget."

"No. I definitely didn't forget. You killed them all for revenge? Revenge for your lost youth and innocence?"

"Revenge? Oh no, *Herr Herman*. I never thought of it in that way for a moment. It was setting things right, you see, making up for my own past failure. War is all about guilt. People talk these days about post-stress something…"

"Post Traumatic Stress Syndrome," I said.

"Ya ya, that is it. Thank you. But it's always about the guilt of killing. They think that's all there is, the doctors. Backwards, for me, all wrong. All those years, all the places I went, I carried the guilt of who I did *not* kill. I should have killed the Gypsy."

Where had I heard that before?

"You could have been killed yourself, trying to," I said.

"Very true. But then, also, I would have been free of the guilt. And the poor man named Gerald Cox might also have lived."

"Might have, could have, should have," I said. "You take all those 'haves' and put them with three dollars, and you can buy yourself another package of these cinnamon rolls. Why bother with it, after all these years? I mean"—I swept my hand around, indicating the shop behind us—"you have a vocation here, a real life. A calling, even. Most poor working stiffs never find that. Couldn't you let the past go its own way?"

"You would think so, wouldn't you? And believe it or not, I tried. But the past would not let me go.

Twenty some years ago, it came to claim me."

"The certificate of authenticity," I said.

"Exactly so. It was 1975, as I recall. The blonde—I forget what she was calling herself back then—wanted me to appraise her old violin, certify it as a real Amati. Which it was, of course. And from what she told me of its story, I knew it had to be the violin from the Ardennes."

"And she was the Gypsy's daughter."

"She said as much, and I had no reason to doubt it."

"Was that when you switched the violins?"

"*Mein Gott!* You figured that out, also? *Wünderbar!* How?"

"I took off the label. Somebody told me once that the real trademark would be burned in the wood, under it."

"Ah, so he did, *Herr* Herman. That's what comes of revealing trade secrets, *ya*? Still, it had to take a lot of confidence to remove a fragile piece of history. But you have surprised me many times now. You are, as you say, not so easy to dispose of. Yes, I switched the violins then. I told the woman I had to keep the Amati for a few days, to do some tests. That gave me enough time to make one of the others in my collection into a very good likeness. It was a small enough bit of sabotage, considering what her family had done. And for a time, I thought it would be enough for me. More brandy?"

"Thank you," I said. "For the brandy and the compliments. Are we out of coffee?"

"I thought perhaps it was time to get down to essentials."

"Maybe it is, at that."

We both took another shot, clinking our cups again.

"But you must have assumed I'd look under the label sooner or later," I said. "And when I saw the burned-in brand of Roger Baldwin, written backwards, it would point me straight to you."

"I assumed later, rather than sooner," he said. "Or possibly not at all. Maybe someday another appraiser would do it, say. In the meantime, it was possible to do one last, um…"

"Con."

"Yes, thank you. A last con in a world of cons. If I destroyed the instrument that you thought was the Amati and made good on your cash losses, then that would be the end of it. The curse, the killing, and even the past. I wanted you to be free of it, you see."

"I picked up on that, yes. Thank you so much. Why?"

He shrugged. "I told you when we first met that I liked you. That buffoon, Evans, died just because he got in the way. I didn't want that to happen to you."

"Are you saying you didn't tip him off that I was in Skokie?"

"Tip him off? Oh, no. I was never in league with him or any of them. As far as they knew, I was just a disinterested appraiser, used once and forgotten."

"You know, that's really rather wonderfully ironic." I had another sip from the tin cup, and it seemed even more so.

"It is, isn't it? The violin that led me to become a fine luthier also led the Gypsy family back to me for a final accounting, and they didn't even know it."

"I believe I led you to Skokie, though."

"On the contrary, I followed Evans to Skokie, not you. He was what the Gypsies call the cop-in-the-pocket, you see. The woman, Amy, was the bait in a sweet fish hook, I think? No, that's not quite right."

"A honey trap."

"*Ya, ya,* that's it. Thank you again. She was supposed to compromise him, seduce him and make him pliable. But I think she succeeded beyond her own hopes. He not only became her lover, he became insanely protective and jealous of her. And he really did think you had killed her. So when you were looking for the Gypsy connection, he was looking for you, to kill you, I'm sure. I was merely looking for her father, looking to be sure that Yonkos *was* her father. And Evans was so very easy to follow. The man couldn't go for an hour without calling somebody or other on the radio or phone. Not like you, *Herr* Herman. You were really very clever."

"Not so clever that you didn't almost trap me and kill me when I went back to the *officia*."

"That was you?"

"Me and a friend."

"Ah, yes, the pretty woman. Perhaps I spent too much time looking at her. Anyway, that was a mistake. I wasn't sure you hadn't given your violin to Yonkos, and I thought it might be more of the Gypsy gang, come back to retrieve it. And to be honest, the killing had almost become a habit by then. It wanted to have a life of its own. An evil life, just like the violin that started it all. The hunter of evil becomes evil himself."

"So you really weren't part of the original con game at all?"

"Never. Not that one, nor any of the others the brother and sister ran over the years. And there were many."

"So how did you know about them?"

"Well, I wouldn't know about the ones before I did the appraisal, would I? After that, I followed their career from a distance, you might say. An insurance adjustor or a policeman would come to me to verify the certificate, and so I would get a new set of bogus names, a new bit of a trail. I never knew exactly how the fraud worked or how they kept getting the Amati back. And I didn't care. I waited and waited for them to lead me back to the father. Finally, when they started using the name Cox for their scams, the name they had stolen, it was just too much. I decided if I couldn't kill the father, I would kill the children instead. After all, they were my mistake, too. He shouldn't have lived to sire them in the first place."

"So you stalked Amy Cox?"

"An ugly word, but yes, I suppose I did. I followed her to your office, and when she finally left with a violin under her arm, I seized my chance. But as you know, that killing was a beginning, not an end."

"It was an end for her."

"True enough."

"Did you really break her neck, or was Evans just telling me that to rattle me?"

"Oh, I broke her neck, all right. I wanted her dead, but I didn't want her to suffer, after all. It was always Yonkos I was after. And when I finally found him, he didn't even remember who I was. Can you believe that?"

"Well, he was under rather a lot of stress at the time. And he was also blind, remember."

"Hmm. Or he pretended to be. I tell you one thing, though: After I finally killed him, I slept without dreams for the first time in fifty years."

"And the real Amati?"

"Can't you guess?" He grinned slyly and chuckled. "A clever fellow like yourself?"

I let my gaze drift pointedly to the Baldwin hanging on his wall, the one he had shown me that first night. Feinstein saw my gaze and nodded in silent confirmation. And it may have been the booze at work, but I felt obliged to chuckle, too.

"Why is it called the Wolf?" I said.

"Because it has a wolf note, of course."

"Say what?"

"You do not know this thing? It is every violin maker's worst nightmare. It is an unplanned harmonic, a note that emerges without being played, a squawk in the middle of an otherwise flawless performance. It is a rogue harmony that the box will produce, again and again."

"But the whole art of making violins is harmonics, I thought. How can this happen?"

"It only happens among the very best ones. It's rare and unpredictable, and it seldom shows itself when the instrument is new. But once it emerges, there is no remedy for it at all. The instrument becomes worthless for professional play. Some museum might give a few thousand for it, since it is still an Amati, but that's all."

"So after that, it's only good for con games."

"Or hanging on my wall. Fitting, is it not?"

And that may have also been the booze, but I had to admit that it was. I couldn't let it stay there, but it was very fitting.

We drank and talked for a long time then, telling each other trivial or monumental stories, both of us avoiding the obvious question. Feinstein produced another bottle and we slipped into it seamlessly. Finally, it was he who broached the unspeakable.

"You talked a while ago about me having a true vocation, I think?"

"I did," I said, nodding with intoxicated exaggeration. "Many people would envy it."

"And I would trade it for a good night's sleep, as it turned out. Amusing. But the problem, I think, is not my profession, but yours."

"How do you mean?"

"You work for the law. You have personal knowledge of four killings. Surely, you have to do something about that?"

"Do I?" I said.

"Don't you?"

"I work for the law, I suppose." I sighed. That's a fact that I've never really come to terms with. "But I'm not a lawman. I'm not always sure just what I am, but it's not that. A referee, maybe. I make sure everybody plays by the rules."

"And the rules in this case?"

"Are simple. The police are entitled to arrest you, and the DA is entitled to try to convict you. But I don't have to help them. I won't lie to them, but I won't do their jobs for them, either. And I won't call them. If they want you, they have to do their own homework."

He looked astonished. Maybe I did, too, since I had just then figured it all out.

"But this is very generous!" he said.

"Not as generous as you think. I do still have to give the violin back."

"Now you joke, I think. The violin you had is dust on the river, and its owner is dead."

"But her people are still alive. And the violin she *thought* she had is still around, too. One way or another, we both need to be clear of it. If you don't pay off all your debts, they just go back to accumulating interest."

"No, Herman, you cannot mean this. You cannot ask me to do this thing."

"That's the deal I made with the *familyia* in Skokie," I said. "And it's also what I owe to Amy Cox. The duty of my office, if you like that better. What you called my vocation."

"They will only use it to swindle more people, you know."

"They will swindle more people, no matter what. It's what they do. I'm only responsible for what I do. And I have to do this."

"I could still kill you, you know." His powerful hand reached deep in the pocket of his smock, and I had no doubt of what it found there.

"You could, yes. Is that the same Luger you had in the forest?" I said. "The one that has kept you from sleeping for fifty years?"

"Of course."

"I don't think you want to let it do that to you again."

"I... But you can't..." The hand came back out of the pocket, and the gun was in it, but he wasn't pointing it at me. He waved it around aimlessly, as if looking for a correct gesture. Then he laid it on a bench and began to weep. Maybe he also trembled, I'm not sure. I turned away and walked toward the door.

"It's been a long night, G.B., and a lot of heavy talk. And I have drunk more than I need or can handle. I'm going out to my car, the gray BMW across the street. I'm going to tip the seat back and have a very long sleep. Maybe I'll have a dream that tells me what to do about you. Good night, and thanks for everything. Especially the coffee."

I waited for the gunshot that would end my life or his, but it did not come. Instead, as I was almost out the door, I heard him say very quietly, "It has been my pleasure, *Herr* Herman."

I went down to my car and did exactly what I had

said I would. The long sleep part was very easy.

The next morning, I found a violin case on the seat beside me. So I knew what to do about Feinstein. Back in the building, his shop was deserted, the walls and benches partially stripped, the door unlocked. He wasn't there.

I never saw the man again.

Epilogue

The police never did come to question me, about Feinstein or Amy Cox, or anything else that had to do with old violins and even older passions. Maybe my uneasy allies, the Rom, had done their jobs, at that. The day after the long night of brandy and soul baring, I met Wilkie in my office and gave him the violin case.

"I've got one last job for you, Wide."

"I'm not going in any more jungles."

"That was a City park, sort of," I said.

"That's its problem."

"This jungle has naked ladies in it."

"Yeah? I'm listening."

"Go find a strip joint in Chicago called the New Lost City, and give this to the night bartender, named Joe Paterno. Tell him it's the Wolf, and it will make him clean if anything can." Joe wasn't really Amy Cox's heir, of course. But then, the Gypsies hadn't really said what they were going to do for me, and in return, I hadn't exactly said who in the *familyia* I was going to give the fiddle back to. Fair is fair.

"Everybody talks in riddles today," he said. But he took the case. "Your girlfriend, Rosie, is talking in riddles, too."

"You saw her today?"

"Just for a bit, this morning at the coffee shop. She says to tell you she's all square with your uncle Fred now. I told her you don't have an uncle, Fred or anything else, but she just laughs, says her markers are all paid off now and she's heading out. What the hell's she talking about?"

"Beats me," I said. "She's crazy." And she had told me as much, more than once. But not as crazy as she seemed at times. Nor was she merely a restless soul running away from a dinky town diner. She was a pro of some kind, one of Uncle Fred's people, and he had sent her to look after me, no less. I always did say he was a good judge of talent.

"When did she leave?" I said. I looked at my watch and suddenly the meaning of the shopping trip in Chicago soaked in. The fancy watch that I would never have bought for myself was Rosie's goodbye gift, given in advance to tell me later that I had not been just an assignment or a debt. Now, when it was almost certainly too late to say so, I was touched.

"About fifteen minutes ago," said Wilkie. "But you aren't going to catch her."

"Why not?"

"She's driving your BMW."

I laughed, in spite of myself. I wouldn't say it to Wilkie, but I felt that she had earned it, wherever she wanted to go with the thing. "Well," I said, "she definitely knows how to do that."

"Yeah?"

"Oh, yeah."

"Whatever," said Wilkie. He left with his signature coattails billowing out behind him. He disappeared into the morning fog, and I watched him do so from the same spot where I had been when Amy Cox had first appeared out of the rain. And I thought about appearances and disappearances and names and labels and illusions and scams and how very muddled they all get at times. I thought about the violin case under Wilkie's huge arm and wondered what was really inside it. Evil? Salvation? Or just an old fiddle? I hadn't looked inside the case, and I didn't intend to.

Finally, I thought about the story Uncle Fred had reminded me of, as I was leaving the visitors room at Redrock, the one he had said to use as my guide. It was an old story, one he had told me many times over the years. I remembered it well.

It happens in the marketplace in ancient Constantinople, a crossroads of commerce and deceit. A young boy, always eager to learn about the ways of the world, is watching the people coming and going when he sees a Turkish merchant, whom he knows, meet a Gypsy who is leading a fine-looking horse. There is lively discussion, money changes hands, and the merchant walks away with the horse. The boy runs after the Gypsy, who is now leaving at a brisk pace.

"Ho, there, Gypsy! Tell me, for my education: did you sell that horse to the Turk?"

"I did," says the Gypsy. "I charged him 54 *sisterces* for it."

"Is that a good price?" says the boy.

"Boy, that is a huge price. That fool of a Turk doesn't know it, but that horse is lame."

The boy then runs the other way and catches up with the merchant, who is leading the horse to a stable.

"Ho, there, Turk! You are the fool of fools. The Gypsy has sold you a lame horse."

"No, no, boy," says the merchant. "It is the Gypsy who is the fool. This horse only walks like he's lame because he has a stone in his shoe. At 54 *sisterces*, I stole this horse."

So the boy runs back to the Gypsy, who is now almost out of town.

"Ho, there, Gypsy! You are the fool of fools. That horse only walks like he's lame because he has a stone in his shoe. The Turk has robbed you."

"Listen to me, boy, for your education. I put that

stone in the horse's shoe so the Turk would think that's why he walks that way. That horse really is lame."

Again, the boy runs back to the merchant.

"Ho, Turk! The Gypsy has cheated you, after all. He put the stone in the horse's shoe to deceive you, and you believed what you saw and became a fool."

"This is true?" says the Turk.

"He told me himself, sir."

"Well. A curse on him for a thief, then. Good thing I paid him with counterfeit coins."

To receive a free catalog of Poisoned Pen Press titles, please contact us in one of the following ways:

Phone: 1-800-421-3976
Facsimile: 1-480-949-1707
Email: info@poisonedpenpress.com
Website: www.poisonedpenpress.com

Poisoned Pen Press
6962 E. First Ave. Ste. 103
Scottsdale, AZ 85251